FRENCH CONNECTION II

Robin Moore and Milt Machlin

French Connection II

Futura Publications Limited

A Futura Book

First published in Great Britain in 1975
by Futura Publications Limited
Published by arrangement with Dell Publishing Co., Inc.
Copyright © Robin Moore and Milt Machlin 1975

ISBN 0 8600 72142
Printed in Great Britain by
Hazell Watson & Viney Ltd
Aylesbury, Bucks

Futura Publications Limited
49 Poland Street
London W1A 2LG

CHAPTER ONE

Popeye Doyle's familiar swagger had become less pronounced in recent months. But as far as Lieutenant Clelland was concerned, the Detective First Grade was still too cocky. Doyle stopped at the Special Investigation Unit chief's desk and stared down at his boss with cold eyes. He didn't bother to remove his pork pie hat.

'Siddown Doyle,' Clelland ordered.

Doyle held his hostile stare for several seconds.

'I said siddown!'

Doyle obeyed, sullenly lowering his posterior into the chair beside the lieutenant's desk.

'I wanted to be the first to tell you, Doyle, that you've been transferred out to the eight one in Bedford-Stuyvesant. You should really enjoy it. There's thirty thousand spades out there you can kick around to your little heart's content.'

Doyle's square face revealed no emotion. He had been expecting something like this for the last few months – ever since his acquittal at a departmental trial. The charge: fatally shooting a federal agent during the chase after the Frenchman who got away. True, they found the shooting was accidental, but a lot of top cops wanted Doyle off the force or pounding a beat in outer Brooklyn or the Bronx. And now the sons of bitches were getting it their way, he thought grimly.

Al Renaldo and his partner Pete Dorrity were loitering within earshot of the lieutenant; they couldn't resist a snicker at Clelland's remark. Slowly, deliberately, Popeye turned from his superior and shifted his angry stare to the two narcotics detectives.

But his voice was soft as he asked, 'Does anybody know how five keys of shit somehow got lost between the time we made confiscation from the Bocca family and the time it was delivered to the property clerk's office?'

The grins faded from the faces of the narcotics officers.

'You're crazy, Popeye,' Renaldo said, a hurt look on his swarthy face.

'Come on, for Christ's sake,' his short, squint-eyed partner Dorrity echoed, 'what's the matter with you?'

'What the fuckin' matter is,' Doyle's voice raised to a shrill bleat, 'is that forty keys – eighty pounds of heroin, were taken from the Bocca brothers by cops in this here unit. Of that eighty pounds, exactly seventy was turned in.'

'And where did you come up with the idea that we grabbed eighty pounds, Popeye?' Clelland thundered. 'We took seventy pounds out of Tony Bocca's basement and put seventy-pounds into the property clerk's office.'

'Look, lieutenant,' Doyle retorted heatedly, 'you, Dorrity, Renaldo and them took the shit down to the property clerk. I was making the collar on Tony Bocca. While you were filling out the forms at the property clerk's office I was writing up the arrest papers on Bocca.'

'So?' Clelland snapped belligerently.

'So me and Tony Bocca had a long, private talk. He was so worried about his father and mother and wife that he finally talked a lot of sense. Why do you think I persuaded the D.A. to drop the charges against them?'

A grim look settled over the faces of the three narcotics officers.

'If it makes you feel better to get all this bullshit out of your system, be our guest, Doyle,' Clelland said.

'How fuckin' dumb do you think I am?' Doyle gave his superior a hard look. 'Bocca told me there was eighty pounds exactly in the stash. Seventy pounds was turned in to the pro-perty clerk, okay?'

'Bocca's just a cheap soldier, what does he know?' Clelland scoffed. But he couldn't suppress the worry-lines about his eyes and the corners of his mouth.

'He knows down to the ounce what he's got because he gets an icepick shoved up his asshole if he's short when his uncle takes the shit uptown to the big nigger.'

Clelland decided to try another tactic with the tough, re-bellious narcotics cop. 'You mean to sit here and tell me that

6

for the past four months you've known about a discrepancy and haven't reported it? I could have you up on another departmental trial.'

'Cut the shit, lieutenant,' Doyle growled disdainfully. 'You know the rules better than me. There's no such thing as a bad cop, right? Right! Ain't that the code? A cop doesn't give any information that can hurt another cop, unless he's a shoo-fly from Internal Affairs. You think I don't know what happened to that ten pounds the property clerk didn't get?'

'Doyle, this transfer's driven you nuts,' Clelland stated flatly. '*I* didn't ask for you to be sent out to Bed-Stuy.'

'Maybe not, but you could have prevented it, lieutenant.'

'In any case, Doyle, it's done. Now if you're unhappy you just do your time out at the eight one. You can put in for early retirement in a year and a half. A Detective First's pension isn't bad. You'll have your gun, you can get a good security job. Just forget all this crazy talk. You know there's nothing to it.'

Doyle felt the hot flush of anger creeping up the back of his neck. What stung him worse than being sent out to a cop's Siberia, was being treated like an imbecile by Clelland.

'Lieutenant, let me tell you that I got better informants than any man in this unit, okay? I happen to know that if someone cut into all the shit that's stashed in the property clerk's office and took it to the chemist's lab you know what they'd find? They wouldn't find no 88% pure heroin, they'd find a hundred pounds, maybe more by now, of milk, sugar and flour. And the shit didn't get taken from the property clerk's office by no Guinea soldier, it took a cop to check it out, right?'

'Are you alleging a felony and asking for an investigation?' Clelland stared through Doyle as he asked the question.

Suddenly Popeye realized he'd made a mistake. He knew he was right in what he said, but he also knew how easy it was for a lieutenant, with the help of a captain or inspector, to frame any cop on the force if he got out of line. Now he'd spilled too much.

'No, lieutenant, of course not. Forget it.'

'Considering that you let the big Frenchman get away with half a million dollars in cash money, which a lot of people

7

around here are wondering about, and then killed a federal narcotics agent all in one hour, I think that the department is being damned lenient with you, Doyle.' The lieutenant's eyes glittered and Doyle recognized the look of a man who would fight to the death if necessary for his job and bright future on the NYPD.

'Forget it, lieutenant.' Defeat and resignation suddenly cloaked him, he seemed to shrink under Clelland's icy stare.

There was a long silence before Clelland sat back in his chair. The lieutenant was thinking hard. Now his expression was more friendly.

'Tell you what, Doyle, I think I have an idea for you. You're too valuable a man to be wasted out in Bed-Stuy. Let me talk to Inspector Terpitz about a job which could win you back the respect of the department. I'm having lunch with him today. This afternoon we'll talk again. Come see me at four. Okay?'

Doyle nodded. 'Anything's better than serving out my time collaring welfare cheque thieves on Mother's Day.' Popeye stood up and walked down the long aisle between the desks of the Special Investigation Unit detectives and clerks. There was no vestige now of the aggressive rolling gait so characteristic of Detective First Class Doyle for many years.

After he had left the Unit's headquarters Dorrity and Renaldo turned their eyes to Clelland who merely shook his head, stood up, and left his desk.

Popeye walked down the ancient creaking stairs to street level of the First Precinct building near the lower tip of Manhattan which housed the Narcotics Bureau of the New York Police Department. Scenes of the culmination of what the newspapers had taken to calling 'The French Connection' case constantly agonized him.

He saw all over again Charnier, Frog One, the big French Connection, insolently waving bye-bye to him through the window of the subway train pulling away from the platform as Popeye stood helplessly watching.

And then there had been a last chance to get Charnier when he took the money from Tony Bocca out on Welfare Island. Somehow during the big fire fight with Bocca's mob, when

8

Popeye had accidentally killed the Federal Agent, the Frog had done the impossible: taken a vanishing pill. He escaped from the island, surrounded by cops, with all the money the Bocca mob had paid for one hundred and twenty pounds of heroin – close to half a million dollars.

As he walked out onto South Street, Popeye shook his head, trying to clear it of the vivid images which tortured him.

At four in the afternoon an anxious Detective Doyle walked quietly through the Special Investigation Unit headquarters and, when bidden, took his seat across the desk from a smiling and friendly Lieutenant Clelland. This time the jaunty pork pie hat was in his lap.

'Got some good news for you, Popeye. The inspector agreed with me that you shouldn't be wasted out in Bed-Stuy.' He paused before continuing.

'Now it happens that the inspector has been getting some high level Federal calls for extra assistance in stopping the continued shipment of narcotics from France, specifically Marseilles, into New York City. As you know we're hearing a lot about cutting heroin off at its source, the laboratories in Marseilles. But the Feds haven't been too successful. The inspector and I figured that nobody knows what the Frenchman, Charnier – who got away from you – looks like as well as you. The two of you had a sort of head to head semi-final here in New York. I figure you'll never forget him as long as you live, Right?'

'That's right, lieutenant,' Doyle asserted eagerly. 'I'd know him any place, with or without his beard.'

'Would you like another crack at getting him?'

'Are you kidding? Would I? It's all I think about. I keep looking for him every place I go figuring maybe he's back in New York.'

'He's in Marseilles, we know that. The French police haven't been much help to us, they don't have anything on him they say. But if you went to Marseilles, worked with the French police, you could find him. When you do you'll get all the

9

backing you need from the Feds working in France and the French police to make the collar and we'll get him extradited.' Clelland paused, gauging the effect of the proposition on Doyle.

'Well, Popeye, what do you say?'

'When do I go?'

Clelland nodded happily. 'That's what I wanted to hear. But it's not going to be that easy. In the first place all we can do is give you a leave of absence and introductions to the Marseilles and Paris police. The Marseilles police will provide you with a desk, semi-official status, and co-operation. The rest is up to you. Any questions?'

'Only one. I haven't got the money to buy a ticket to Hoboken, much less France.'

'You will be provided with tickets and whatever expense money we can squeeze out of the budget. That will be damn little, and you may have to dig down into your sock for some of the dough. But it's better than the Congo patrol in Bed-Stuy isn't it? It'll give you a chance to get the old job back again.'

'I'll get the Frenchman, lieutenant. You can bet your sweet ass on that!' Doyle's square jaw took on a rock-like set. His eyes had a hard, almost fanatic glitter.

The lieutenant seemed satisfied with Doyle's grim determination. 'We'll give you all the help we can from here but once you get on that Pan American jet for Paris you're on your own.'

Nearly twenty years as a detective had given Doyle that ultra-sensitive ability to smell danger that cops called 'street savvy'. But this time his natural protective instinct was shorted out by his eagerness to square his beef with 'Frog One', and restore himself to his proper function with the Narcotics Bureau. The amalgamation of sensory clues, body language, the lieutenant's tone of voice, his sudden reversal from hostility to friendship, didn't flash the instant warning it should have.

Why was the lieutenant being such a pal? Doyle did ask himself that. Maybe he just wanted Doyle far away and out of his hair. Maybe he had some other shenannigans he was afraid Doyle would stumble on. Maybe it was his way of paying Doyle off to shut up about the diluted heroin stash in the property clerk's office.

This was a gift horse whose mouth Doyle didn't plan to inspect. As a matter of fact he was betting every chip he had on that horse to win.

CHAPTER TWO

A WORD OF ADVICE. You are about to visit France. You will find that your enjoyment of your stay in France will be increased many times if you speak French constantly with the people you encounter. Nothing is so flattering to the natives of a country as when a visitor good-naturedly uses words and expressions in their language to make known needs. Do not be afraid to use these words, pronouncing them according to the phonetic key that follows each word and sentence in this book . . .

Popeye Doyle nodded over the little red, white, and blue pocketbook and, unnoticed, the book *French for your Travels* fell to the floor of the compartment. Outside the green of Durance gave way to the paler southern buff colours of Provence. The train began to pass through villages of tiled roofs huddled under a brilliant blue sky. Cypresses stood straight as black fingers against the horizon and the sun bounced in silvery rays off the leaves of olive trees. As it approached Marseilles, the train passed long rows of enormous, modern apartment buildings and supermarkets with names like Mammoth and Casino. Doyle lifted a groggy eyelid to glance through the window. It didn't look quite like the outer reaches of Queens but it didn't look much like his idea of southern France, either. The compartment had long since emptied. The last passenger, a teenaged blonde in blue jeans had left the train at Aix-en-Provence. Doyle had tried her with a few phrases from the Berlitz book without success and the girl had moved to a corner of the compartment to immerse herself in her book. After eight hours on the train, the detective felt cruddy from head to toe. He rubbed his hand along the back of his neck and rolled up little balls of dirt that he threw out the window. His beard felt scratchy and greasy and the pork pie nylon fibre hat that he pulled down over his eyes failed to keep the brilliant August sun from burning through the lids.

Doyle lifted his belt and reached down a grimy hand to pull his jockey shorts out of his crotch, where they had become wedged in a damp mass. He pulled the cuff of the double knit green sports slacks down over his socks. It had ridden up almost high enough to reveal the ankle holster strap there with the small-calibre Browning he had bought especially for the trip. It was a flat, light job, unobtrusive, yet with a good punch.

The conductor, who spoke a little English and had called out the stops from time to time, stuck his head through the door. 'Marseilles one half hour,' he said. 'Okay?'

'Okay,' Doyle said.

The conductor smiled as though he had passed his Regents exams and continued down the corridor. Doyle staggered down to the wash basin at the end of the car and tried to freshen himself into a semblance of decency. Returning to the compartment, he stowed the Berlitz book in his pocket and pulled a folder from the black plastic attaché case on the seat next to him. It contained several pages with listings of the contents of the pockets of Charnier's tan cashmere overcoat found in his hotel suite. Also it listed bits and pieces picked up from the dresser and the ashtray, some match books, a couple of pari-mutual tickets, and rubbings from the telephone pad beside the bed which revealed several phone numbers that were meaningless to Doyle. The guy had not left much behind when he skipped town.

With a hiss of air brakes, the train now slowed to a crawl and was easing into the giant shed of Gare Saint Charles. Doyle pulled his phrase book from his pocket and turned to the section called 'If You Travel By Train'. He could only find two phrases of any use; '*Where is the porter?*'

'*Oo eh luh pohr-terr?*'

'*How much is it for each piece?*'

'*Kohn-b'yahng ess pahr koh-lee?*'

But he had already figured out that he would give the motherfucker a quarter a bag. There was a coin marked one franc that was just about the size of a quarter and he figured that had to be right. Those frogs would rip you off if they had a chance anyway. He'd just give it to 'em and fuck 'em. But when he had pulled two Samsonite grey cases from the compartment he found there were no porters, only little shopping carts like they had in supermarkets back home. People were grabbing the carts and pushing their bags down the long *quai* towards the exit, so Doyle grabbed one for himself and loaded his bags and raincoat onto it, placing the attaché case containing his .38 and holster in the little tray in front of him. He had got very little out of the DEA agent in Paris, only the name of the man to contact at the US Consulate in Marseilles, Frank Kilian, and the name of a hotel, the Terminus. 'It will be the easiest one for you. It's right in the station. You'll see big signs. You'll be able to get yourself settled without too much hassle.'

The young fed talked as though his teeth had been wired together by some East Side orthodontist. Doyle had wondered how a kid his age could have got such a soft job. He didn't look much over twenty-four and had gone straight into the Bureau of Narcotics and Dangerous Drugs just before its designation was changed to the Drug Enforcement Agency. Never had a day in the street. The kid probably wouldn't know a key of shit if it hit him in the face. You didn't get street savvy from sitting on your ass in the Consul General's office in Paris.

Doyle pushed his little wagon past the brightly coloured rows of refreshment stands and news kiosks. He stopped for a minute to look at one of the news stands but couldn't see one single publication in English, not even a copy of *Time*. He left the wagon at the end of a corridor with a neon sign pointing to the Terminus Hotel and lugged the bags down the long bleak hall. To his surprise, the lobby was modern and clean-looking. He dragged his bags up to the desk that said 'Reception' (that sounded like the right word) and banged on the desk.

'Anybody here speak English?'

'Of course, m'sieur. What can we do for you?'

'You got a room for a couple of weeks, single?'

The woman behind the desk, grey-haired, middle-aged, reminded him of his high school biology teacher, Miss McNally.

She looked at him as if he were a paramecium on a slide, as she flipped through the cards in a file before her. 'We can let you have a single-bedded room with bath for 160 francs.'

Doyle knew a franc was worth about twenty cents. Divided by five, that made more than thirty dollars a night! 'For chrissake, is that the cheapest you got?' he asked. 'I'm paying my own bills now.'

'I'm sorry, m'sieur, that's all we have. The hotel is practically complete. If you want a cheaper room, I can make some calls for you.'

'Yeah, would you do that?' Doyle said. 'Something more like fifteen dollars a night, maybe ten?'

As she spoke on the phone Doyle looked around him. There was a Polynesian-style bar in the corner and a grill room behind. Several of the men passing seemed to be speaking English but with a Scottish or English accent. The woman returned in a few minutes. 'I have a room for you. I'll write the name of the hotel on a card. You will give it to the driver, or if you want to walk it is just at the base of the steps, those that run in front of the station.'

'I'll walk,' Doyle said. 'Just point me in the right direction.'

'Just go down the big steps and there'll be a big square in front of you, Place des Marseillaises. On the right you will see this hotel – Hotel de l'Univers. It is like your word universe. You'll recognize it. Give them this card. They know you're coming.'

'Well, thanks a lot,' Doyle said, hoisting his bags.

As he came out the door a taxi pulled up. A dark faced kid with a thin moustache was at the wheel. He flashed a big smile and Doyle could see that he had stainless steel molars.

'You want a taxi, fellow?' the driver said in English.

'Forget it,' Doyle said, 'I'm walking,' and started off toward the big staircase that ran down from the station. The driver shrugged and drove off. The staircase must have been 200 yards long and Doyle was beginning to regret the fact that he had decided to walk. But he didn't want to get into any hassles with Marseilles cab drivers until he knew the ropes. Halfway down the steps he put down the suitcases and the attaché case,

14

and wiped his head. There was a bar with tables on a terrace and he was tempted to stop for a beer but he didn't even know how to ask for one. He figured he'd better get settled before he started figuring that sort of thing out.

From where he stood, he could see the sign for the Little Palace Hotel and a little further down on the right, a sign for the Hotel de l'Univers. It had two stars on it. Doyle wondered if that was good. He had noticed that the Terminus had four stars on its sign. Finally he hoisted the bags again, staggered down the rest of the stairs and into the narrow hall that served as the vestibule to the Hotel de l'Univers. A heavy-set, balding man in a grey cardigan was at the reception desk reading *Le Provençal*. From the lists of figures and the pictures on the page, Doyle guessed he was figuring out the ponies. He handed the card to the man, who looked at it for a minute scratching his unshaven chin, then opened the door behind him and yelled 'Coco! *Viens!*'

A red-haired girl about five foot three with a round little bosom and a bright smile popped out of the room. The heavy-set man gestured with his thumb toward Doyle. '*Amerique,*' he said.

'You weesh room?' the girl said to him, smiling.

'Yes, I wish room,' Doyle said. 'Not more than ten bucks a day. Fifty francs, right? With a bath.'

'Your passport, please,' she said.

Doyle produced it. The girl filled out a small slip of paper referring to the passport. 'You are detective?' she said.

Too late, Doyle remembered the passport contained the designation under the place for occupation. 'That's right, just taking a little holiday.'

The girl pulled a key attached to a large brass check from a board full of similar keys next to the desk. 'Follow me,' she said.

They crowded into the small cage of an open elevator and the girl closed the folding gate by hand, then pushed the button marked '4'. The elevator groaned slowly upward. Doyle felt strangely exposed. He could see out through the brass bars of the elevator and people on the stairs could see in. The girl wasn't bad looking, a little too much make-up, but good teeth. 'You speak English,' he said as the elevator creaked up.

'A leetle,' she smiled.

'What do you do in this town for action?' Doyle asked.

'*Pardon?*'

'You know, action. Drinking, dancing, screwing.'

The girl looked puzzled. 'Action?' Then she smiled brightly. 'Marseilles very good action!' she said.

The brass cage shuddered to a halt. Coco pulled the gate open and led the way quickly down a hall covered with a worn-out green carpet. The doors had little white enamel ovals on them with blue numbers. The room was about twelve by twelve, not big and not small. There were high ceilings and a double window, with a narrow balcony outside, not big enough to stand on. The girl pulled the drapes and showed him to a curtained alcove. She pulled back the curtain, and gestured inside. 'Zee bath,' she said. Then in a flash, she was gone.

Doyle put his bags on the floor and looked around the room. There was a double bed which had a modern white headboard with shelves and a cubbyhole. There was an old-fashioned inter-com-type telephone on the wall, a bureau with a big mirror, a couple of old chairs, and a pink and blue pastel painting of a girl with bare tits on the wall.

His kidneys were bursting from the long trip. Doyle stepped into the bathroom and looked around. In one corner was a tub. To his right, a sink and a mirror. Next to it, a long oval-shaped china thing that looked like a toilet bowl but had no seat. A goddamned bidet. There wasn't any goddamned toilet in the room. Doyle unzipped the fly of his wrinkled slacks and aimed a yellow stream into the white bowl of the bidet.

He was just zipping himself up when there was a knock at the door. A skinny kid about twenty-two was in front of him, tall, dark-faced, with crooked yellow teeth. 'Mr Doyle?' he said.

'Yeah.'

'Police. Will you come with me?'

Doyle wondered who had got the word out ahead of him.

16

'What do you mean, come with you? I'll go down in the morning.'

'You will come with me now, please,' the kid said.

'Where's your fucking badge?'

'I have it here.' The kid reached inside of his baggy blue pin-striped jacket and Doyle found himself looking down the barrel of a 9 mm. Beretta.

CHAPTER THREE

A Citroen DS-19 was waiting outside, motor running. At the wheel was a short, dark man with curly, crisp grey hair. He wore a light brown leather sports coat that matched the colour of his swarthy skin. His eyes were dark with long, curling lashes that gave him a girlish look, but the pupils were bright and shiny.

'A cokie,' Doyle thought.

The young kid nudged him into the Citroen with his Beretta, and Doyle regretfully got in and sank down into the deep, soft cushions as the car pumped itself up to driving height and glided off smoothly down Boulevard d'Athenes. At the corner it turned into the broad street which was the Canabiére, the busy main thoroughfare of Marseilles. The kid sat across from Doyle, his back in the corner, the Beretta held loosely in his lap. 'You speak English?' Doyle asked.

'Enough.'

'Where are we going?'

The kid smiled, but didn't answer.

As the Citroen approached the old port, Doyle could see the masts of the fishing boats and yachts sticking up into the sky. Ahead were the cranes and diggings for the new Marseilles Metro. Suddenly, the Citroen was locked tightly in a traffic jam that made rush hour on the Long Island Expressway look like a Coney Island dodge-em. A cop in a round, white pillbox hat was blowing his whistle frantically, trying to disentangle the mass of homeward-bound traffic.

'You know what, kid?' Doyle said. 'I think you pulled the wrong time of day for this snatch. At this rate we ain't never gonna get anywhere. I want you to think twice about what I'm gonna say. I'm gonna grab that door handle and I'm goin' out the door. There's no way you're going to be able to get away with this car, so you'll have to leave it and it's going to be traced to whoever owns it. I don't think that this is the time to shoot me, right kid? So just be calm, don't get excited. You'll probably get another crack at me. See you around the pool room.'

With this, Doyle reached forward, grabbed the chrome handle of the Citroen, opened it and stepped out into the traffic, leaving a pair of dumbfounded Frenchmen in the shiny black car. They had been in the Citroen only a little over five minutes and Doyle had no trouble retracing his steps to the Boulevard d'Athenes.

At the hotel he told the surly concierge to call the girl.

'The girl Coco,' he said. 'The one that speaks English. Get her.'

'Coco,' the concierge echoed dimly. 'Ah, Coco!' He yelled back through the door for the girl who came out in a few minutes.

'Tell this fuck to telephone me if anyone comes and asks for me, right? Telephone, you understand?'

'If somebody asks for you, you want telephone your room,' Coco said.

'You got it, kid. You're really smart. You really got it.'

'Il veut qu'on lui donnes un coup de fil si quelqu'-un lui demand.'

The concierge nodded vaguely. Doyle hoped he got the message.

Upstairs, he inspected the room. He was on a high floor and there was no access to it from the outside. The balcony stopped short just outside the window. The door lock was flimsy and anyone could put his foot through it, but Doyle figured if someone was going to rub him out in the room, he would have done it in the first place. Still, he moved the dresser against the door. Then he opened the attaché case, took out the folder, put it on the bed beside him, took out the ·38, and put it under his pillow. From the Samsonite suitcase, he took one of the two fifths of Jack Daniels he had brought with him. He thought of calling down for ice, but wasn't sure he could get the message over on the telephone. Besides, it would have meant pushing back the bureau from the door. Too much trouble. He was exhausted by the long train ride and though it was still early, he couldn't keep his eyes open long enough to review the contents of the folder or even to figure out what the young kid had been after. He took off the wrinkled slacks, smoothed them out and put them under the mattress, hung his coat over the chair and got into bed in his skivvies, pulling the fat, thick French comforter over his shoulders. Sleep came immediately.

CHAPTER FOUR

Marseilles had been a seaport for thirteen centuries when the Arab sailors first introduced opium to the Orient. Through the ensuing hundreds of years millions of addicts were created, first opium smokers, then morphine users, and finally heroin addicts. In fact heroin – first invented as a cough remedy – was ultimaely introduced as the miracle drug which would break the morphine habit, much as methadone is touted today.

Despite its ancient history of prominence as a Mediterranean port – a centre not only for commerce, exchange of culture and ideas, but for piracy and smuggling as well – Marseilles only became the principal base for heroin refining in the fifties. This came about after a long war between powerful Sicilian gangs.

Control first rested in the hands of the Guerini brothers – two Corsicans who achieved wealth and power by helping the Gestapo combat the wartime Communist resistance movement. After the war Guerinis and their allies, powered by undercover CIA financing, helped break the power of the Communist CGT – France's most important labour union confederation. They also were instrumental in seating Gaston Deferre as Marseilles' semi-permanent Socialist mayor. As a result of the powerful political connection, the Guerinis and later their Corsican rivals the Venturis, gained control of the Marseilles docking area, and ultimately of the enormously profitable heroin trade with America.

The Guerinis had discovered at an early stage that morphine base was an ideal smuggling material. A powder, it is virtually indestructible and can be moulded into any shape and fitted into any type of container. When pressed into flat cardboard-like sheets, it slides beautifully into a double-bottom suitcase. It can be moulded to fit into a spare tyre, a truck's air brakes, or a hollowed out space in a T'ang dynasty idol.

The province of Afyon in Turkey had been the centre for growing the opium poppy almost since its introduction to the civilized world. But in the late sixties the Turkish government announced that with the help of three million in American money, it planned to cut back and ultimately eliminate the cultivation of the white, drug-producing flowers.

The commercial assembly line channelling opium and mor-phine base from Turkey to the highly proficient laboratories of Marseilles for conversion to high-priced heroin, had to be retooled to meet the new situation. The Corsicans who had handled the operation between the Middle East and Marseilles by agreement with the Sicilian-American Mafia were ready for the challenge. Thousands of the compatriots had gone to Indo-china in the beginning of the Vietnam war, when the French were fighting to preserve their foothold in the Orient. Many had stayed on to establish lucrative legitimate import-export businesses, and even more profitable enterprises involving the smuggling of cigarettes, stolen antiques, and above all opium. So the Turkish decision to cut poppy production meant only increasing the oriental production of morphine base (which is ten times more compact to ship than raw opium) and finding additional ways of shipping it.

Certainly among the thousands of tons of cargo arriving from ports all over the world at Marseilles' new deep-waterport of La Joliette, a ton or so of contraband morphine base could be concealed without attracting undue attention. After all, it isn't as though the traffic were something *new*. Simply an expansion of shipping 'bottoms' to meet the new needs of commerce, and the Corsican-Sicilian axis was nothing if not ingenious.

While Popeye Doyle was sweating out the results of jet and train lag, an example of this ingenuity was wallowing in the mistral-driven sea-troughs west of the islands guarding the entrance to Marseilles harbour. Beyond the fifteenth century tower of Saint Jean and the breakwater a small Japanese freighter was bustling through the Mediterranean at its top speed of eight knots.

Watching it from a white turn-of-the-century villa on the Corniche John F Kennedy was a slim young man, elegant in the way only the wealthy French can be. He wore Gucci shoes, a Skye tweed jacket and a black cashmere turtleneck sweater. A powerful pair of Zeiss binoculars was mounted on a tripod near the window with big lenses for night vision. The young man watched the boat with satisfaction and turned towards the older, grey-haired man mixing his scotch at the butler's tray in the corner. '*Ça va! Elle arrive,*' he said.

Smiling, the older man crossed the floor and stooped to peer briefly through the glasses. Then he picked up the two drinks and retired to a room somewhere in the rear of the villa, leaving the young man to watch the progress of the boat.

The freighter steamed steadily westward, till it was out of sight around the corner marked by the monument to the dead of World War II. Placidly it steamed past Fort Saint Jean and Fort Saint Nicolas, around the bend and into La Joliette, the bustling commercial harbour of Marseilles. By morning the freighter had unloaded its cargo at one of the long, finger-like docks stretching from the quais of La Joliette and was locked beside a vast dry-dock. A huge pump began to lower the water level in the basin of the repair dock as longshoremen busily attached stanchions and thick wooden supports to the ship from the dock side to keep it upright once the water was gone.

The freighter's captain, a grizzled Japanese in a soiled white cap watched the proceedings. From his place high atop the ship's bridge he could see the approach of a grey Mercedes

220 SL. The car bumped across the intersecting loading rails of the shipyard and parked opposite the drydock. The elegant young man in the cashmere sweater dismounted, came to the edge of the drydock and caught the eye of the Japanese captain. He tipped his finger to his head and nodded once. The freighter captain's return nod was barely perceptible. Then with a tiny smile he moved to the other side of the bridge to check the work of the dockers. Without expression, the young man climbed back into the Mercedes, circled around a giant crane, and drove away from the drydock.

CHAPTER FIVE

Doyle woke at about eight, staring at the unfamiliar blue and pink print of the girl with the bare tits. The displaced bureau against the door gave the room the disorganized look of an attic storeroom and it took a few seconds for Doyle to register where he actually was. Groaning, he reached over and finished the remains of the warm Jack Daniels by the bedside and shuffled into the curtained bathroom. Glumly he urinated in the bidet again, thought about getting another room, even another hotel – one with a crapper in it. Just as he finished patting the aerosol shaving cream on his face, there was a knock at the door.

'Who's that, for crissake!' Doyle yelled.

'*Petit déjeuner*. Breakfast.'

It was Coco's voice. Doyle wouldn't have minded getting next to her but he eyed his wrinkled skivvies and the bureau braced against the door and thought about the problem of getting the shaving cream off his face. 'Leave it outside the door!' he yelled.

He remembered what his friend Feder had told him before he left. Feder had spent a vacation in Europe. He told him they left a goddam breakfast of frog coffee and some kind of rolls whether you wanted it or not.

Doyle wondered if there was somewhere in Marseilles like

the Market Diner on West Street where you could get a glass of real orange juice, a couple of eggs looking at you with English bacon and a cup of good coffee. Somehow, he doubted it.

Sure enough, the coffee was lukewarm, bitter and tasted of chicory. Even adding some of the hot milk that was in the second pitcher on his tray didn't help and the little rolls that looked like salt sticks from Max's deli just weren't. They had no taste at all to Doyle's palate. The coffee was about the same temperature as the dribble of water that came out of the weird, telephone-like device that hung over the tub in place of a shower.

Somehow Doyle managed to scrub the grime of the railroad trip from him. He threw his soiled skivvies in the corner of the bureau drawer after he had moved it back into place, pulled his rehabilitated slacks from under the mattress, strapped on the ankle holster and stuck the .38 into his clip-on belt holster. Then he slipped into a fresh sport shirt, and took his jacket from the chair where it was hanging.

After some trouble, he managed to make the concierge call the number of the consulate and get instructions about how to get there by taxi. The consulate was on rue d'Armeny near the Place de Prefecture. It was hard to miss because there was a big American flag hanging out front. The meter read 4.60 and Doyle gave the driver six one-franc coins, which seemed to make him very happy. He decided to give less next time.

The consulate was in a grey stone building in a row of small shops. The girl at the desk asked Doyle's name and called up to John Hyde, the DEA man whose name had been given to Doyle by the creep in the Paris office. In a few minutes Hyde came down and introduced himself.

'Hi. I'm Johnny Hyde, DEA. You're Doyle?'

'Right,' Doyle said.

'Sorry about this business of coming down to get you. Security, you know,' Hyde said. In the elevator he pulled a little chrome-plated key from his pocket, and stuck it in a keyhole next to the button to the third floor. When the elevator arrived at the third floor, he used the same key to open the door.

'It's all bullshit really,' Hyde said apologetically, 'but that's the routine.'

He was a tall, good-looking guy, around twenty-five with a blond goatee. He was in his shirt sleeves and was wearing a vest with lapels. 'The kid ain't here a year,' Doyle thought to himself, 'and he's turning into a frog already.'

'I'll introduce you to my boss,' Hyde said. He let him into a large, light, airy office. There was a map of the world on one wall with pins in it. A sign on the door said 'Department of Justice – DEA'. Underneath it said 'Department de la Justice'. On the other wall was a large grey safe and a fireplace. The mantle of the fireplace was covered with little toy animals, which Doyle realized suddenly were all frogs. In the corner of the room he noticed a case of Beefeater and a case of Smirnoff's vodka. Behind the desk was a small, sharp-faced man with long sideburns and a pair of little half-rimmed glasses that he was using to read a report. When Doyle came in the man took off the glasses, stood up and held out his hand.

'You're Doyle, right?' he said.

Doyle had the feeling that the man had already been briefed. 'Right,' Doyle said.

'Have a seat.'

Doyle sat down in the leather-covered armchair opposite the desk. Not a bad set-up, he thought. A lot better than the Narcotics Bureau. These feds really live good.

Harry Lawton, the DEA Chief, leaned back in his chair and pressed his fingers together. 'What can we do for you, Doyle?' he asked.

Doyle pulled the letter from his pocket introducing him as a member of the department and of the Narcotics Bureau. Lawton looked at it without much interest. 'What are you planning to do here?'

'I'm going to find that motherfucker Charnier,' Doyle said.

Lawton allowed a very thin smile. 'You must be kidding. You know there's a million and a half people in this town? How are you going to find Charnier? You have no authority here, no contacts. You can't speak the language and if you

24

start fooling around, you are liable to screw up some of our operations. I don't get it.'

Doyle's face coloured with anger. 'Look', he said, 'you do your job, I'll do mine. You know what that sonofabitch Charnier did.'

'Sure,' Lawton said. He got up and looked out the window. 'I also know that when you made the bust, you got one of our best agents killed.'

'What the fuck are you talking about?' Doyle said. 'That wasn't my fault!'

'The guy is dead,' Lawson said flatly. 'I don't see what help we could give you.'

'Look, just tell me where the police headquarters is. I'll work it out myself.'

'Hyde, write it out for him,' Lawton said. He turned to Doyle. 'Listen, I don't mind your trying to spot Charnier, although how you're going to do it is beyond me. But don't get involved in anything and don't get in our way. It took us a couple of years to get where we are here and we don't want anybody messing us up. Get it?'

'They must really fit you guys up with paper assholes when they turn you out of that fed school,' Doyle said, taking the paper. 'I'll let you know if I find anything.'

'Thanks a lot,' Lawton said.

Doyle slammed out of the office. 'Wait a minute, Hyde's got to take you down in the elevator!' Lawton yelled after him. 'Security, you know.'

In the hallway at the elevator the young DEA man put a sympathetic hand on Doyle's shoulder.

'I know we came down heavy with you, man,' he said. 'But this is very frustrating duty. These new guys they assigned to the "stupes" – that's what they call the agents from the Bureau of Stupefiants – they don't really have that much experience. And then half the time we give them the tip, they make a collar, and the guy is suddenly sprung mysteriously on orders from Paris. The only thing we can do, we can pay for information – about five hundred bucks for every kilo we recover. The "stupes" can't do that. Against French law, and besides their budget is peanuts. I don't know whose idea it was to send you here, but you're strictly on a wild goose chase.'

The elevator arrived and Doyle crowded into it with Hyde.

'You know something?' he said as they creaked down to the street floor. 'You fucking feds couldn't find your ass with both hands!'

CHAPTER SIX

Police headquarters was on rue Antoine-Becker, down near the old port behind the big, candy-striped cathedral. It was a sprawling old grey building that had a strange family resemblance to the First Precinct and the Narcotics Bureau on South Street. They must have had some special architect that designed police headquarters in all the different countries, Doyle thought.

As he approached the tall, black, pointed iron railing that surrounded the headquarters, a strange sight greeted his eyes. Big refrigerated trucks were pulled up inside of the wide courtyard. From them cops in shirtsleeves were unloading crate after crate of frozen fish and dumping them onto rows of trestle tables, erected in front of the building like a giant marketplace. Arranged along the tables were more cops and plainclothesmen who were searching through the fish, cutting open the slimy bellies, sticking their fingers inside, pulling out the guts and tossing what remained into the trash barrels. Other cops were pounding at the part of the catch which was still frozen or using saws or knives to open the fish. Some were dipping the rest into bowls of hot water to thaw them quicker. Dead eyeballs were rolling all over the courtyard and the cobblestone surface of the court was slimy with ice and scales. The cops were all yelling, complaining and joking but it was obvious that nobody liked the messy job, especially as the sun heated up the remains of the fishy cargo.

From his pocket Doyle took his police notebook in which he had written the name of the man in charge of the Narcotics

Bureau in Marseilles, Rene Barthelmy. There was a cop standing guard by the gate. Doyle went up and pulled his sleeve. 'BAR-THEL-MEE?' he said as clearly as he could.

The cop looked at him blankly and shook his head. Doyle opened the notebook to the page with the name and pointed to it. The cop nodded and pointed to a stocky man with black, curly hair in his shirtsleeves. Though his torso was thick, Doyle noticed there was no telltale bulge of fat where his black belt dug into the meticulous but fishstained yellow-tinted shirt. The pudgy fingers sorting their way roughly through the gleaming entrails were hairy and muscular. Working with him were two plainclothesmen, a small, wiry, grey-haired man and a younger athletic looking detective who was checking the cargo against a ship's manifesto. Doyle crossed to where the stocky inspector was working, pulled out his badge and waved it at him. 'Doyle,' he said. 'New York.'

Barthelmy wrinkled his nose a little. Doyle wasn't sure whether it was from the smell of the fish or the sound of his name. 'I am Barthelmy,' the stocky man said. 'We've been expecting you.'

'You speak English. That's a relief,' Doyle said.

Barthelmy took one hand out from the fish, dripping with slime. He held it out for Doyle to shake. Doyle looked him in the eye and then reached out his hand, grabbed the slimy fingers and pumped them firmly. 'What are you doing here, working overtime?' Doyle asked. 'It isn't even Friday.'

'Narcotics,' Barthelmy said.

Miletto and Diron bent over their fish. They wanted no part in the exchange.

'They're hidin' it in the fish?' Doyle shouted above the noise of the other cops. 'That's sure a new way of popping shit. Eating it. It beats mainlining.'

If Barthelmy got the joke, he didn't react. His cool grey eyes had laugh-lines at the corners, but at the moment they were as cold as the fish's belly before him. Nodding his head towards the two men on either side, he introduced them. 'Inspectors Miletto and Diron. They'll help you in your work.'

Doyle stuck his hands in his pockets so he wouldn't have to

go through the slimy handshake routine again. Silently, the two men nodded acceptance of the introduction and went back to their job. Doyle stood watching the searching procedure for a while, not knowing quite what to do.

As Barthelmy worked, the men on his team began to come over to him, all shaking their heads and holding their arms up to show that there was nothing in the fish. Angrily, Barthelmy sent them back to search for more. With disgust, they returned to the messy job.

Behind the police, a group of fishermen were protesting vociferously in Moroccan patois. It was obvious that the plain-clothesman talking to them could barely understand what they were saying, but finally he got the message. Nodding grimly, he placated the angry fishermen and went over to where Bar-thelmy was working. Briefly, he gave a report on what had been said. Doyle listened, but couldn't get the drift of the message. 'What did he say?' he asked Miletto who apparently knew English.

'He said somebody played a joke on us. It's the first of April. Do you have that in your country?'

Doyle broke out in a grin, but Barthelmy's face was grim and tight-lipped. It was obvious he was having trouble control-ling his temper. Miletto tried to hide a rueful smile. Barthelmy turned to the plainclothesman who was able to speak the Moroccan argot.

'Send them back in their stinking boat to Africa. If we see those bastards in Marseilles again, they're finished,' he said.

Turning to Raoul he said, 'Get this crap back in the trucks.'

There was a big, muddy washroom inside the headquarters building where the disgusted plainclothesmen and uniformed policemen were able to clean up. As Barthelmy finished wiping his hands, Miletto bustled into the room with a buff folder which he handed to his superior. From where he stood, Doyle could see the initials of the New York Police Department on the folder and the seal of the City of New York. Barthelmy read from the folder:

28

'Doyle. Forty-two years old. Nickname Popeye. Hmm. Spinach, no? Popeye.'

Doyle was furious. 'How come you're reading my file in this shithouse?'

'I like reading it here,' Barthelmy said. He went back to reading the folder. 'Well, well. Thirty-five kilos of heroin. A big arrest, no? *Regardez*, Miletto, we have a real cowboy from the far *ouest*.'

Doyle started to grab for the file but Barthelmy slid it under his arm. Doyle was furious.

'Where the fuck did you get that?'

'Listen, Mr Popeye,' Barthelmy said. 'I was asked to help you. I did not ask for you to come here. Naturally I asked who it was I was helping and I found out right in this file.'

He looked into the file again. 'After this big heroic arrest of yours, the thirty-five kilos, it disappeared, no? Right out of police headquarters, it says here. It was maybe some friends of yours?'

'My friends are still on the force,' Doyle said flatly.

But it was apparent to the New York detective that Barthelmy had some kind of pipeline to the NYPD. The story of the ripoff of the drugs from the property clerk's office had broken only the day before Doyle left New York, and with very few details.

Barthelmy closed the folder. 'How many men have you killed?' he asked.

It was clear to Doyle that he was already in the shithouse with this frog narc.

'Just a fucking minute. Am I being interrogated, or what? I'm supposed to be working with you, right? Or am I some kind of goddamned suspect?'

'It says in your folder you've killed five men,' Barthelmy said. 'Isn't that quite a lot?'

'Listen,' Doyle said, 'I've been a New York cop fourteen years. The dope that comes out of your town killed a lot more people that I ever did.'

Barthelmy started to answer but Miletto, apparently anxious to cut off the argument, took the folder from Barthelmy. 'I'll show you to your office,' he said. 'Follow me, please.' His voice was softer than Barthelmy's, maybe a little apologetic.

Just as Doyle was about to leave, Barthelmy yelled after him, 'Two of the men killed during your big bust were policemen, right?'

Doyle looked back bitterly. 'Just read what it says, Henry,' he said, and left.

The grey-haired detective led him out of the washroom around to the other side of the partition and indicated a battered brown mahogany desk pushed against the outer wall of the washroom. Over the partition the noise of flushing could clearly be heard. Miletto looked apologetic. 'You know, we have no budget for extra men and very little space. As for a telephone, it's impossible. However, we have found a phone book for you, see?'

He pulled open a drawer and indicated the red and white Bottin. 'And this drawer, the top right-hand one, it locks. Here's a key.'

He pulled it, an old-fashioned skeleton key, from a tray inside the drawer. 'You're joking, aren't you?' Doyle said. 'This looks like the reception desk in a fuckin' Bronx junkyard!'

Miletto exposed his palms in a gesture of resignation. 'Come on, I want to talk to Henry about this,' Doyle said. 'Where's his office?'

Miletto led the way, through an outer office with anti-drug posters and a few waiting chairs into Henry Barthelmy's inner sanctum. He had to admit that it was not exactly a palace and had no resemblance to the offices of the DEA at the US Consulate. Still, there was a modern steel desk, a new safe in the corner, a glass case that apparently contained souvenirs and evidence from past capers, a map of the harbour of Marseilles on one side and a world map on the other with little red strings that seemed to indicate the major heroin routes between Turkey and the United States. The heaviest line of marking tape ran from Istanbul to points along the Mediterranean – Lebanon, Athens, Munich. Most of the tapes again converged on Marseilles, although a few went directly from Munich to Amsterdam. Doyle wasted little time inspecting the decorations. 'Henry, do you realize that you've got me practically in the shithouse? And just a desk with no privacy, no walls, no telephone – what is the deal?'

Barthelmy smiled. 'I suppose you are already homesick for your Yankee offices, but here in France we have very little money for fancy furniture. Besides, you're not on our budget. We didn't send for you. It's all we can spare.'

Barthelmy's voice was flat and uncompromising. 'If you are homesick, Popeye, maybe you want to go home again. Or should I send for some spinach?'

Doyle's face flushed with anger. 'Look, Barthelmy, let's cut that chickenshit out right now. I'd rather be a harness bull in Bed-Stuy than the President of France, but I got a job to do here. I'm gonna find that Charnier and put him where he's never gonna see daylight again, even if you guys can't find him – even if you *won't*.'

Barthelmy leaned back in his swivel chair and clapped his hands in a slow, methodical imitation of applause. 'Bravo!' he said. 'It's D-Day in Marseilles. The Yankees have landed. Lafayette, we are here.' But suddenly, the mocking tone was gone from his voice and Henry Barthelmy was all cop. 'Listen, Doyle, this character Charnier that you claim you can find – in the first place, there is no such person. It is obviously not his name. There is no record of him in our files, no record in Paris. There is no record among our informants in the street of anybody who has a name that sounds anything like that, or even looks like your description. At least, there are so many that do that we could never find him.

'In fact,' Barthelmy said, his voice rising, 'there is more of a record on *you*, and it is not very nice. Do I have to remind you that it was *you* who let Charnier escape!'

Doyle bit his lip in frustration. 'You don't have to remind me,' he said. 'I know too fucking well.'

The admission seemed to soften Barthelmy's cold hostility. 'Come on, I have to work. You can come along, but only to observe. You carry no gun? It's illegal for foreigners, you know, even for cops,' Barthelmy said.

Doyle felt the guilty weight of the .38 on his hip and the small Browning on his ankle. If Barthelmy had not already spotted the hip holster, he was no cop. He decided that the question was only a formality. He looked into the division inspector's eye with all the open frankness he could muster. 'No,' Doyle said, 'I have no gun. I go by the book. You read my file.'

'That's why I asked,' Barthelmy said.

CHAPTER SEVEN

In the courtyard of the prefecture, Doyle and Barthelmy piled into the shiny, black Citroen DS-19 that belonged to the Police Judiciaire. It was unmarked, but carried a roof-light and siren, which cleared the way with its hee-haw braying as Miletto drove it swiftly through the streets. Diron at his side was communicating by radio with the police crew already on the scene. Despite the vigorous use of the siren, it was a while before the Citroen could push its way through the narrow, old streets to the Panier Quarter, where the Cour Saint Eloi was already busy with a hectic tableau reminiscent of the earlier scene in the courtyard of police headquarters. There were about six Peugeot 404 wagons with flashing blue rooflights blocking off the ancient courtyard, which was surrounded by buildings that could have gone back to the Phoenician origins of the ancient town. These leaned and sagged at crazy angles, the windows bulging from the walls. The old houses seemed to support one another; as though if one stone were removed, the whole square would fall into a heap. In most of the windows, jeering heads appeared, shouting down at the cops working below on the terrace of Manfredi's Pizzeria, which occupied the main corner of the plaza.

The police were hard at work when Barthelmy's car arrived. Fish were cascading over the pavement tables and chairs of the restaurant. The customers were still scattering, most taking advantage of the raid to disappear without paying, others even profiting from the occasion by grabbing a fish or two and wrapping it in newspaper before disappearing. Manfredi, a short, stocky Italian with a cascade of chestnut curls and a soup-strainer moustache was screaming like a maniac at the cops who were busily dumping fish all over the premises – some were not too fresh, to judge by the smell. Doyle wrinkled his nose in disgust. It wasn't just the fish, but it was the mouldy, musty, miasma of the ancient quarter, compounded of hundreds of years of layered filth. '*Cochons salauds! Sales espèces des cons!*' Manfredi screamed.

Doyle watched with a half smile. The whole thing reminded him of certain busts uptown in New York. An overripe melon thrown from the roof landed only a few yards away and Doyle moved into the shelter of the terrace's awning. Just like Harlem, he thought, except there they put it into a garbage can before they throw it.

Barthelmy bowed in mock courtesy to the raging Italian. '*Un joyeux premier avril à toi, aussi.*'

This was the payoff for this morning's fishy gag, Popeye assumed.

'It was not my joke, I swear it,' Manfredi said, 'on my mother's life.'

Barthelmy looked over at the fat lady with a mole like a coffee bean on her right cheek and a moustache almost as luxuriant as her son's. She was waving a fish knife and screaming louder than anyone from behind the display of oysters and sea-urchins in front of the restaurant's window.

'At least you *know* who your *mother* is,' Barthelmy said.

He gestured with his head to Miletto and Diron who picked up four of the chairs that had been knocked over by the police and set them up around the table, two facing the street and two facing the restaurant. Barthelmy gestured for Doyle to take his seat.

'What will you eat, Popeye?' Barthelmy said.

Doyle looked at him in astonishment. 'You mean you're goin' to *eat* in this joint after the stunt you pulled? You gotta be crazy! In Harlem they'd piss in your soup.'

Barthelmy ignored him. 'The bouillabaisse is very good. It's a fish soup, you know.'

'Listen, the stink of all this fish is making me puke already. If you don't mind, I'll have a pizza. This *is* a pizzeria, isn't it?' Doyle said.

Although Manfredi was standing nearby, Barthelmy got out and shouted loudly to Mother Manfredi inside, '*Trois bouillabaises et un pizza pour notre copain de NEW YORK!*'

It sounded to Doyle as though Barthelmy was leaning hard on the word 'New York' and he could sense that several of the men lounging around watching the action turned their heads to zero in on him. It was obvious that there were a lot of people in that neighbourhood who were curious as to who this foreigner was with Barthelmy and his team. It was also apparent that Barthelmy was going to a lot of trouble to let them know.

Doyle didn't comment. He just said, 'Tell them to hold the anchovies, Henry.'

Behind him and on the other side of the street, Doyle could already spot four or five people slouching aimlessly, darting glances over to the table to make him. *What the fuck*, Doyle thought. They already had him spotted once anyway and perhaps sitting here as bait might be the best way to find Charnier. He didn't know any other way.

As they waited for the order, Manfredi, his customers now all gone, slumped, deflated and dejected, but still smouldering, into a seat at Barthelmy's table. He started to protest angrily, but in a quiet voice. Doyle couldn't make out the words, but he got the music.

'You cops come in and ruin my business,' Manfredi said. 'I'm finished. Now you expect me to tell you things. Why should I ever tell you anything again?'

'Because,' Barthelmy said very sincerely, 'if you do not I will close this place down. I will kick you out into the street, and I will tell everybody in the "milieu" *who* tipped me off.' Just 'cause you give us information doesn't mean I have to take any garbage from you. Now you have some information today, what is it? I want it, and I want it *now* or this little party we

34

had today will look more like the first of May than the first of April.'

Manfredi was swallowing hard. His eyes darted about, trying to avoid the neighbours peering from the windows, the dark faces slouching on the corners in apparent unconcern. He leaned his elbow on the table and rested his chin in his hand, so that his fingers concealed his mouth even more than the moustache did.

'I'm not sure what it means, but my cousin is a water inspector in Aubagne. He tells me that they're using a lot of water up on rue Galice.'

Miletto took the chance to explain to Doyle. 'He's giving us a tip. He says that there's a little house in the suburbs here where they're using a lot of water. You know, they use it in the labs to purify the morphine base.'

At this point, Mother Manfredi arrived and unceremoniously threw a huge tray of fish and a pot of soup down on the table, along with Doyle's pizza. The pizza looked to Doyle exactly like the kind they served along Times Square or Bleecker Street. The first bite tasted reasonably good, although the crust was on the soggy side, but then he felt a stab of grit between his teeth that nearly punched out his $200 inlay and another which cut sharply into his gum. Angrily he spit out the grit, along with a mouthful of blood onto the slimy pavement. 'What's in this goddamn thing?' Doyle said. 'It tastes like glass!'

Looking closely at the pizza in front of him, he picked several pieces of shiny clear crystal out of the cheese. 'It *is* fucking glass,' he said.

'I thought they might do something like that,' Barthelmy said. 'See, it's in the bouillabaisse, too. They don't just hate Americans.'

Behind her cooking fire, Mother Manfredi smiled blissfully. They asked for lunch. She *gave* them lunch.

CHAPTER EIGHT

The Japanese captain had removed his soiled white cap and merchant marine uniform. He emerged from his cabin on the top deck dressed in a tight-fitting grey tropical wash-and-wear suit. A pair of thick prescription sunglasses perched uncertainly on his flat nose. Across his shoulder was the strap of a Nikon EF with several spare rolls of 35 mm strapped to it in leather cylinders. Hanging from a criss-crossing strap was another leather tube containing his auxiliary 135 mm lens. The whole outfit was crowned with a peaked golfing cap in Stuart-tartan cotton. All in all the captain gave the impression of being a typical middle-aged tourist on a Lindblad tour of the Mediterranean.

He descended the gangplank of his freighter sedately with a casual wave at the Yugoslav first mate who had taken over the bridge. The Kyoko Maru, long since unloaded of its cargo, was propped up in one of the port's half-dozen dry-docks for repairs and painting. The dock itself had already been drained and workers with scaffolding, paint buckets, acetylene welding and cutting torches were already descending into the huge basin of the dry-dock to begin work on the exposed hull.

Against the wall of one of the warehouses adjoining the dry-dock was a booth with a pay phone in it. The captain entered the booth, slid down on the steel corner stool and extracted a tooled leather Florentine change purse from the pocket of the wash and wear suit. From it he poured a wild assortment of international currency onto the metal counter in front of him – Japanese yen, Taiwsanese sen, Vietnamese and Lebanese piastre, Portuguese escudos, Deutschemarks, Swiss francs and American nickels and dimes, along with a handful of French pièces. From the miniature numismatic collection, he selected after some thought, a dime-sized half-franc piece. From a side pocket in the change purse he produced a tiny piece of tissue paper with a number on it which he carefully dialled after studying the instructions on the plaque screwed to the wall before him.

When a cultured voice answered, the captain identified himself in almost faultless French. (The Captain had after all spent most of World War II on a minesweeper operating out of Hanoi.)

There was a brief conversation in which the captain identified himself by his code name. *Capitaine Nemo.* Following verification of his identity, the cultured voice on the other end dictated careful, if cryptic, instructions which the captain copied down in Katakana characters on the back of the tiny bit of tissue paper on which the phone number had been written.

When the call was finished, the captain hung up, selected another coin from his collection, and referring to a sticker on the wall of the booth, phoned for a taxi.

When the taxi arrived the captain directed it in his sibilant French to the Quai des Belges, which was a short distance away in the old port. Strolling curiously and without haste along the quai, the stockily built Oriental seaman made his way through clusters of Moroccan and African street merchants hawking ankle bracelets, chains of beads, ebony woodcarvings and intricately worked elephant tusks, past wagons selling ice cream, clusters of balloon and peanut vendors, and a woman who thrust her blind and crippled baby at passers-by with mindless disinterest. Ignoring them all the captain pushed his way through to the Chateau d'If tourist boat.

There were two docks. The dock on the left was filled with a line of passengers who were waiting to board but the Japanese ignored this departure and strolled aimlessly around the pier until a second ship came in and tied up at the right-hand dock. He waited until the boat on the right was almost completely filled with tourists; then he took a seat at the very edge of the stern. This section of the boat, away from the awning that covered the forward part of the craft, was usually avoided by seasoned passengers. It got all the spray on the trip across the choppy Bay of Marseilles to the medieval island prison where the fictional Count of Monte Cristo had lived out his incarceration.

The captain gazed happily at the scene around him as the ship pulled out of the sunny harbour past the rows of pleasure yachts and fishing ships, past the gates of the castle of Saint Nicholas and under the brow of Napoleon the Third's castle of the Pharo, which the Emperor built but never lived in. If the Japanese knew anybody on the ship, it was not apparent. He seemed unaware that the handsome young man in the black turtle-neck and the Skye tweed jacket had taken a place next to him, carrying a blue flight bag.

The boat splashed out on the choppy fifteen minute ride across the bay to the rocky island where a group of people waited like stranded refugees to be taken off again. As the sightseers crowded to get off the boat, nobody paid any attention or indeed even saw the captain or the elegant young man since they were behind the rest of the crowd. Calmly the young man got up and mixed with the crowd, leaving behind the flight bag on the seat next to the captain. As he stepped ashore, he paused, lit a cigarette and checked to see whether anybody had noticed his actions, but all were busy mounting the narrow stairs to the ancient cylindrical stone tower above them.

Casually, the captain picked up the flight bag and joined the eager crowd, pausing from time to time to take souvenir photos of the ancient castle. The flight bag fitted in with the camera and the rest of his holiday equipment, as though it had been his from the start.

CHAPTER NINE

In New York the police don't bust many heroin purification labs. That's because most of the heroin arrives there already purified. Purified heroin is a lot more compact and therefore more easily smuggled into the country than raw opium or the heroin which arrives from the Orient (now called 'brown sugar' because of its colour and texture). There is nothing that can compete in purity with the genuine Marseilles product. The most famous 'chemist' that ever converted a key of heroin was

Joe Cesare, a Corsican, but the lot the Bureau des Stupefiants had the tip on couldn't be Cesare's because Cesare, arrested and convicted a year before, had hung himself in La Baumette Prison after a few months. They used to call him Monsieur Jo, and he was a rich man. However, he never had much chance to spend his money. Since 1964 he had been in jail and had only been out less than nine months when he was caught, out at Aubagne in his laboratory, La Suzanne. Monsieur Jo learned his technique from Louis Albertini, who was the founder of the French school of 'chemists' but in a short time Cesare knew more than his master. Before his first bust back in '64, 'Monsieur Jo', with two or three assistants, was said to have been able to convert more than 17 kilos of morphine base into an equal quantity of heroin every day. Street price in New York today – probably about eight million dollars. Cesare was the biggest producer that ever existed, but like many chemists, by the time he hung himself (just short of his sixtieth birthday) his body was eroded by years of inhaling acid. He had ulcers, indigestion and all the other ills of his trade.

It doesn't take a graduate industrial chemist to purify heroin, Miletto told Doyle as he briefed him prior to setting up the raid on the lab in Aubagne that Manfredi had told them about. Basically the chemistry of it is simple. But it still requires seventeen different steps and those seventeen steps take a whole day. The work, furthermore, is dangerous. That's why the chemist gets from $500 to $1500 for every kilo that he purifies.

Probably the most dangerous part of the process is the first one, in which the morphine base, fresh from Turkey, is dissolved in acetone and then heated gently, *very* gently, in a water bath. This usually means a flask is immersed in a big tin pail and the water is heated, because if the acetone ever gets above 212 degrees, the boiling point of water, there is usually one hell of an explosion. After the heating process, a vacuum pump is used to suck off the acetone fumes. Here the problem for the secret lab is that the vacuum pumps wheeze loudly and they have to be muffled. That's usually done with styrofoam. Then the base is filtered and treated with carbon black to whiten it. After that, it's neutralized with hydrochloric acid.

Next it's baked into sludge. Then it's dried in tin bakery pans, usually in an ordinary closet, with electric or butane heaters under it. It comes out in dry pieces that break into pebble-like chunks. These are crushed in a Moulinex blender, dried and sifted and then the whole process is repeated until a satisfactory degree of purity is reached.

Jo Cesare was said to have achieved more than 95% purity. In the trade, if anybody asked about the quality of a batch of H, they'd say it's 'Cesare pure' if they wanted to indicate it was top stuff. Most chemists today are lucky to get 60 to 70% purity. All this work takes a long time. Cesare had produced as much as 17 kilos a day, but for the others generally it's considered that twelve kilos would be a maximum for a day's work. Most chemists would be happy to produce four or five. This means that when a big load is being prepared, it takes weeks and weeks to get it all together, in order to achieve a shipment of, say, a hundred kilos.

Doyle absorbed most of this information in the car on the way out to Aubagne. Already, a number of police vehicles, most of them unmarked, had moved discreetly into the village.

Diron was already on the scene, directing the dispersal of the police vehicles. Miletto was at the wheel of the Citroen. Barthelmy was issuing commands in staccato bursts via the two-way radio, maintaining a constant check on the fleet of vehicles blocking all escape routes.

Doyle could sense a surge of almost sexual excitement, charging up from his groin as the car approached Rue Galice.

Aubagne was a small working-class suburb on a hill about fifteen miles east of Marseilles. Rue Galice was in an isolated once-elegant neighbourhood. A few gracious old houses, and the remnants of some country estates, still not cut up by real estate speculators, survived amongst a cluster of houses – almost shacks – often referred to as 'Bidonville', because of the number of 'bidons' or tin cans used to piece out the siding of the workmen's hovels. It was not essentially a neighbourhood involved with high-level crime, but it was like all ghettoes, an area without enormous affection for the minions of the law. Already curious eyes noted the unusual assemblage of motor vehicles around the old Chapelle estate, where it was rumoured that old 'Fan Fan La Tulipe' Chapelle would summon neighbourhood girls to his 'bridal' cottage in order to exercise the *'droit de seigneur'*. Rumour locally was that old Chapelle had never bedded the same woman more than once (he had only one son who had died in Indo-China) and that he insisted that each companion be a virgin.

In any event the estate had always remained a mysterious area, set back in an open field apart from the workers' shacks.

Its patrician main house and three outbuildings (including the notorious 'bridal cottage') were surrounded by a high stone wall, topped by the shards of broken glass so frequently employed to insure privacy.

It was probably its isolation from the rest of the village that made the estate so attractive for the processing of morphine base into heroin. It is almost impossible to operate a lab near any concentration of houses because the distinctive smells from the acetone, hydrochloric acid and other chemicals used in the process would soon cause complaints, and ultimately, investigation by police.

The fact that the Chapelle estate was the only site in the neighbourhood that seemed feasible for location of a heroin lab, made it fairly simple for Barthelmy's investigators, who had checked out the neighbourhood the day before, to pinpoint the scene of the criminal activity.

Certainly, to the casual eye, there was nothing sinister about the old place – apart from the jagged glass-topped wall, which local people said had been installed only in the past year.

Children played among the fruit trees in the shaded front yard. A gardener regularly raked the gravel into neat patterns like a Zen garden, according to the bread and wine delivery men interviewed by Barthelmy's informants.

Across the field from the Chapelle place was a tired sagging old hotel, ironically named Le Beau Rivage, which in the more glorious days had served largely to accommodate the swank overflow of the Chapelle house-parties.

Barthelmy left a plainclothesman with the worried looking concièrge-proprietor, who now operated the place largely as a low-priced house of assignation, renting beds by the hour. The inspector was taking no chances that a warning phone call would alert the heroin chemists. With Miletto and Doyle he climbed six steep flights of stairs to the roof, from which, with the help of binoculars, Barthelmy was able to make out the façade of the main building over the top of the wooden gate. Doyle was impressed that neither Barthelmy nor the older Miletto was even breathing hard after the long steep climb, which had left the New York detective at least a little winded. Barthelmy had a stocky well-rounded form which gave a deceptive impression of obesity, but under his striped business suit his body seemed to be as solid as a medicine ball. Miletto, though he was obviously not far from retirement, seemed on the other hand, frail, but like a lot of thin men, he had enormous endurance and a whip-like strength.

'The local people,' Barthelmy explained, examining the house through his glasses, 'think it is only a suburban retreat for some rich man from Paris. They know nothing of his work. There are children around – that removes suspicion. But here – do you see on the side of the wall there where it's dug out a bit – there's a meter?'

Doyle took the glasses. 'Yeah. I see it.'

'You can see there's all new plaster around it. It's obvious that they took the meter from inside the house and put it outside so that the meter reader wouldn't have to go inside. They've probably by-passed the actual electric connection anyway, and are feeding current directly off the mains because they know that we watch for a sudden rise in current usage, but the water is harder to check. We probably wouldn't have caught it without the tip from Manfredi. Those are two of the main ways we catch them – the water, the electricity. Sometimes it's the smell.'

'But usually it's a stoolpigeon,' Doyle said. 'Right?'

Barthelmy smiled. 'Usually. Yes.'

With his binoculars, Barthelmy scanned the edges of the walls, the area on three sides of the little estate that he could see. Every exit road was blocked with some sort of disguised car – a fruit delivery truck, a moving van, some small three-wheel delivery wagons for cleaning and drying. Methodically, he checked out each station with the two-way radio, then signalled to the other two men to go downstairs and launch the raid.

As they emerged from the hotel and climbed back into the Citroen Barthelmy gave the signal to Diron who was waiting at the gate in a cesspool-pumping truck. At the signal, Diron nudged the driver, who instantly threw the truck into gear, and crashed it right through the wooden doors, splintering them flat, as agents of the Police Judiciaire threw heavy blankets over the glass-topped walls and swarmed over them on all sides.

The children who had been playing under the trees looked startled and ran for cover towards the house. Barthelmy again gave his warning to Doyle. 'You do nothing, Popeye, you understand? Say nothing. Just stay close to me and observe. Do I make myself clear?'

'Do anything?' Doyle said. 'Me? I'm naked, remember? You must think I'm some kind of a hero. Forget it. I'm just gonna watch and see how you pros do it.'

As they walked towards the house, Miletto picked up the bullhorn and shouted through it. '*Haut les mains!* Everybody come out – it's the police. You're surrounded.'

As he spoke, two of the agents of the Bureau of Stupefiants kicked through the wooden door and rushed inside. There was a sound of scrambling, running feet. Heads appeared at the windows and disappeared quickly. There was the splintering noise of smashing doors as the agents broke in from the rear and the side of the house.

Minutes later some of the agents reappeared, one of them leading a stout, violently protesting housewife in an apron, her arms still covered with flour from her baking. Suddenly there was a groaning rumble and the sound of an explosion from the garage attached to the side of the building. Green smoke belched from the roof in great gusts. A twelve-year-old girl who had been sitting near the tree beyond the garage was blown over by the blast. She fell to the ground, then picked herself up and ran screaming, her hands held over her face. Barthelmy, Doyle and Miletto started towards the source of the

43

explosion, but the smoke soon enveloped them.

'Jesus,' Doyle said. 'They broke their acid!'

The people already in custody were shrieking in panic and now crowds were forming in the road outside, attracted by the smoke and the noise. Barthelmy signalled for his team to rush the garage. He and Doyle stuffed handkerchiefs over their faces and tried to penetrate the room. The green smoke was everywhere, almost impenetrable. Hanging over the counter, the top of his hair singed into a black, prune-like mass, was one of the chemists. The second was on his hands and knees on the floor, blood rushing in a violent red stream from his throat.

Turning from the lab, Doyle caught sight of the twelve-year-old girl. One side of her face had been peeled away by the heat of the blast and corrosive hot acid. Beyond her, enveloped in a cloud, he caught sight of another dark figure moving swiftly towards a small iron door in the wall. Street instinct over-rode caution, and Doyle started after him, forgetting that he had been ordered only to observe.

Barthelmy, coughing from the gas, tried to call Doyle back. The iron door in the wall appeared unguarded and the dark figure, after fumbling at the latch, managed to swing it open and quickly slip through. Doyle, ignoring the cries behind him, plunged ahead at full speed. Outside, there was no one at the iron gate and the man started running across the field towards the narrow street leading into the workers' quarter, with Doyle puffing fifty yards behind. Because he knew he would be working with the police that day, he had left the .38 behind, afraid that it might be spotted and cause him embarrassment. The ankle holster, since he ran at full speed was no use. The distance would be too great to risk a shot by the time he got the Browning out and aimed it. The man was pulling away from him as he approached the cluster of tin-roofed workmen's shacks and Doyle was hardly aware that Miletto and Diron were chasing across the field about a hundred yards behind. As the man reached the narrow street leading into the quarter, his way was temporarily blocked by the crowds beginning to surge out of all of the doors in the narrow passage, attracted by the noise and commotion.

The man dodged anxiously through the crowd, but Doyle closed fast, and the mob, already alerted by the distant hee-haw of sirens as police cars closed in from all sides, grudgingly gave way. Just as the running figure was about to turn the corner into the ancient marketplace, Doyle caught him against the old stone wall with a waist-high running tackle.

The man began to yell and scream violently in French. Doyle tried to get him in an armlock and reached vainly for the cuffs that he wasn't carrying. Finally he managed to get his quarry under control. He hoisted the screaming fugitive to his feet, almost breaking the man's arm which he had pressed up behind him, nearly to his neck. Doyle slammed his captive against the wall, rattling his teeth with the impact. 'You just stand there, you sonofabitch. We'll get the cuffs on you any minute.'

Risking a look back at the opening of the street, he could see Miletto and Diron bearing down hard. 'Hurry up, you bastards. I've got him here!'

But at that moment, as he turned back, the dark-faced stranger suddenly bent his head and butted it full into Doyle's face, almost ripping his nose from its roots. Suddenly Doyle's eyes went blurry with tears, his nose emitting a drenching stream of arterial blood and his hands opened in reflex as the dark figure butted him again, this time in the stomach, stamped on his instep with excruciating force and darted fast for the market place.

He heard, rather than saw Diron and Miletto come puffing up, wheezing heavily from the exertion. 'He went around the corner! You can still get him. I think I gave him a couple of good ones and he's probably punchy.'

Miletto and Diron lumbered after Doyle's assailant in the direction Popeye had indicated. Doyle stopped to dab at his nose and eyes with the red bandana he pulled from his pocket. 'Sonofabitch,' he thought, 'I never figured on getting hit in the face by somebody's *head*. These foreigners have weird ways of fighting.'

It took about ten seconds, not much longer, for him to clear his vision and get the bulk of the blood away from his nose.

Then he dashed after Diron and Miletto into the market place. The two men had the swarthy figure against the wall as Doyle ran up. 'That's the bastard – arrest him! I want him collared, do you hear?'

But what he saw was not an arrest. Rather he saw what looked like Diron slipping a wad of franc notes into the swarthy man's hand. There was a brief conversation and Doyle started towards the little group, only to feel his arm tugged by Barthelmy, who came up behind.

From the windows above the market several sets of eyes were watching the action as the swarthy man pocketed the money, turned and ran deeper into the workers' quarter.

'What are you guys up to?' Doyle said. 'You're paying the spook off for beating my balls in and nearly busting my head?'

Barthelmy pulled him around to the corner, out of the view of the market. 'He's *ours*, you idiot. How do you think he got out of there?'

Doyle looked at him with shock. 'Oh Christ! I'm sorry. I didn't realize . . .'

But before he finished the sentence there was a high-pitched urgent scream, followed by a gurgle. Barthelmy raced around the corner into the market and saw Miletto and Diron racing for the small street that led further into the quarter. A circle of men clustered around a huddled figure on the ground. Parting the crowd, the police pushed through to the centre of the action.

Miletto, who was the first one to get there, spit on the ground and said, '*Merde!*'

The swarthy man was on his knees, holding his throat, but unable to keep the blood from seeping through his fingers from the cut that ran across his neck from ear to ear. Every pocket in his mismatched jacket and worn blue pants had been turned inside-out and the police money was obviously gone.

Barthelmy turned furiously to Doyle. 'Why don't you go back to New York and kill cops, since that's what you do best? You just ruined an agent that took us two months to infiltrate and it's all wasted through your insanity. *Merde!*'

Miletto and Diron raced further down into the quarter. But

it was hopeless. The killers would long since be gone.

Barthelmy knelt by the body, but the informant was now beyond any comfort. He signalled to a uniformed agent to dispose of the body and strode off angrily towards Rue Galice. Doyle, still dabbing at his nose which was now clotting painfully, trotted after the inspector.

'Listen, Henry, you didn't put me in the picture,' Doyle protested. 'If you'd put me in the picture, the guy'd still be alive. If you told me about the operation, right? Right?'

Barthelmy continued angrily towards the Citroen parked near the courtyard where the suspects were now being assembled. He didn't even give Doyle a backward glance.

CHAPTER TEN

In the courtyard, the occupants of the heroin-processing plant were lined up. One body lay covered with a rubber sheet on a stretcher. The second chemist had already been taken off in the ambulance, along with the little girl whose face had been ruined in the explosion. Left behind were the little bourgeois family which had served as a front, supplying their children to give an air of innocence to the operation; two more chemists and several other men who apparently acted as guards at the lab.

Miletto, who had been questioning the men, turned towards Barthelmy and Doyle as they approached. 'The explosion ruined everything. It was an accident. The acid burst and they had not yet processed any amount of heroin, although we had found quite a bit of morphine base here. But nothing like the whole load – maybe twenty kilos.'

Doyle and Barthelmy went in to look at the remains of the lab which was just beginning to clear itself of smoke. 'Looks like they were just setting it up, Henry,' Doyle said. 'Nothing in it yet. Look at all that acid they spilled. There must have been enough there for a hundred keys – maybe more. You screwed up. You busted in too soon.'

Barthelmy whirled on him angrily. 'I have a job for you,

47

Doyle. You want to know about the case? You want to find out what's happening? Why *don't* you talk to the suspects?'

'Who, me? What, in sign language? You know I don't speak any fucking French.'

'We'll give you Miletto for an interpreter.'

'Shove it,' Doyle said.

'No, my friend,' Barthelmy answered. '*You* shove it. You don't help us, Doyle. You fuck up. What do you know about Marseilles? You think this is Harlem where you can go kicking niggers around in the street?'

Now it was Doyle's turn to get angry again. 'Listen, you sleazy bastard. You know damn well you kick them around in the slammer instead, just like every other cop.'

Barthelmy turned away, obviously fighting to control his temper. He turned back, seemingly icy calm again. 'You want to help, Doyle? Get depositions from each one of them. I don't give a damn what they say, but I want it in writing. Miletto will help you.'

'Listen,' Doyle said, 'I came to nail that frog Charnier son-ofabitch and it's not part of my plan to sit around beating my meat while you French narcs get the credit. That's what you want, right? You stick me in office next to the shithouse so you can pull down medals for the job when I find him.'

Barthelmy looked at him coldly. 'That's right. You give me any trouble, Popeye, and I'll call Paris. In five minutes we can have you deported.'

He turned and strode off towards the Citroen, leaving the detectives and Doyle in the courtyard.

Although the patient grey-haired assistant inspector seemed to try his best to keep Doyle in the picture, the questioning frequently went too fast for the New York detective to follow, and he realized that it was not always simple for Miletto to stop for explanations.

The only thing that emerged clearly was that this was a sizeable operation. From a capacity of the lab set-up and the large supplies of acetone and acid it seemed likely that a large shipment had been planned, a shipment even big enough to

48

interest Frog One. But there was no chance of making a definite link. Even if these chemists were connected to Charnier's operation, it was doubtful that they knew him personally. In all probability his contacts would have been through an intermediary. If he were down on South Street Doyle would have had informants who could have pointed the way. He could have threatened to toss these crumbs in the Bastille and throw away the key. But here he was gripped with a feeling of frustrating impotence. At the end of the third hour he gave up and accepted a ride from Diron, the younger of Barthelmy's two assistants in his Renault 16.

When he got back to the hotel, Doyle was bone tired, both from the work and from the emotional strain of the day. His nose was swollen and bruised, and his teeth felt as though they had been separately tapped loose with a mallet. He picked up a *bagnat* down at the sandwich stand, had them wrap it up to take out.

Crossing the street, he went into the *Bon Coin*, a small bar on the square where workmen were having their daily *pastis*. He stood around until someone ordered a beer, then pointed to it, and after some frantic semaphoring, he was able to convey the idea that he wanted a bottle of beer to take out, six of them, in fact. The bar could not supply any paper bags so he distributed the six bottles around in his jacket and trouser pockets. Clutching the sandwich in the bag, he returned to the Hotel de l'Univers, planning to spend the night going over his notes, reviewing the material he brought from New York and getting quietly pissed.

Downstairs he picked up a copy of the local paper to see if he could make any sense out of it at all, even though the fucking thing was all in French. On the front page was a picture of Barthelmy with the remains of the lab, and another of him talking to the two suspects. The headline said 'GROS DROGUE LABORATOIRE TROUVE A AUBAGNE!' Underneath was a smaller headline that said 'Deux Maître-Chimistes Arrêtès, Etudients de "Professeur" Cesari.'

Doyle could figure out the word 'drogue' was 'drug' and he

49

certainly could make out Barthelmy's name, but the rest of it didn't make too much sense. 'Laboratoire' — that had to be 'laboratory'.

The story was continued on an inside page, but Doyle could make even less sense out of the main text. He banged his palm against his already bruised head in frustration. Most of the rest of the paper seemed to be devoted to want ads, football news and pictures, horse racing, television and movies.

As he opened the third beer, staring morosely at the incomprehensible garble of letters on the pages of *Le Provencale,* he heard a knock on one of the doors out in the hall, and the voice of Coco, who apparently was delivering a message or a packet. All of a sudden a lightbulb flashed over his head, just as they did in the comic strips. He rushed to the door in time to catch Coco standing before the brass elevator cage.

'Hey, Coco!' he said, 'can you come in a minute? I want to talk to you.'

The little redhead's face lit up in a bright smile. 'You want see me?' she said. 'You want see Coco?'

'That's right. Come on in,' he said.

Grinning mischievously, she tapped her way across the tiled floor on her old-fashioned stiletto heels. Inside, Doyle closed and locked the door.

'I'm sorry about all this mess,' he said. 'I just decided to eat in and I didn't have a chance to clean up.'

Smiling, Coco sat on the edge of his bed. 'You have an accident, yes?' she said, pointing to his still bruised nose.

'Yeah, it was nothing,' Doyle said. 'Listen, you speak English, right?'

'A leetle,' she said.

'So maybe you could help me. I could even give you a few bucks. I need some help in . . . well, like readin' the papers and things like that.'

'You want Coco help you?' she said, moving her little rump over on the bed.

'Yeah, well, I'm not sure you're getting the right idea,' but eyeing the two pleasantly pouting mounds of flesh now and the lovely pink swelling where the low-cut blouse cut into the skin, Doyle thought maybe his ideas would change.

'Your nose,' Coco said with concern, 'he is terrible! I fix.'

She led him by the hand to the washbasin and then filled it with lukewarm water. Taking the little towel hanging on the side of the basin, she dabbed carefully at the end of his nose which was still filled with blood and at the cut on the bridge of his nose. Even the gentle action of the warm soap and water was painful.

'Take it easy!' Doyle said. 'That really hurts.'

But he was conscious of her warm breasts pressing against him as she worked seriously and carefully. The large brown eyes were close to his, and he thought he detected an amused glint beneath their glassy surface. As she continued to work on his face, he casually put his hands around her waist, which had a very nice, developed curve from the edge of the hip, inward.

Coco's only reaction was to move her pelvis a little closer to his. Methodically he took the towel out of her hand, dried his face, still holding to her hip with one of his hands, then bent his head and carefully lowered his lips to hers. There was no sign of resistance, but Doyle winced at the contact.

'Shit!' he said. 'The inside of my mouth is all cut up. That really hurts!'

'Coco hurt you?' the girl said with concern.

'Listen, skip that. Let's go in the other room and talk a little. You want a beer?'

Coco smiled shyly. 'I like a Jack Daniel like you have in your drawer.'

Doyle looked up angrily. 'You been goin' through my drawers?'

Coco shrugged. 'I fix rooms, no? I see the bottle, the drawer is open.'

Here Doyle thought, 'Bullshit – she's probably been through everything. But I suppose there's not much she could understand.'

'Okay, okay,' he said, taking a tumbler from the bathroom. He poured her three fingers of the valuable stuff. It was hard to get over here, and expensive, but what the hell, it would

51

probably be worth it, the way things were working out.

With a grin of childish delight, Coco took the half-filled tumbler in both hands and buried her nose in the glass.

'It smell funny, no?' she said.

'Are you kidding?' Doyle said. 'That stuff is like Channel Number 5. It's beautiful. You ought to put a little behind your ears.'

'No,' Coco said, giggling, 'I put it inside my stomach.'

At this, she belted back about an ounce of the Daniels. Doyle opened up another beer and sat down on the bed beside her.

'Take another slug,' he said.

'I cannot drink so fast,' Coco said, wrinkling her nose.

'Okay, just take a small slug and put down the glass.'

'Okay,' she said, tilting her head back like a bird as she swallowed another finger of Daniels.

'Okay,' Doyle said, 'now lay down and let's talk. Maybe my mouth's out of commission, but the rest of me works pretty good.'

Coco put the glass down and stood up.

'Wait a minute, where are you going?' he said. 'I mean, you don't have to get pissed off. I just figured, well, you know, there in the bathroom, it seemed like we could get together.'

'Coco she is not going anyplace, but I must take off the dress, no? Otherwise it get all . . .' She gestured hopelessly, unable to find the word, then began to unfasten the dress, which had a row of buttons running straight down the front to the bottom, like a shirt.

'Listen, I can give you a hand with that,' Doyle said.

Coco said, 'No, no, I do it myself.'

Doyle felt a very sudden and insistent warmth rising in his groin and his pulse began to accelerate in excitement. This was the best he felt since landing in France. He lay back against the headboard and watched as Coco carefully removed the dress and hung it over a chair. Underneath she was wearing a red lace bra and garter belt, but no pants. Her pubic hair spread in a soft jungle and its colour almost matched that of the scarlet stocking-supporter. Doyle hadn't seen anything like that since pantyhose came into style, and there was something about it he really liked.

Coco started to unfasten the bra, but Doyle held up his hand.

'No, just hold it that way for a minute. Get into bed here. I'll help you with the rest.'

Coco shrugged.

'Turn out the lights,' he said.

'Why?' said Coco. 'You no like to see me?'

Doyle smiled and took another slug of the beer.

'You know, maybe you're right. I never did it with the lights before, but I'd like to see you, all right. And leave that funny thing on that's holdin' up your stockings.'

'Okay, Popeye,' the girl said.

She tiptoed in her stocking feet to the edge of the bed, sat down beside Doyle, took the beer bottle out of his hand, and kissed him very tenderly on his bruised mouth.

'It not hurt now, *cherie*,' she said.

'No, honey, that don't hurt one bit and I bet you can do a lot more with that beautiful mouth.'

'You like Coco mouth?' she said brightly.

'Honey, I love it,' Doyle said.

'You just be comfortable, cherie,' the girl said, smiling. 'Coco make you happy.'

Doyle lay back on the pillow and closed his eyes. He felt the butterfly touch of her warm lips on his neck and throat and her fingers gently working at the buttons of his shirt. There was nothing about this he could fight, but, in back of his mind he wondered how she ever found out that his nickname was Popeye.

CHAPTER ELEVEN

Afterwards, Coco led him to the sink where she moistened the washcloth again, still stained from his nosebleed, and scrubbed his sexual parts vigorously. Then she filled the bidet beside the basin and cleaned herself thoroughly in the little porcelain bowl.

53

'Well,' Doyle thought, 'that's one way they're cleaner than we are, these French.'

Later they sat up in the bed, sipping the Jack Daniels and smoking.

'You have the cigarettes *americaines*. Very good. Cost much money in Marseilles,' she said, inhaling deeply and blowing two langorous streams of Yankee smoke from her nostrils. 'In Marseilles, ten francs *le pacquet*. You *comprenez*?'

Doyle did a quick calculation. Christ, at those prices he would go broke smoking three packs a day the way he did.

'Wait, I show you,' Coco said, leaping nimbly from the bed.

She ran to her dress hanging on the chair and from it took a pale blue pack of cigarettes. She jumped back beside him, her small rounded breasts bobbling agreeably.

'These French cigarettes – Gauloises,' she said. 'Not so good. Very strong. Only two francs. You like?'

Like Paul Henreid, she put two of the loosely-packed French cigarettes in her mouth. Doyle could see that the tobacco was much darker and coarser than the Yankee product. After lighting them both, Coco ceremonially presented him with one.

'My present for you,' she said, smiling coquettishly.

Doyle took a deep drag of the Gauloise and instantly broke into a retching cough. The tobacco was sharp, burning and strong and had a powerful, strange smell, almost like marijuana.

'For crissakes, these could kill you!' Doyle said. 'Ain't you got a surgeon general in this country?'

Coco looked disappointed. 'You no like?'

'No, no,' Doyle said, 'it's great, great.'

He coughed again into his hand and spit up some blood. At first he thought it was the tobacco, but then he realized that his mouth was still sore from the beating it had taken and also from the mouthful of glass he had taken aboard in Manfredi's.

'Your teeth bad?' Coco said with concern.

'You said it, baby. Yours would be, too, if they'd been through what mine had,' Doyle said.

He decided to save the question about how she knew about his nickname for later. Meanwhile, whatever her motives, she could probably give him some help.

He pulled the paper from under the bed and asked her to read the story about the bust in Aubagne, but it was soon obvious that the whole thing was over her head. She read very haltingly and seemed puzzled by many of the words.

'I am sorry,' Coco said. 'I am not good at reading. I come from a small country town. Not learn much reading.'

Shit, Doyle thought, she's not going to be too much help. However, he had her go through the paper page by page and explain what she could. A little column in the corner of an inside page caught his attention. It was headed '*MOUVEMENT DU PORT*'.

'What's that?' he said.

'That is the boats, how they come and go.'

'No kidding,' Doyle said, 'let me look at it.'

The column was divided into four sections. One was headed '*Arrivées*', *the other* '*Départs*', another '*Attendus aujourd'hui*' and the other '*Enpartante Aujourd'hui*'. Coco said that '*Arrivées* (obviously) meant boats which had arrived, '*Départs*', boats which had left, '*Attendus Aujourd'hui*' meant boats that were expected to arrive that day, '*Enpartante Aujourd'hui*' were boats that were expected to leave that day.

The names of the boats were in capitals and were not hard to decipher and he could see that the names of the town of origin of the boats and the hours during which they could take on mail were listed after. The lists for departing boats gave the hours of departure. Of course, it was all on a twenty-four hour clock; but Doyle had learned that years ago in the army. In fact, having had the column explained to him, he could now almost understand it without help. Of course, it meant nothing to him that the fourth ship down on the left under '*Enpartante Aujourd'hui*' was the Kyoko Maru.

On the same page with the story of the drug bust, which included a head shot of Joseph Marro, who was apparently the boss of the lab operation, was a story that seemed to interest Coco. She read it painfully slowly, her fingers following each word, clucking with pity, as she deciphered word after word.

'What's that story?' Doyle asked.

'It is a boy I used to know, a young boy, twenty-four years

55

old. It says here he died here with much pain because he took the drug . . . Like this.'

She made the familiar gesture of the plunger in the arm.

'Too much, he took. He dies very bad. Very much pain.'

'Heroin? An overdose of heroin?'

She shook her head and referred back to the paper.

'No, not heroin, palfium. It say here he break into drug store. He take the palfium, but she is too strong. He not know how strong. He kill himself. It is an accident, no?'

So they got junkies here too, Doyle thought. You wouldn't know it, to talk to Barthelmy and his friends. According to them, it was only an American problem.

'This guy a real buddy of yours, an *amigo*?' Doyle asked.

Coco shrugged. 'I know him. He come sometime to the bar downstairs. Not a good friend. I just know him sometimes.'

That could mean a lot of things, Doyle thought. He also thought that Coco knew a lot of people.

CHAPTER TWELVE

In a field near Calas, about ten miles northwest of Marseilles, toward Aix-en-Provence a shotgun blast reverberated through the flat, rolling fields. A low-flying pheasant plummeted out of the sky and hit the ground with a thud. The man with the shotgun had a deeply tanned face and a white, grizzled beard. He took the gun from his shoulder with an attitude of pleasure, as the two field dogs dashed towards the fallen bird. He was wearing a Scottish tweed shooting jacket with suede leather shoulder and elbow patches, smart brown shooting breeches and the sort of half canvas, half leather shooting boots favoured by the French. His American companion, William Ball, was dressed casually in weekend country clothes and a pair of trousers that looked convincingly like officers' pink twills. He was tall, trim, and had a light tan with the slight yellowish undercast that comes from long exposure to tropical anti-malarial drugs. The chin was classic, the mouth strong and straight. Sterling character shone from every pore. The eyes were bright, steely blue and direct.

Behind them a Landrover was parked and in front of it a tall, slim, graceful brunette was arranging a picnic on a folding table, with the help of two African servants, their faces ornamented by striped tribal scars. With the checked table cloth, the small bowl of freshly-picked wild flowers, the vintage wine reclining in its basket, the red napkins and glistening silver set for three and the graceful wine glasses at the head of each setting, the table would not have looked out of place at an elegant country inn.

Ball turned to his bearded friend as he took the bird from the field dog's gentle mouth.

'Listen, we've got to talk.'

The bearded man grinned, ruffling the elegant feathers of the dead bird.

'Ah, Bill, relax. You are too American. There is no rush. We are here for the day. Enjoy the shooting. It's already two days past the end of the season, and . . .'

'Listen, Alain, I haven't got that kind of time.'

The bearded man handed the bird to an African bearer, who added it to the kill bag lying two yards away.

'I will not be hurried, Bill,' the bearded man said. 'If that's the ultimate purpose of your visit . . . Do you know how long it takes to prepare a two hundred kilo order? It takes time, even with a double shift of chemists, we could not turn it out in less than two weeks, and we must be careful. If we try to operate day and night, it attracts too much attention. That extends the time.'

'Well, your suppliers are awful goddam slow,' the American said.

'Yes, they're slow,' the bearded Frenchman answered, 'but they are good, they are the best. That's why we've been successful and have not been caught.'

'Our money is also the best,' Ball said. 'It took a long time to find all that American money, clean, small bills. It took patience too. It wasn't that simple, and I've got to get that money back into the PX account in Thailand in less than a month.'

The bearded man's smile disappeared.

'Then you can pull out. I won't hold you to the deal. Money is not a problem when you have a product like ours. There are always people waiting.'

Ball let the challenge go, scanned the horizon where the beaters were trying to flush a few more birds.

'Alain, you know how nervous my people can become. They're all big men. They're risking a lot. They know about the business. They read everything. They read that a laboratory in Marseilles has been raided, a man killed. Then they don't hear from you. It makes them nervous. That's understandable. They don't like delay. They've got a whole chain of delivery with people waiting and every change of schedule means complications. Complications can lead to trouble.'

The bearded man shrugged.

'Neither they, nor I, nor you have any choice in the matter. Delay is part of the business. We have no mass production methods to produce our product. That's why it's the best in the world.'

'You want me to tell them that?'

Charnier paused. He took a yellow handkerchief from his breast pocket and rubbed a thumbprint from the chased gold-plated receiver of the shotgun.

'Just tell them all will be well. Tell them the first half of the shipment of morphine base arrived from Turkey the other day. The rest of the base will be here in a few weeks. Processing will take another few weeks. That's all I have to say, all right?'

He flashed a brilliant smile to erase the tension of the previous moments. It had its effect on Ball.

'All right, I suppose,' he said. 'But let us know what's happening, Alain, from now on. It's the secrecy that breeds distrust.'

The bearded man smiled again.

'If we have no secrets, mon General, we have no business. *Voilà!*'

As he finished the sentence, a bird rose swiftly, flapping in a flat trajectory from the field of grain. The African handed him the loaded shotgun. He started to swing the barrel in a trajectory after the flight of the swooping bird, then dropped it as the slim brunette, Denise, approached them. She too was dressed in tweeds and brown canvas. It was a mannish outfit, but on her, it only emphasized the extreme femininity of her movements. Still she carried her shotgun at a correct angle and handled it like a man.

Charnier slipped his arm around her and whispered something in her ear. She smiled and nodded and squeezed his manicured hand gently in hers.

A brace of pheasant rose again from the field where the beaters had been advancing through the deep grass. The bearded man, playing the role of gentleman, held his fire as Denise and Ball each let go both barrels.

The bearded man applauded.

'Excellent, both of you. You make me feel humble.'

Denise turned to Ball and said, '*Magnifique*, Bill. Your timing was superb.'

Ball shrugged. 'I'm not used to the gun. It's just a Winchester that I borrowed from one of the guys in Bangkok. But that piece of yours – I'd give my share of the deal for it.'

The bearded man patted his gun proudly. It was a Holland & Holland under and over, with a magnificent chased receiver. On it were the initials HRH Maharajah of Jodhpore.

'I wouldn't want to put a price on it,' he said, 'but it might well be worth your share.'

He handed the gun over for Ball's inspection and turned to look with an intimate smile at Denise. His glance went to the Landrover which had a curtained back partition. The girl smiled back, handed her gun to the bearer, and left them for the vehicle. Ball and the bearded man handed their guns to the bearers who reloaded them.

The bearded man turned to the American.

'We have to decide the matter of the rendezvous, where we meet after you have arranged the delivery.'

'New York?' the American said.

The bearded man smiled, and then chuckled.

'William, you must know better than that. New York is

hazardous to your health, and certainly to *mine*.'

The American grinned.

'Of course. I love it, you know. It's a very amusing city.'

'How did you get out,' the American asked, 'if that's not a secret?'

The bearded man shrugged. 'Actually it was simple, even droll. Eighty-three policemen wanted to talk to me. Fifty-two of them chose to talk to my money instead. I love a city where you always know where you stand.'

'And the sixty kilos,' Ball said, 'it disappeared right out of police headquarters. Three quarters of a million dollars worth. Did you . . . ?'

The bearded man shook his head ruefully.

'I'm afraid not. It seems that there are eight New York detectives who made themselves very rich. If they thought I was coming back to New York, they would not be amused. Nobody wants competition.'

He chuckled. Ball nodded his head appreciatively.

'Of course,' the bearded man said with some bitterness, 'they were not all that co-operative. There are men so stupid that they can't distinguish from duty and self-interest. There is at least one of them who almost ruined the entire thing. I think you know who that is.'

Ball nodded.

'Yes, I think I know. You know, I haven't lost all contact with the other side. I get my information, and it's not an important thing, it's a nothing, but that same stupid American *flic* still has an idea he can interfere. Still it's nothing for you to worry about.'

'I guess not,' Ball said. Then, after a pause, 'Incidentally, Alain, when did you stop using the name Charnier?'

The bearded man smiled. 'You mean when did I start?'

Denise was waving from the area of the table that the meal was almost ready. The two men walked towards her.

'Let's see what my lovely Denise has prepared for us,' Charnier said.

He signalled to the African aides to relax, and with a gracious gesture indicated to Ball to join him near the Landrover for the meal. Spread over the table was a superb cold collation of *paté de compagne*, small pickled onions, fresh green salad, a little rack from which a selection of sausages was hanging. On a tray beside the table was a selection of at least ten cheeses. A big basket of fresh bread, brought only an hour before by one of the bearers, was in the centre of the table, and sweet butter. Resting in the shadow of the Landrover to avoid heat were several bottles of red wine.

Charnier gaily kissed the girl's reddish auburn hair.

'Denise, you've surpassed even your own talents. *Bravo!*'

And he held the chair for her to slip in as the American joined the French couple for their noon meal.

On a hill nearby, the Africans squatted around a cut-out kerosene can and cooked their meal of lamb and rice.

A troubled frown passed Ball's smooth, tanned face as he rolled the freshly poured wine over his palate.

'The wine is nice – from your cellar?'

Charnier smiled.

'No, no. It's just a Gicondas. It's a nice Côtes du Rhône not far from here. But for an afternoon collation like this, it's perfectly adequate.'

Ball hardly heard what he said.

'About that American cop. You said he still might make trouble?'

Charnier waved his hand deprecatingly.

'Don't even think about it. It's being taken care of.'

CHAPTER THIRTEEN

Doyle sat at the battered mahogany desk shoved against the wall of the office washroom. His fingers drummed impatiently on its gouged and battered top. Miletto was next to him, standing, sometimes pacing, as they interrogated the figure opposite them huddled against the wall in a stiff wooden chair. The man was a Corsican and spoke in a rapid, strongly-accented patois that would have been impossible for Doyle to understand even if he had known French. As it was, the question and answer volley between Miletto and the suspect was gibberish with pantomime. Doyle leaned back in his creaking swivel chair and put his feet up on the desk. The ankle holster could clearly be seen, but Doyle was beyond caring. Let them take it, let them send him back, let them do what they wanted. The endless strain of merely going through the motions of daily life, ordering a meal, making a phone call, taking a ride in a taxi, finding his way through the streets – they were all jobs now, more like puzzles than the automatic processes of life to which he had become accustomed.

The desk in front of him held a large plastic café ashtray lettered with the words 'Pastis 51°'. It was full of mashed and shredded cigarette butts, mainly Gauloises. Economics had forced Doyle to rely on the French cigarettes, and he was even coming to like their harsh, honest taste. Crumpled sheets from the note pad, doodled sketches, notes and dozens of inept drawings of a bearded face littered the desk and surrounding floor.

Idly Doyle opened the yellow police file in front of him and stared uncomprehendingly at the columns of typewritten figures. A few words he had come to know. 'Stupefiants' he now knew meant drugs. They called the French narcs something like 'stews' – at least that's what it sounded like to Doyle but that must have been short for 'stupefiants'.

The guy they were questioning was named Gordoni. Miletto had told Doyle that he was part of the mob of Albert Bistoni. Bistoni, in turn, was a close associate of Jean-Baptiste Croce, a Corsican and a captain in the Francisci-Venturi syndicate, who were widely regarded as the biggest dealers in Marseilles. For some years Gordoni had been making a living by peddling information to the Bureau de Stupefiants, much of it reconcocted. He was suspected of having set up several phoney drug labs in order to cash in on the bounty offered by the American DEA. Now his information had become even more unreliable, and the suspicion was either he'd been scared into keeping his mouth shut or he really knew something this time. Miletto came over to the desk to extinguish his cigarette in the cluttered tray.

'This type – Gordoni – he has three arrests for burglary, one conviction. No record of drugs.'

'Let's see his arms,' Doyle said.

Miletto told the man to pull up the sleeves of his tattered cardigan. Up and down the battered arm were the telltale purple lines, needle tracks.

'I knew he was dirty,' Doyle said. 'Ask him how he'd like to spend the next three nights here.'

Miletto rattled off the question in French. Gordoni rolled his head wildly in negation.

'Then ask him,' Doyle said, 'if he knows Charnier.'

'Look, he's got a beard like this.'

He grabbed a pencil and sketched another bearded face on the yellow pad. He knew it was meaningless. It looked nothing like Charnier except for the beard, and beards certainly come and go, but it was all he had to go on.

Miletto rattled the question off in fluent Corsican patois. Gordoni stared at the picture and shook his head hopelessly.

Doyle gripped the edge of the desk in impatience. His impulse was to give the little rat a backhand that would loosen up the teeth in his mouth, but it wasn't his stationhouse. Besides he really didn't think that the stoolie knew anything. He turned wearily to Miletto.

'Lock him up,' he said. 'We'll get back to him.'

'But there's no law against addiction,' Miletto started to protest.

Doyle flashed in anger.

'Make one up! Suspicion, consorting, conspiracy, impersonating a human being – any fucking thing. You guys know how to do that. They can't get bail for four days, right, under your system?'

'Right,' Miletto said.

'Okay, throw him in the slammer. Who's next?'

Miletto led the Corsican out towards the corridor where a uniformed policeman would take him across the hall to the lock-up.

Miletto turned Gordoni over to two younger cops standing smoking in the hallway and turned back to Doyle.

'Let's take five and open the windows, for crissake.'

He rubbed his hand in a tired gesture over the hardening scab on the bridge of his nose.

'You know this is fucking useless, don't you? What have they got us down here for?'

Miletto didn't answer. Instead he said, 'You want a sandwich?'

'Yeah, okay,' Doyle said. 'Listen, I'm going nuts from those goddamn *bagnats*. Would you try to get me a hamburger – onion, rare, with mayo and ketchup and mustard.'

'Mayo?' Miletto said.

'May-uh-naze. You know, the white stuff they put on sandwiches. They got Hellman's here?'

Doyle knew Miletto hadn't the slightest idea of what he was talking about, but he had to get some of this out of his system.

'Listen, I don't want Miracle Whip, you understand? Only Hellman's if they got it. And tell him to really *schmier* it on.'

Miletto shrugged and wrote on his pad *'un hamburger garni'*.

Alone for the moment in the cluttered space designated as his office, Doyle walked to the window and stared out into the streets of the panier. Above it rose the lights in the hills surrounding the city. The magnitude of the raid at Aubagne indicated that a big deal was going down. It had to be a Charnier deal; it was too big for anybody else. Charnier was the man behind the Francesci-Venturi syndicate. Feds he knew in the States had complained to him that in the past they'd got close to the syndicate leaders, only to have the thing killed by politicians in Paris. Hyde had also hinted at a fix from the top. It was the same in all the countries – nobody cared if you nailed the bottom guys, but the top guys were surrounded by a fortress of influence. He was determined, however, that this time Charnier would not slip through his fingers. But this endless questioning of low-level stoolies was a waste of time. He wondered why Barthelmy had assigned him to the job. To keep him busy? To drive him out of his mind? Stoolies on that level wouldn't have heard of Charnier, even if that was his real name. They would never lay an eye on the guy.

They had to get through to somebody on a higher level than these two-bit operators.

Restlessly, he paced into the long hall where the night duty cops were lounging and gossiping. Down the corridor, through the anteroom, he peered into the open door of Barthelmy's office. The Inspector Divisionaire was slumped over his desk reading files in deep concentration. Doyle stared at him wordlessly, until the inspector, sensing Doyle's presence, looked up. Neither man said anything, but there were big questions in Doyle's eyes. Something smelled very bad about this set-up they had him in, but he knew he wouldn't get the answer by just asking.

Wordlessly, Barthelmy returned to his papers and Doyle turned away sourly. As he left, Barthelmy looked up, smiling grimly. Returning to his office area, Doyle slumped at his desk, rubbing his eyes. He felt as though they had been rolled individually over the cobblestones of the rue de Panier. He knew he had to think, not about Gordoni or any of those other idiot suspects, but about how to get out of this rat-trap and into the real job of chasing Charnier. He wondered if these cops just hated him, or were they covering up for Charnier? If they were part of the deal, how could he ever nail the big man? He wondered if the DEA men would co-operate if he really had a fix on the guy. Or would they be blocked by politics too? His mind was barely ticking over. He knew he needed time and rest to get his head together for some kind of new approach.

Miletto returned briskly with the sandwiches which he placed on the desk and signalled to the two young cops to bring Gordoni back from the lock-up. This time they decided to leave the cuffs on the slight Corsican.

Doyle, frustrated, shoved Miletto aside and grabbed the man by his collar, shoving his head back against the wall. The Corsican's eyes rolled wildly from side to side seeking escape as Doyle hissed angrily in his ear, 'Listen, you motherfucker. I'm goin' to take you in an alleyway, see? I'm gonna start with your throat, see, and I'm gonna bust everything in it. Then I'm gonna hit your belly. I'm gonna hit you so fuckin' hard in the belly that your back will break. Then I'm gonna put your arms over the curb, see, and I'm gonna use them for a trampoline. Then I'm gonna get your legs. I'm gonna make oatmeal out of your kneecaps. By then you'll put me right in Charnier's lap.'

Miletto's voice interrupted the concert.

'Eat the food, Popeye, before it gets cold.'

The flat voice broke the tension and Doyle let the little informant slump back in the chair, his face grey with fear.

Miletto had placed the tray of food on the desk and Doyle examined it curiously. A charred and sinister slab of meat curled on a short section of French bread. Doyle flipped it disgustedly with his finger.

'Did they have to cremate the goddamned thing? They got the mayo and the mustard on it, but no ketchup.'

Disgusted, he wrapped both hands around the thick French version of a hamburger and gnawed his way aimlessly into it. The bread, at any rate, tasted good. Miletto had ordered the same thing, and bit into his with curiosity, obviously believing that he was sampling an American delicacy.

Doyle tasted the sour bile that was climbing up his throat, leaving in his mouth a strange metallic taste. He was coming close to some kind of a breaking point. Angrily, he threw the half-eaten hamburger at Gordoni and followed it across the room. He grabbed the informer by the front of his soiled shirt.

'You rotten little fink! You ever pick your feet in Poughkeepsie?'

The Corsican leaned away as far as he could from Doyle's unexpected, impetuous assault.

Miletto echoed the question, 'Poughkeepsie?'

'Ah, fongu,' Doyle said, 'that's it! I'm gettin' out of this goddam sewer.'

He grabbed his jacket off the chair and started angrily towards the exit. Miletto called after him in a worried tone.

'Doyle! The orders . . .'

Doyle made an obscene gesture with his fist moving back and forth rapidly across the front of his fly.

'You know what you can do with your orders – right here . . .'

Miletto signalled for the young cops to take Gordoni away again and trotted after Doyle who was striding angrily towards the door.

Barthelmy, still reading, caught a quick glimpse at the angry American, dropped his papers and picked up a phone.

As Doyle strode through the massive nineteenth century stone portals of the Hotel de la Police, Miletto came to the door behind him and nodded to two plainclothesmen who were lounging near the steps. One was tall, young, innocent, wide-eyed and wore a sweatshirt with a picture of the Chateau d'If on it. The other was an old pro, dressed in a rumpled, unnoticeable suit and battered felt hat, a man you could never remember once you'd seen him.

As Doyle strode rapidly down the rue de Panier away from the Hotel de la Police, the two peeled off inconspicuously down the street and followed him in the shadows. Miletto stayed long enough to watch the departure, turned back and stopped at the door of Barthelmy's office. He nodded once to his chief, a sorrowful expression on his face, and Barthelmy nodded back, once, with satisfaction. Miletto shrugged and returned to put the office area into a semblance of order.

Doyle, striding angrily up the street, took a right towards the Canebiére. Already from his rides around the city with the cops he knew that all the action was over near the tall columned neoclassical opera and in the winding shadowed streets around it. In his heart he knew it was hopeless. Charnier was not likely to be seen in these seedy bars, yet he felt a tremendous urge to get his own ear to the ground, unfiltered by Miletto's hesitant translations. He wanted to throw his eye over the faces, use his street savvy, to follow his battered nose to see if it could lead somewhere.

In New York that had worked, but New York was his own playground and this was some kind of a weird, strange zoo. As Doyle pushed through the crowded streets of the Canebiére, across the little fountain square where the sign said that some frog had killed a Yugoslavian king or something, past the 'Scottish and American Bar' that he had checked out ten times without finding anybody who'd speak English, let alone a Scotsman or an American. Once into the narrow streets of the opera quarter he registered subconsciously the two shadowed figures slipping behind him and he knew they were cops.

For the moment he didn't give a rat's ass.

No more than five minutes after Doyle hit the street, Barthelmy was on the phone to New York.

'Hello lieutenant, how are you? . . . Yes, the weather here is very sunny . . . No I don't think Doyle is really enjoying it . . . Well, he's not getting anywhere in his investigation, as I warned you . . . Yes, your plan is going as you suggested. He is annoyed with us and beginning to walk around Marseilles by himself, just like, as you say, a sitting duck.'

The voice on the other end sputtered in explanation, but Barthelmy's expression remained sour and dissatisfied.

'Frankly, I do not like your plan, but I have orders from Paris to follow your instructions. If this Charnier, or whatever his name is, sees him here on the streets it could be very dangerous . . . I have two men on Doyle night and day but he is unpredictable. I can only repeat this is not my way to do it . . .'

Again came a chorus of explanations from the other side of the Atlantic. Barthelmy responded with his own plan.

'Me, I would tell Doyle at least that he is, how do you say it? bait . . . Well, he is your man, not mine, but I don't want to be responsible for . . . Yes, he is very evident. Very visible . . . merde! . . . On a été coupe! . . . Allo? . . . Yes operator we were cut off . . . What do you mean it is the French operator's fault? What? . . . Hello? Hello? Merde!'

The French inspector hung up, folded his hands in front of him, and sat there lost in unhappy thoughts.

CHAPTER FOURTEEN

Without throwing a glance over his shoulder at the two shadows, Doyle strode purposefully into the first bar he saw, a PMU Tabac where horseplayers huddled over their *pastis* marking up their racing forms with spit-moistened pencils. It was different, certainly, from Third Avenue, but Doyle felt a certain kinship in this place of the players.

Absently, he said to the bartender, 'Four Roses, water on the side.'

'*Comment?*' the bartender said with a puzzled expression.

Doyle, distracted, had forgotten for the moment that he was still in France. Now grinning weakly he inspected the bottles on the counter behind the barman.

'Shit, let's see – bourbon,' he tried pronouncing it in French, 'Boor-bone, you know, Jacques Daniel!'

The barman shrugged. Doyle craned his head past the white-jacketed shoulder and looked at the bottles again. There was nothing that looked like bourbon. But there was a bottle of Grant's Stand Fast on the shelf.

'Okay,' he said, 'el scotch-o.' He pointed to the triangular bottle.

The barman followed his pointing finger and smiled. 'Ah, whee-ski.'

Doyle smiled happily. 'That's right, pour it in there. Mucho, mucho. Plenty of ice.'

The barman finally understood Doyle's frantic pantomime and built a fairly respectable drink. Doyle grabbed it and threw a ten-franc note on the bar. The bartender rang it up.

'Say, where's my change?' Doyle said. 'Ten francs is worth two bucks. Change-o.' Doyle tapped his finger on his drink and pointed to the cash register.

The bartender shrugged, beckoned with his finger, and led him towards a chart on the wall printed with figures hardly larger than a phone book. At the top it said, 'Tarif des Consommations'. Doyle couldn't understand the heading but he got the idea it was a price list. The bartender ran a finger edged in mourning down the list to the word 'scotch' and ran it across the line to the figure 10 F. He shrugged.

'Wheeski *dix francs*.'

Doyle got the idea. He slouched into a chair behind a marble-topped cast-iron table next to the window overlooking the street. He sat there soaking up scotch and atmosphere. The drink was strong but short and it didn't last very long. Doyle reached into the side pocket where he fingered a mass of crumpled monopoly money and pulled out another ten franc note and threw it on the bar. 'Hit me again, pal', he said. 'More whee-ski, *otra vez*.'

The barman took the glass, filled it with ice, whisky, and soda from a siphon on the bar. In the mirror over the bar, Doyle spotted two girls coming in, one in a sweatshirt labeled 'Princeton University', the other in tight-fitting blue jeans and tall wedgies. Both had long, straight blonde hair. Doyle downed a half of the Grant's in two gulps and turned to the girls.

Approaching their table, he tipped his plastic fibre pork pie hat. 'Hi girls. Which one of you went to Princeton?'

The girls stared up at him blankly.

'How's about I buy you mademoiselles a drink, what do you say?'

The girl in the Princeton sweatshirt said, '*Je vous en prie, m'sieur. Laissez-nous tranquilles!*'

Doyle stood there, understanding the tone of the dismissal, but not willing to accept it. 'Listen, what the hell, come on. We can just have a jar together, right? A whee-ski.' He held up the glass and signalled by pointing to his chest and to the two girls.

But they understood perfectly. They didn't want to play. 'No, no. No English,' the Princeton girl said. '*Foutez-nous le camp, hein!*'

The girl in the jeans found a crumpled note in her blue bag which was made of matching denim and threw it into the saucer on the table as two young men on motor scooters pulled up outside in French versions of Hell's Angels jackets. One of them even had a crushed leatherette billed chauffeur's cap. He leaned his head in through the bar and held up a finger to the girls who smiled and left wordlessly.

Doyle looked hopelessly after them and muttered, 'Kiss my Irish ass.'

He threw down the drink and walked decisively from the bar, determined that if he found no clues to his quarry, he would at least find some action. Anyway he knew what drink to ask for, as long as his money held out. The two patient shadows, one a half block behind the other, detached themselves from the doorways in which they were leaning and ambled aimlessly after the New York cop. They seemed to be looking everywhere but at him.

Already with the two large scotches under his belt and away from the grey, dreary atmosphere of the Hotel de la Police with its oppressive feeling of being manipulated, Doyle began to feel better. Under his breath, he began humming to himself the only French song that he knew,

> *'The First Marines bought the beans*
> *Parlez-vous*
> *The Second Marines cooked the beans*
> *Parlez-vous*
> *The Third Marines ate the beans*
> *Shit all over the submarine*
> *Hinky, dinky, parlez-vous.'*

He laughed softly to himself and stopped as he passed a curtained window with the word 'Bar' over it. It looked more promising than the *Tabac* anyway, and he could see inside there were girls sitting at the bar that didn't look as though they'd be as fussy as the Princeton girl and the bluejean hippie.

Doyle went in, took a stool near a tall, slim girl who looked like she had more than a touch of the tarbrush in her (good-looking though). He threw a ten franc note on the bar and asked for a whisky. The bartender looked for a moment un-comprehendingly at the bill, and then pushed it back at Doyle.

'Not enough,' he said in English. 'Whisky twenty francs.'

He smiled coldly and pointed to a sign over the bar, 'Scotch whisky — 20 francs'. Doyle looked around. He could see a couple of blond guys with crew cuts who didn't look French, but then they didn't look American. It sounded like they were talking German, or maybe Dutch. They were crocked out of their minds. Each had his arms around two girls. On the table in front of them was a heap of crumpled bills and every once in a while one of the girls would take a bill and either wave it at the barman for another round of drinks or look questioningly at the sailor. The crew-cut man who looked like old Marshal Hindenburg would take the bill and stuff it into the top of the girl's dress which barely covered the nipples of her ample bosom.

The scene registered on Doyle. A sailor's clip joint. There were millions of them like that down on Sand Street, in Red Hook and a couple along West Street. More than anything, it reminded him of some of the joints in the West Forties and along Eighth Avenue in Manhattan. That accounted for the signs in English. They probably never got a Frenchman in this fucking place in a year. All sailors, merchantmen, people like that.

Now he looked around and saw another sign on the wall in English 'Ice Cold Beer 3f50'.

'Okay, never mind the whisky,' he said. 'I'll have a beer.'

No sense in pissing away money entirely. Besides, he didn't want to get stoned out of his mind; only a little happy.

The tall brown girl turned towards him with interest and said, 'You American? You buy me a drink?'

'Sure, sure,' Doyle said, 'have a drink. But no scotch, huh?'

'*Un menthe*,' the girl said to the bartender who took a teeny, thimble-sized glass and filled it with a thick green liquid.

'Let me see that,' Doyle said. He took the glass and sniffed it. It smelled of peppermint. He tasted it. It had alcohol in it all right.

'Jesus,' he said, 'how can you drink that stuff all night?' The girl shrugged indifferently.

'Twenty-five francs,' the bartender said.

Christ, Doyle thought, I would have been better off springing her to a scotch.

He turned to the girl. 'You speak English?'

72

'A leetle,' she said.

'How about you and me go out and do some swinging?'

'*Comment?*' the girl said blankly.

'I thought you said you spoke English. "You" (he put his finger against her tawny breast) "and me" (he pointed to himself) "outside" (he pointed to the door) "drink" (he held his thumb up with his fingers in the first and pantomimed drinking from a bottle), "maybe sleepee together" (he held his two hands together and put his head against them in a gesture of sleep).

The girl smiled bleakly. 'No, no. Me stay here. Drink.'

'Oh yeah,' Doyle said, disgustedly, 'well not with me, baby, not at these prices.' The dumb broad, he thought, she don't even make an effort to entertain me. Otherwise maybe I'd stick around and buy her a few. She just doesn't look interested.

He looked again at the face. The girl had thick, soft African lips and a thin nose that flared at the nostrils. The hair was dark and frizzy. The skin was caramel-coloured with cream undertones and certainly looked good enough to eat.

'You from Africa?' Doyle said.

'Af-ri-ca?' she pointed to herself. 'Me Madagascar. Father Italian sailor.'

'Yeah, well that's really interesting,' Doyle said. 'Madagascar – that's Africa, isn't it?'

The girl had lost interest again. It was obvious she found conversation in English a chore, but maybe she'd just run out of vocabulary. Doyle figured if he sat around with her all night making a kind of conversation and blowing maybe a hundred, a hundred and fifty bucks, he might get her to go home with him, and God knows what *that* would cost extra. He was better off with the chambermaid in the Hotel de l'Univers. Disgusted, he scooped up his change and left without leaving a tip.

The cold beer (it had been a Beck's, a good German beer) had gone down nicely over his dry tonsils, but you couldn't get a buzz on with that sort of stuff. He decided that he'd tank up in the cheap bars on whisky at two dollars a shot and only drink beer in the B-girl joints.

Without looking back, he sensed that his mini police squad

was still behind him, lurking in the darkness down the street. He thought about asking them in for a drink but then figured, *Fuck 'em. Let 'em learn the business.* He remembered the aching hours in the freezing cold in some Manhattan doorway, endless hours of stakeouts that always seemed to take place on the coldest, dampest, darkest days of winter. Hours without a break for a cup of coffee, a drink or a sandwich. *Well, it was just tough shit for those frogs. Popeye Doyle, anyway, was going to have a good time that night.*

CHAPTER FIFTEEN

As he proceeded further into the Opera quarter, there seemed to be more and more bars with beckoning women sitting on their stools, but Doyle knew his money wouldn't last long if he kept drinking in those bust-out joints. He stopped at another corner *tabac* and decided to try the cloudy liquid *pastis* that all the rest were drinking. He pointed to a glass on the counter beside him and to himself. The bartender nodded wordlessly, poured the yellowish, clear-fluid into a tall glass and placed a water carafe marked 51° beside him. Doyle pushed a ten-franc bill at him and the bartender returned a saucer in which there was a large round five franc coin about the size of a half a dollar, two of the ones that were like a quarter, one franc each, and some small chickenfeed. The stuff sure cost a lot less than scotch.

It had a cool, pleasant, licorice-y taste. It seemed almost harmless at first, but Doyle could feel a warning flash of heat as it hit the stomach. The flavour reminded him a little of the anisette he would drink sometimes down in Mulberry Street with the dagos. He wondered if he could get used to the stuff and what kind of buzz you could get off it. It sure would save money.

He turned off the street flanking The Opera building on to Rue Molière. There he was pleased to see a joint called 'Le Speakeasy'. The door was locked and there was a little peephole in it just like there were in the old speakeasies or in the fag after-hours joints in New York. Doyle rang the bell and a pair of black, beady eyes regarded him from behind the small window. There was a grating sound of sliding metal and the door swung open.

Inside was a long bar with about ten girls in it, some guys in uniforms who looked like naval officers, some other guys with short haircuts who had to be krauts or Russians or something. They had white skin showing around the napes of their necks, where their hair had been cut recently, probably for the trip ashore. At least it looked a little more like the kind of place Charnier might hang out in. Doyle noticed nobody was drinking *pastis* in the place; almost everybody was drinking whisky, some were drinking champagne. He ordered another beer.

There was a girl about two yards down the bar wearing a tweed skirt below her knees with buttons up the front. They were open from the hem almost to the crotch. She wore a short yellow sweater with puffed sleeves that didn't quite reach her waistline, revealing a nicely-tanned strip of skin. Her hair was done in two careful rolls, like a pair of Danish pastries, one over each ear.

'*Tu prends un verre, cheri?*' she said.

'You want a drink, right?' Doyle said.

'Ah, you are American!' she said, as though it were a great discovery.

'Yeah,' Doyle said. 'You speak English?'

'A leetle,' the girl said.

Christ, more of that crap. So far every girl who said she could speak 'a leetle' had a vocabulary of about seven words.

'Okay, have a drink,' he said. 'But no champagne, huh?'

The girl gestured for a scotch. It cost twenty-four francs, almost five bucks. It was rotten not having an expense account.

'Listen, kind of nurse that one, will you, baby?' Doyle said.

The girl looked at him without comprehension.

'Ah, never mind.'

The German beer was good, strong and cold. Doyle drained a half a glass with his first sip, then decided he'd better coast a little if he was going to find anything out before he got stoned.

75

'Listen, can you come out with me?' he asked the girl. Maybe if he could get her out of there it wouldn't cost him so much.

'No, no, I must work here,' she said.

'I mean, I'm willing to pay you if you go out with me.'

'No, no,' she said, 'I must work here. I must sell drinks.'

'Oh, you get a cut on the drinks, right?'

She smiled. 'They give me half of what I sell. You'd like buy me another drink?'

Doyle looked with astonishment to see that she had already finished the scotch. He picked up the empty glass and smelled it. There had been scotch in the glass, all right. At least she wasn't drinking tea.

'Okay,' he said, 'I'll buy you another drink, but I'd like some help first. I'm looking for a friend of mine, a Frenchman. He said he'd meet me around here somewhere but I can't find the place. He's got a beard, a white beard.' He pantomimed hair around his face.

'*Une barbe?*' she asked.

'Yeah, right, a "barb". He's like about fifty years old, maybe sixty, about so high (he held his hand up just above the bridge of his scarred nose). Nice-looking guy, plenty of money. You ever see him? Here, I'll draw you a picture.'

He pulled a stub of pencil from his pocket and attempted another rough sketch on a bar napkin. The girl looked on it with interest.

'No,' she said. 'I do not know him.'

'I'll bet you don't,' Doyle said. Angrily, he drained the beer and strode from the club.

He passed a few bars on Rue Molière, looking for a place that had the right feel. He was expecting nothing; mainly he was just letting off steam, but he felt that he had to cover a lot of ground, that he couldn't spend too much time in any one place, at least for that night. He had to get the lay of the land.

The next bar, the Perroquet Bleu, had long, yellow drapes in the window. He had to duck his head to look through the narrow vee of the opening inside. It looked lively. Several couples were dancing. There was a big colourful jukebox in one corner

76

and several alcoves with divans and curtains, giving a certain amount of privacy.

Doyle opened the door and stood watching the scene for a while. There were maybe four or five guys there who looked like they might be Frenchmen. The rest were sailors also, or maybe tourists. The more he looked, the more he realized he was in the wrong quarter. This was not Charnier's stamping grounds. He might go to some joints that had broads in them, but they wouldn't be like this. But you could never tell. Some of those Mafia big shots in New York would hang around in the sleaziest dumps, where you'd least expect them.

He slouched into one of the divans and his head snapped back at the unexpected softness. The couch was at least six inches shorter than he expected it to be. A girl with frizzy, ginger-coloured hair and a tan pant suit came up and took his order. Doyle was tired of beer, and pastis and all that crap. Even the scotch didn't seem like a great idea.

'Listen, you got any bourbon, American bourbon? You got any Jack Daniels or anything like that?' Doyle said.

The girl smiled. 'Of course. You would like Old Forester or Jack Daniels?'

Civilization at last! Doyle sighed. 'I'll take a Daniels, on the rocks, plenty of ice, huh?'

The girl smiled and Doyle could see from the way she moved as she walked towards the bar that she was a butch from way back.

The girl put down the drink with a little saucer of pistachio nuts which Doyle cracked absently and munched on. Before he took his second satisfied sip of the Daniels, he found himself looking into a pair of silk-covered knees. His eyes continued up and he liked what he saw. The girl was wearing a tight-fitting knitted black jumper with a white blouse and puffy sleeves. Her hair fell in soft, chestnut folds to her shoulders and hung over one eye in a peek-a-boo style reminiscent of Veronica Lake's early movies.

'Okay?' she said, indicating the seat beside him.

'Oh-KAY!' Doyle said, patting the seat beside him. 'Make yourself comfortable. What's your name, baby?'

'Babette,' she said, 'what is yours?'

'Pop . . .' Doyle said and stopped himself. 'Bill. My name is Bill,' he said. 'Pleased to meet you, Babette.'

'You are English?'

'Nah. I'm American.'

'Good. I do not like the English,' the girl said. 'I like the Americans.'

'Yeah, I bet,' Doyle said.

This time he didn't wait for the girl to ask him for a drink. He signalled to the butch.

'What'll you have, baby?'

'Is champagne all right?' the girl said.

'How much is it?'

'I'll get a small bottle – only fifteen dollars.'

'*Only* fifteen dollars,' Doyle said. 'For chrissake, you think I'm a Yankee millionaire?'

'No, no.' The girl put her hand on his knee and the touch sent a tingle clear up to Doyle's navel. 'It is just something I like. If you want, I will have a mint.'

The thought of watching her drink another one of those green slimy concoctions nauseated Doyle. He reached into his hip pocket and took out the black wallet of traveller's cheques, ruffling through them. At the rate he was going, he'd have to find Charnier pretty soon, or he'd be flat on his ass. Still, there would be a salary cheque from the police department coming to him at the Consulate in a day or so. He had about a thousand in traveller's cheques, all fifties. He reached his hand into his other pocket and felt the diminished roll of French francs.

The girl's eyes carefully caught the blue flash of the traveller's cheques. 'It is all right,' she said. 'They will take traveller's cheques here.'

'Great,' he said and waved at the butch again. 'A bottle of champagne and two glasses.'

He pulled a felt-tipped pen from his pocket and signed the cheque. 'Here, take it out of that.'

The girl sat very close and Doyle could feel the warmth of her thigh against his. He reached his hand down casually and put it on her knee. The girl didn't seem upset. She acted as if

78

it wasn't there. What the hell, a guy had to get *something* for his money!

The butch arrived with the champagne in a Piper Heidsick bottle.

'Hey, I thought you were drinking a *small* bottle,' Doyle said.

'Well, the girl get mixed up when you gave her the cheque. That's all right, a big bottle is only twenty-five dollars. You save money that way.'

'Yes, I save money. At any rate I'm gonna be in one of those welfare hotels by tomorrow.'

The girl smiled brightly without comprehension. She took the dripping bottle from the bucket, and poured two foaming glasses of the champagne. Doyle had to admit it tasted good once you got used to it. She clicked her glass intimately against his.

'*Cin-cin,*' she said.

'Right,' Doyle said. 'Over the teeth and over the gums, look out stomach, here she comes!'

The girl laughed, flashing a beautiful set of choppers.

'That is your American toast?' she asked.

'Sure. I know a lot of them,' Doyle said. He took her by the chin and tried to kiss her but she turned her head away smiling. Then she looked back apologetically.

'We are not supposed to do that here,' she said.

'Yeah, but you can't leave here, right?'

She smiled enigmatically. 'Not until later.'

'What time do you close?'

She shrugged. 'Maybe two, three o'clock; maybe four.'

Oh great, Doyle thought. I'm supposed to keep slugging down this twenty-five dollar a bottle stuff for the next four hours. He drank silently, calculating. He'd been around enough to know the score. It probably worked the same in every country. You sop up the booze for three or four hours, get crocked out of your mind and the girl ducks out the back door and that's it.

Doyle took his felt-tipped pen from the pocket and tore a page from his notebook. This time he tried to draw something remotely recognizable.

79

'You ever see a guy like this?' he said. 'White beard, plenty of money, a Frenchman? He's a terrific pal of mine. I was hoping I could find him and we could go out doin' some drinking. I think he hangs around here a lot.' The girl looked at it with interest.

'Yes, I think maybe I know him. He comes in here sometimes.'

Doyle felt a sudden tightening in his chest.

'*You know him*? He's a big man, right? Like Father Christmas?'

'No, no,' Doyle said in disgust. 'He's only about this big.'

He held his hand up across the bridge of his nose.

'And he's kind of skinny.'

'Oh,' the girl said, disappointed. 'Then it is not him. It is important to you to find this man?'

'Listen, I'd give a couple hundred bucks if I could lay my hands on him, because we're such great pals.'

'There is another man – I think he looks like what you say. Will you tell me again how he is?'

'He's about this tall. He's got a kind of a good tan, like he's been out on a boat or something a lot. He's got a white beard all around his chin and he's got a white moustache, too. His eyes, I think they're brown. Weighs maybe a hundred and fifty pounds.'

'One hundred and fifty pounds? How much is that?'

'Oh yeah, kilograms. Well, he weighs like a little under seventy keys.'

'*Comment?*'

'Seventy kilograms, maybe, he weighs.'

The girl looked thoughtful.

'Perhaps I know him. You say he has plenty of money? He drinks in the expensive bars?' She touched his knee again gently.

'Wait, I telephone.'

Maybe it was the liquor, but Doyle didn't feel the excitement he should. He'd been on too many wild goose chases. But still the lead was better than no action at all. He sipped thoughtfully at the champagne and looked at the people around him.

The cashier, a tall girl with a mass of black curls and big luscious-looking red lips, was deep in conversation with the butch. It was obvious that they were girlfriends. Babette had disappeared through a pair of curtains leading back to the ladies' room. She was back in five minutes, smiling.

'I think maybe I have found him, but we must wait. We will finish the champagne first, no?'

'He's not gonna go away, is he?'

'No, no,' she smiled, 'I think I know where he is. He always eats in a Chinese restaurant called the Asia. It is over near the Canebiére. *Très élègante*. But he has not come in yet.'

'How do you know he's coming?'

She smiled tolerantly. 'I called the restaurant. I asked for him. But I do not tell him his friend is looking for him. That is right, is it not?'

'Yeah, right,' he said. 'Well, when is he coming?'

'Very soon,' she said, 'very soon. He has booked a table for eleven o'clock.'

'Isn't that kind of late,' Doyle asked, 'to be having dinner?'

The girl shrugged. 'Your friend has strange habits and the Chinese restaurants stay open very late.'

Idly, almost without looking, she rested her hand on his leg. She ran her fingers in dainty arpeggios up his thigh, close enough to the crotch that he could feel the heat of her hand.

'Then after we find your friend . . .'

'I thought you couldn't get out of here?'

She smiled and pulled his head close. He could feel the hot breath against his ear as she whispered.

'You will give Yvette, the blonde, twenty-five dollars. You have it from your cheque. She will be happy.'

'And what about you? You don't look like you'd go for nothing, baby,' Doyle said.

She winked mysteriously. 'We can talk about that later.'

It must have been the champagne getting to him. Normally Doyle wouldn't have let that go. He would have settled it first. But looking at the girl's deep grey eyes from so close, feeling the flutter of her perfumed breath against his ear and the little dance her fingers were doing on his thigh, he was not inclined to bargain. In fact, he almost forgot that he was supposed to be going to find Charnier.

'Well listen. First we've got to find my little old pal, right?'

'Right,' she said. 'By the way, what's his name?'

'Never mind his fucking name. We'll just find him. It probably isn't even the right guy you've got fingered over there.'

The girl shrugged. 'He is like the man you describe.'

Doyle took a handful of bills from his side pocket, threw twenty-five dollars worth of francs on the table with a couple of bills from the loose wad in his pants pocket, and folded up the rest into a neat package. He helped Babette to her feet out of the low divan and for a moment she lost her balance and tumbled lightly against him, her breast brushing against his arm. He was inclined to forget the bearded man entirely.

'I am sorry,' she said. '*Pardon.*'

'Yeah, baby, *pardon*,' he said.

As they left, he deliberately put the wad of franc notes into the top of the butch's blouse, but if he expected any reaction, he didn't get one. The girl simply smiled and said, '*Au revoir m'sieur.*'

CHAPTER SIXTEEN

Outside there was no action, except bars. All the shops and other stores had rolled down their steel shutters, and there were blocks with no lights at all, especially as they began to walk out of the Opera quarter.

'Listen, why don't we take a taxi?' Doyle said.

'No,' Babette said. 'It's not very far, and it's a nice night for walking.'

She put her arm through his and pressed her breast against it. At the corner of the Rue de Paradis Doyle stumbled against the kerb and apologized.

'I'd better tie my shoelace,' he said. As he knelt down he reached under his cuff and loosened the small pistol in its ankle holster. He wasn't at all sure what he was getting into and the liquor had blurred his judgment a little. But there were a lot of long streets up this way and now there were no lights at all, just empty closed buildings and dark doorways. Then, again, if the girl were right and it were Charnier, which he doubted, there might be some action. He figured he'd worry about that when he got there.

He couldn't see them now, but he was pretty sure that those two shadows were still back somewhere in the darkness behind him. He straightened up and offered his arm again and they walked pressed against one another up the Rue Pavillion, across the Cours Saint Louis and into the Rue du Musée. This was the area that, in the daytime, was a busy fruit and vegetable market. Doyle had passed through it the day before on his way to get a sandwich and he remembered the sausages and piles of fruit. But now it was dead as yesterday's news.

'How the hell far is this place?' Doyle said.

Babette patted his arm reassuringly. 'It's just another few streets. Just past the market place.'

They crossed the wide area fringed with the rotting remains of the day's commerce and went into another street even darker and narrower.

'It is just a little way up here,' she said, reassuringly.

Doyle, meanwhile, to be on the safe side, had pushed into the middle of the street which was now free of traffic.

'Why are you walking in the street?' Babette said.

'It's just something I learned in New York,' Doyle said.

At this point the street was narrower and darker than ever. Ahead, at the corner, silhouetted in the dim light was what might have been a man, leaning against the wall, or it might have been a roll of canvas or a pile of old garbage. Doyle slowed down to size up the figure, but before he could get a fix on it, there was a sound of quick footsteps from a doorway behind him. He turned in time to catch only the dim flicker of shiny steel and was aware of the sound of footsteps running, from the other end of the street.

Babette tried to hang onto his right arm but he sent her

flying against the steel shutter of the fruit and vegetable shop and almost in a single movement stooped to reach for the ankle holster.

His sudden drop took the advancing silhouetted figure by surprise and threw it off pace just enough for Doyle to come up under the arm and catch the man across the temple with the flat part of the automatic. He fell back cursing just as the second figure came running down the street and threw himself on Doyle's back. Doyle ducked again, this time throwing the man sideways and over his shoulder in a judo throw. The first man was already up and advancing on him with a knife and Doyle didn't waste any time in apologies. He raised the angle of the Browning ever so slightly and pulled the trigger. The bullet glanced off the upper part of the knife-carrier's forehead and sent a little patch of hair and blood flying through the air.

The second man, seeing the gun, scrambled to his feet and ran for the open area of the market place. Babette was nowhere to be seen. She had, no doubt, scuttled into one of the many doorways of the street. Doyle dropped to his knee and holding the tiny automatic in both hands took aim at the running mugger's back and squeezed the trigger. The man seemed to stumble, ran several steps more, and crashed into a boarded-over pushcart, slumping to the ground with a moan.

Then there was the sound of more running steps as the Old Pro and the Young Shadow arrived on the scene finally.

'I thought you guys were supposed to be looking after me,' Doye said. 'What the fuck kept you?'

The older man knelt by the fallen figure and examined the wound. It had passed into the upper shoulder, but the bullet velocity wasn't enough to make it emerge from the other side.

'He's not bad,' the older man said. 'René, you send for the ambulance. There will be a car parked at the Canebière that can radio in.'

He pulled the cuffs from under his seedy jacket and pinned the man's arms together behind him, giving him a fast but careful frisk. Then he pulled the man to his feet and pushed him across the wooden cart, smashing his head into the painted surface. It was a style Doyle could appreciate. From some-

84

where in the baggy folds of the shabby jacket the Old Pro had produced a Luger. He turned it now towards Doyle.

'May I have your pistol, please, sir?' he said.

The voice was cold, hard and businesslike.

CHAPTER SEVENTEEN

The Old Pro and the curlyheaded kid dropped Doyle off at the Hotel de l'Univers.

'I suggest you discuss this matter with Inspector Barthelmy tomorrow,' the Old Pro said. 'It is serious, you know.'

He took Doyle's hold-out gun from his side pocket. 'I will give this to him and he will decide about its disposition.'

His ankle felt naked without the extra protection of the holdout piece. He had the police .38 in a drawer up in the room, but there was a good likelihood that he would have to turn that over pretty soon, after what had happened. All the exhilaration of the drink had passed through his system, leaving him only with the incipient hangover he knew would face him in the morning.

For once the thought of some of the strong black French coffee appealed to him and as he passed the desk, he asked the bleary-eyed concierge if they would send some up.

He was already in his skivvies when Coco arrived with the coffee, rolls and sympathy.

'You have been in trouble again, no? Bad boy!' Coco said. She took his coat and pants from where he had thrown them on the chair and dusted them carefully with her hand, smoothed them out and hung them on a hanger. The Hawaiian sport shirt he had worn almost since his arrival was soiled at the collar and stained with dust from the scuffle on the street.

'I will wash this for you,' Coco said. 'And give me those, they are filthy too.'

She gestured toward his skivvies. With some embarrassment Doyle took them off and handed them to her. She threw them with his socks into the bidet and ran warm water to

85

cover them. She ducked outside for a moment and returned triumphantly with a box of soap flakes which she added to the mix in the bidet.

'Now you lie down. Coco make you happy,' she said.

Doyle climbed naked between the sheets holding the warm saucer and coffee to his chest and tried to eat the roll so the crumbs didn't fall in the bed. Coco busied herself in the bathroom, humming, scrubbing, rinsing and finally hanging the laundered garments over the tub. From the pocket of her apron she removed a small bottle of cologne, put a few drops on the washcloth, moistened it with warm water and came to the bedside to wipe Doyle's dusty and battered face.

'You look like somebody play *petanque* with your head,' she said soothingly.

Doyle pushed feebly at the rag. 'Hey, you want me to smell like a fag or something? What is that, perfume?'

Coco kissed his ear and whispered, 'Sshhh, be quiet, rest. You get into too much trouble, bad boy.'

Her hand made soothing circles on his chest – widening circles that gradually reached to his navel and below. Gradually Doyle felt as Coco had predicted, warm and comfortable. As he started to doze, Coco turned the light out and there was a rustling sound as she slipped out of her clothes and into the bed beside him.

In the morning she was gone, and the socks, underwear and shirt had been ironed and folded and placed on top of his bureau.

I wonder what she wants from me, Doyle thought. But whatever it is least she's better than that Babette bimbo. With *her* I got fucked *without* a kiss. He picked up the wall phone as he wiped the shaving cream from his face and had the concierge call Barthelmy at the Hotel de la Police.

'Good-morning, Popeye,' Barthelmy's voice said, and there was a crisp, official air to it. 'Can you come in to talk with me? As soon as possible, please.'

Doyle sighed with frustration. 'Yeah, I guess so.'

'Or better yet,' Barthelmy said, 'meet me in about an hour. Is that too soon?'

'No.'

'At the Samaritaine. You know where it is. It's on the Quai des Belges. On the Vieux-port.'

'Yeah, I know. Down by the boats, right?'

'Right,' Barthelmy said.

'What's the idea, Henry?'

'I think it's better that we talk informally . . . first.'

It was not unpleasant waiting on the terrace of the Samaritaine. The Arabs passed regularly through the crowd with their funny little homemade banjos or ukeleles or whatever they were, the carved ivory tusks, the long chains of beads, the carved statues of the girls with the big tits and the big asses, the ebony elephants and the rest. Behind the sound of the squealing of brakes and the honking of horns there was a constant pop, pop, pop machine-gun patter of the little drums with tympanic balls attached that the Africans constantly rotated to produce a sound like the one Doyle had heard so frequently in the score of television suspense dramas. From the streets ringing the forests of masts in the old port came the smells of the Mediterranean – tar, salt water, garlic, grilled fish (stale and fresh) and the faint effluvium of clogged drains.

Over on the far side of the quai, Doyle spotted a tall, striding figure in a grey tropical suit that looked vaguely familiar. The clothes had an American cut, and in a moment it clicked in Doyle's mind that it was the young DEA agent, the one with the beard. He wondered if it was an accident that he was there at that moment. In any event, he didn't turn his head. He just kept walking out towards Fort Saint Jean.

Barthelmy was a few minutes late, and Doyle ordered a *pastis* while he was waiting. The slightly perfumed taste of the licorice put a soothing, anaesthetic blanket on his tongue. At five after eleven, the black Citroen pulled up outside the cafe without sirens or lights. Miletto was behind the wheel, and he took off as soon as Barthelmy jumped out of the car.

'I'm sorry I'm late,' Barthelmy said, breathlessly. 'The traffic was incredible. I should have walked. It would have been faster.'

'Yeah, it's like that in New York, too,' Popeye said. 'Have a pistachio nut, Henry. They're good for the digestion. Got lots of Vitamin E, gives you plenty of *cojones*, you know?'

Barthelmy pulled a seat up the tiny marble-topped table and signalled to the waiter. He noticed Popeye's glass.

'I see you're taking up at least some of our customs, *hein*, Popeye? Perhaps you are growing to like Marseilles?'

Doyle grimaced. 'Fat chance.'

An African, his face carved almost as deeply as the statues he was carrying, approached them with an armful of souvenirs but when he saw Barthelmy he moved on without making a pitch.

They sat in silence, watching the scene before them until the waiter had brought the *pastis* and left.

'So,' Barthelmy sighed, 'again you're making trouble! You are some kind of cowboy from the far west, hein Popeye? But this is not the far west. What can we do with you now?'

'What do you mean?' Popeye said, 'what can you do? If those fucking guys mugged me they probably would have killed me. And that broad – aren't you going to nail her? You could find her easy enough in that bar.'

Barthelmy shrugged. 'Who would be the complaining witness. You? And how could you prove that she had tipped off those men? No, it's hopeless. You should keep your sexual adventures at home, at the Hotel de l'Univers.'

Popeye looked up curiously. 'What do you mean by that crack?'

Barthelmy shrugged again and gave a half smile. 'This is my city, Popeye. There is nothing that happens here that I don't know about. Not that I mind, as long as it's legal.'

He cracked a salted pistachio with his fingernail and flipped the little boat-shaped shell into the gutter. 'The first man got away in the darkness and, I don't think we're going to look for him too hard. The second man is not too badly hurt. We're holding him until we decide what we can do. Maybe if you had wanted sex, you should have asked me, or stayed at the hotel.'

Popeye exploded in anger. 'Look, you sonofabitch, I wasn't interested in sex. The broad said she knew where Charnier was.'

'And you believed her?'

'Look, at least I was *looking* for him. That's more than you guys are doing, sitting around with your thumbs up your ass.'

'I assure you, Popeye, that in New York you would not have fallen for the oldest game in the world. How on earth could she have known who the man was when all you have to go on is the fact that he's got a beard and he's French?'

Barthelmy's face softened. 'Popeye, you know you are wasting your time, don't you? Do you not understand that?' You are being set up . . .' Barthelmy started to say, then bit his lip.

Doyle looked up curiously. 'What do you mean?'

Barthelmy hesitated, taking a long drink of the *pastis*, as though to clarify his thoughts.

'Nothing. I meant only that your superiors would be glad to see you fail.'

'How do you know that? You don't even know them.'

Barthelmy smiled. 'I know police work. It's the same all over. Understand me, Popeye, I have no hatred for you. In some ways, I even admire you. I suggest very strongly that you go home. This trouble that you were in last night would be sufficient reason.'

'Trouble,' Popeye said, 'What do you mean trouble? Because those guys tried to mug me?'

'No, because you had a pistol and you shot it off and you wounded a citizen.'

Barthelmy turned to snap his fingers to the waiter to refill the *pastis*. As he did, a girl in a smart print dress cut just above the knees and a big straw sun hat came weaving through the tables toward them.

'Ah, Monique, *viens chèrie*!' Barthelmy said, beckoning to the girl. He got to his feet as she came to the table. Doyle reluctantly lumbered to a standing posture also.

'Popeye,' Barthelmy said, the essence of Old World graciousness, 'I present to you Mademoiselle Le Fevre.'

'*Monique, je te presente detective Doyle de New York.*'

The girl held out her hand and smiled radiantly. '*Enchanté*,' she said, as Barthelmy slid a chair under her.

Doyle looked at the girl appreciatively. 'Well, Henry, I was trying to figure out why Charnier likes this burg so much and

I guess I found out.' His eyes sized up the woman appreciatively.

'Ah, m'sieur Doyle,' Bathelmy said, smiling, 'you're beginning to acquire an Old World patina. In any event, before we digress into social chit-chat, I would like to remind you of what I said just before Monique came up.'

'Right. You want me to split for New York. While Charnier walks around like a goddamn playboy and you sit around having lunch with beautiful bimbos, I'm supposed to be chewing my nails out in some beat in Canarsie.'

Barthelmy favoured him with a bleak smile. The woman put her hand over his protectively.

'Can I get you a taxi to the airport, Doyle?' Barthelmy said.

'I think I'll stick around,' Doyle answered.

The French detective shrugged. 'As you wish. And now, if you will excuse us, we have a lunch rendezvous.'

He got to his feet, threw some bills on the table, and offered his arm to the girl. Doyle sat, steaming, with suppressed rage.

'I'm staying, Henry! And listen – those two tails of yours, you ought to dump them. They couldn't follow a red-headed midget riding a camel. Who's that tall, curly-haired guy? Your brother-in-law?'

Barthlemy's eyes went cold. 'Listen, Doyle,' he said.

But Doyle interrupted him. 'You listen to *me*, buster. 'I'm here to find that fucking Charnier and believe me I'm going to find his ass. I could do it a lot easier if you put Sacco and Venzetti over there back guarding school crossings or whatever they do.' Doyle gestured across the street where the two men were lounging without much effort at concealment. 'The way it's going, they're liable to get run over by a bicycle. If they'd have been on the job, I wouldn't have had all that jam-up last night at all. On the other hand, I suppose they could have got hurt if they'd come up too soon and I wouldn't want to have *that* on my conscience.'

Doyle added a bill to the pile on the table, disregarding the fact that Barthelmy had already picked up the tab, and walked off like a man hanging up a phone.

'*C'est une drôle de type,*' the girl said, gazing after Doyle as he strode off.

'*Oui,*' Barthelmy said, '*mais il peut lui arriver quelque chose de plus drôle que ça!*'

CHAPTER EIGHTEEN

Doyle walked back to the hotel, his angry stride serving to cool his resentment. He stopped at the sandwich stand to pick up a bagnat on his way back.

Discouraged, Doyle slumped into the room's one shabby armchair and poured himself a Daniels from the dwindling supply. One bottle was already gone, and he was halfway into the second. He was all but convinced that his mission was hopeless. The French cops were obviously out to tangle him up and give him a lot of bullshit work to do, anything except to help him find Charnier. The goddamn feds were protecting their own ass, probably afraid he might succeed. Trying to cope with the language every day was driving him around the bend and the chances of spotting Charnier in a city of a million and a half without having any contacts, ins or knowledge of the society were becoming increasingly difficult.

Doyle polished off the Daniels, stuffed the remains of the sandwich into his mouth, and wiped his fingers on the doily atop the bureau. Then he went to the small dressing table, opened the drawer, pulled out his folder, shook out the manila envelope that he had brought from New York and tried to assemble some clues. There were phone numbers; some of them might be Marseilles numbers, but what would be the use if he called? He wouldn't be able to identify the person at the other end anyway! There were the parimutuel tickets. There was nothing written on them. They were losing tickets. Doyle didn't know even why he kept them, except they were just something he found that connected to Charnier. There was a matchbook from Divonne les Bains. It had a picture of some kind of a hotel. Underneath, it said 'Ces bains ces charmes' and 'sa casino'. There was nothing else written on the matchbook cover, but it was obviously a French matchbook. There were a couple of New York phone numbers too, but he had not been able to tie them to anything significant back in New York.

One of the Manhattan numbers had a Canal six exchange, which would have put it somewhere down on Mulberry Street, not far from headquarters.

There were a few butts from Balkan Sobranie cigarettes. They would make great clues, if he actually had Charnier in his sights, but not much use now. The sonofabitch was probably smoking those fat imported cigarettes while Doyle was choking his way through another pack of Gauloises.

Hopelessly, he put the meagre clues back in the manila envelope and slid it into the drawer, not bothering to lock it. Slamming the drawer, he reached for the porkpie straw hat and the key to the room and left, not knowing entirely where he was going, but feeling that he had to walk and think. He thought about putting on the .38, since he felt strangely naked without the ankle holster, but it would have been too easy to spot under the sport shirt and the weather was hot for the jacket. Besides, he didn't anticipate any problems just walking around the city in broad daylight.

He strolled down the crowded streets of the Canebière, past the Mono Prix, the Place Charles de Gaulle toward the sea and then turned left on the Corniche John F. Kennedy.

Here the buildings were newer and cleaner and brighter and the atmosphere reminded him more of some beach town out on the island, except there was no beach, nothing but rocks and the mountains rising all around with the Chateau d'If on its rocky island in the background. He walked about a mile, thinking deeply and trying to find some way to make sense out of his position. There was an iron rail on his right and now there was a small sandy beach and an inlet. Doyle leaned over it, aimlessly lighting another Gauloise. Below were eight or ten people, men and women, in shorts and bikinis, laughing, shouting and running in a highly competitive game of mixed-sex volleyball. It was in a small pavilion of a restaurant called Calypso. Above the volleyball courts was a sign that said 'club privée', which Doyle took to mean private club.

The girls were well tanned, and generally speaking, well built, although one or two were on the chunky side. The bikinis were the briefest possible, and when the girls stretched for a particularly difficult shot there was never a white mark showing under the straps. Doyle watched the game idly. The last time he recalled having watched a volleyball game like that was in Washington Square Park, where he had been staked out to watch a bunch of junkies who used the game as a contact point. But it would have been hard to hide anything more than a nickel bag in the clothes that bunch was wearing. Even the men were wearing 'le minimum' – teeny trunks that barely covered their balls.

There was a shout and a giggle as one of the men caught the padded volleyball on the palm of his hand and sent it soaring over the iron fence into the street. Dutifully, Doyle trotted after it and returned to the fence. A girl with long, streaky blonde hair, her chest heaving attractively with exertion, held up her arms to him.

'Please, sir, the ball,' she said.

How the fuck did everybody know he was an American, Doyle wondered?

Doyle watched for another fifteen minutes or so and then, on some signal, the game seemed to break up. The players all returned to lockers lined up underneath the overhead walkway. Doyle strolled off down the road as far as the monument to the dead of World War II, overlooking the Islands of the Fereoles. It was a hot, bright day and the Mediterranean sparkled until the glare hurt his eyes and it was hard for him to believe that he was really at work. It seemed more as though he was in Miami Beach or some resort goofing off, and in fact he wasn't accomplishing much more than that.

Passing the Calypso again on his way back, he decided to go in and have a drink. Certainly it was more the sort of place that a Charnier would inhabit than the places he'd been in the night before. He was feeling hot and sweaty from the walk and his stomach still had uneasy rumbles of the drinking of the night before. About the only thing he thought he could hold on his stomach then was a big, tall, cold, spicy Bloody Mary.

The room was bright and had the salty marine-type decoration of a beach resort. Doyle approached the ample bar surmounted by a giant stuffed Maco shark and sat at the modernistic rattan bar stool.

'Give me a Bloody Mary,' he said. It seemed to Doyle that in a classy place like that the bartender should speak English, but he didn't. He simply stared blankly at Doyle.

'*Bloody Marie?*' he said.

Doyle looked desperately around him for help. A girl with a familiar swatch of sun-bleached blonde hair and the briefest of bareback sundresses was on the phone in the corner. Doyle gestured to the bartender to wait and when the girl hung up he went over to speak to her.

'Listen, honey, you speak English, right?' he said.

She looked at him with amused curiosity. 'That is right. Can I help you?'

'Yeah,' Doyle said, taking the girl by the arm. 'Come over here and explain to this guy what a Bloody Mary is. You know what it is, don't you?'

The girl laughed. 'Yes, I know what it is.'

She climbed up on the bar stool next to Doyle and explained to the curious bartender the construction of the exotic American drink.

'Tell him don't forget the hot sauce, will you,' Doyle said. 'Make it plenty spicy.'

'*N'oubliez pas le Tabasco,*' the girl said to the bartender.

'Listen,' Doyle said, 'how would you like to have one yourself?'

The girl smiled and shook her head. When she did, the bleached blonde hair swirled attractively around her face.

'No, but I will have a small vermouth-cassis.'

'Sure, whatever,' Doyle said.

'You from Marseilles?' he asked.

'No, Paris,' the girl said. 'But I'm working here now.'

'What kind of work do you do?'

She smiled deprecatingly. 'I work for Avis. You know, the car people?'

'Oh yeah, right. Avis. You talk pretty good English, you know that?'

'Well, I used to be a stewardess with Pan Am, so I've been in New York many times.'

'No kidding,' Doyle said, thrilled at last to meet someone who could connect to the life that now seemed so far away. 'You know Jilly's and Jimmy Ryan's? You know Jack Delaney's in the Village?'

The girl shook her head. 'Those are not the places I went to. Remember, I only had very little time to turn around. Mostly, we just went around the East Side, around First Avenue, Second Avenue, Maxwell's Plum – those places.'

'Right, the single-o joints,' Doyle said. 'Maybe I could have seen you there sometime. That would have been funny, right?'

'Right,' the girl said.

'Listen, what's your name?'

'Françoise,' the girl said, 'Françoise Charpentier.'

'No kidding?' Doyle said. 'There was a great frog fighter by that name, George Charpentier. You're not related to him, are you?'

The girl smiled. 'No, no. Charpentier is a very common name here. And what is your name?'

'My name is Doyle. They call me Popeye.'

'Oh,' the girl said, 'you are a sailor?'

'No, I'm sort of a government consultant,' Doyle said. 'Yeah, a government consultant. Public relations.'

He drained the Bloody Mary. It was a good one, spicy, the girl had given the bartender all the instructions correctly, the lemon, the worcestershire, the tabasco, the salt, the pepper. He pushed his glass forward for a refill.

'Listen,' he said, 'you busy? Maybe we could go around, do something, catch a movie or something. Have a couple of drinks, bounce around?'

The girl smiled. 'I'm afraid I have an appointment.'

'Well listen. Can I see you sometime?' Doyle said, almost in desperation.

'Well, you can always reach me at Avis, at the airport.'

'Okay, right, I'm gonna do that. You'll hear from me,' Doyle said, as the girl walked out.

Watching her pass through the glass doors, Doyle thought it was the trimmest ass he'd ever seen, and the legs were so evenly tanned that there wasn't even a white patch at the back of the knee. *That broad*, Doyle thought, *is all class*. And meeting her gave him one more reason to stay in Marseilles.

CHAPTER NINETEEN

Doyle spent the rest of the day wandering around the city, trying to get the feel of the place, trying to gain some independence of movement. He felt trapped by his inadequacy. Taking a taxi was still a problem; telephoning was impossible. Public transportation was out of the question, since he couldn't find his way to the right bus or even ask his way.

He walked out along the broad boulevard that reminded him of the upper reaches of the West Bronx and then found himself at a small arch, something like the one in Washington Square. He was at Porte d'Aix. Turning left from the arch, he found himself looking down a hill into a long, narrow street. It seemed to be crowded from wall to wall with human beings. He'd never seen so many people in one place in his life. It was the Rue des Chapeliers, sometimes called 'a corner of the Casbah' in Marseilles.

The faces were, without exception, dark, ranging from light brown to dark brown. The clothes were a weird assortment of cast-off suits, mismatched jackets, African jellabas, kaffiahs. Even in Spanish Harlem, Doyle had seen nothing to match this for crowds. The closest comparison he could make was New Year's Eve in Times Square.

Both sides of the street were lined with shops that hung their merchandise outside as if in a Levantine bazaar. Row on row of suitcases hung up to a height of ten or twelve feet above the street. Other stores displayed racks of leatherette and plastic jackets lined with mock sheepskin. Others had shoe displays stacked high above the street.

As Doyle pushed his way cautiously through the crowd, he found himself towering almost a head above the rest. He felt suddenly like a giant, but a naked giant, without the holdout pistol or the .38. Most of the people in the crowd pushed past him blankly, but from doorways he was aware of hostile eyes, a stranger in their 'paradise'. Almost subconsciously he reached into his pocket and clutched a ballpoint pen he used for taking notes and sketching beards. In his mind he had always felt it would be North Africans and Algerians that would be the core of the drug trade, but looking around he saw none of the pimp chic which he had come to associate with successful drug traders.

If anybody around here was in the drug business, they had to be damn poor at it because there was nobody who looked like he had two francs to rub together. One thing was certain – Charnier would never be found dead or alive on this street.

Doyle turned to push his way onto the boulevard again and felt a hand snaking into the pocket where he kept the note-books. His left hand lashed out and closed on the wrist of a slender seventeen-year-old dark-eyed, curly-haired kid. His face looked like the Christ in some of those old churches around Europe and he looked scared, but not scared enough.

Suddenly a shiny switchblade gleamed in his hand. Almost automatically, without a thought, Doyle's right hand lashed out with the ballpoint and plunged into the large black-lashed brown eye of the teenage pick-pocket. There was a scream of anguish as the boy dropped the knife and clutched his hand to the bleeding eye socket. Doyle didn't lose a step, but kept going. He knew what would happen if the kid had a chance to point him out.

The crowd quickly closed around the boy and Doyle was out of the narrow street and into the big square with the third century Roman arch before anyone had a chance to figure out what had happened. When he crossed over to the other side of the square, Doyle pulled the ballpoint pen out of the pocket again and saw that the tip was greasy with coagulating blood.

97

Disgustedly, he wiped it off with a ragged Kleenex still crumpled in the bottom of his pocket from New York.

Now Doyle was anxious to get back to the hotel to rest and to do some thinking, but he had no idea where he was or what direction he was walking in now. All of a sudden, he felt ripped by panic. There was no one there who could help him and he had no way of explaining where it was he wanted to go. He started on the route that he figured would lead him downhill towards the water, towards the sea. He knew that if he got down to the ocean he could find his way to the port and then back to the hotel.

Now he was on a street almost as crowded as the other, but here the faces, instead of being brown and beige, were black — a purply black, a blue black, a dead black colour that he never saw in Harlem. Many were carved and striped with scars, tattoos, cicatrizations.

The heads didn't move as he walked down the street, but the eyes followed him warily. Reflexively, Doyle reached again for his only weapon, the ballpoint pen. In general, the people of the quarter tended to remain immobile as he went past and none came close enough to cause trouble. But certainly if he felt a stranger in the Canebière or the Vieux-port, he felt like a man from Mars here, where hardly a white face showed to break up the threatening tribal pattern.

Now he found himself in an open square and on it there was a tall signboard with a map. There was a small circle on the map that said 'vous êtes ici', and Doyle could dope out that it meant that this is where he was. After some scrutiny, he was able to make out the crisscross pattern of the railroad tracks leading to Gare Saint Charles and from there could find the Place des Marseillaises where the hotel was. He had been walking in exactly the wrong direction.

He turned around, took an angle to bring him away from the narrow, crowded old streets and back on to the broad boulevard leading to the centre of the city. Now he could even see road signs pointing towards Centre-Ville. If he could find a goddamn taxi, he could probably even explain to the guy that he wanted to go to the Hotel de l'Univers on the Place des Marseillaises, but there were none around. Still, he couldn't be too far away because he had walked there in less than an hour. It took him only about a half hour to get back to the hotel.

Too late, he realized that he must have been shadowed the whole time of his walk. Obviously, they'd switched off plain-clothesmen. He wondered if he hadn't lost the tails when he passed through the crowded rue des Chapelliers.

Lighting Gauloise and putting the blue packet handy beside him, he poured a finger of Daniels into the bathroom tumbler and diluted it heavily with water. There were now only about four inches of the precious bourbon left in the one remaining bottle. But he didn't want to get crocked; he just wanted to think.

In a sense, he had learned a lot on the walk. He'd learned where *not* to look. There's no way that Charnier would be in those streets with black and brown people and there was no signs of the flashy kind of wealth that comes out of the drug trade, no night clubs, no broads, no fancy cars. If anybody down there was dealing, they were dealing retail – nickel bags. But where *would* Charnier be? Not in the cafes around the port, not in the shabby nightclubs and bars of Opéra; that wasn't his style. Aimlessly, Doyle fingered the cigarette butts, the matchbook, the pari-mutuel tickets. There *was* one thing that almost all of them did – suddenly the pari mutuel tickets and the word 'Casino' on the matchbook began to jell in his mind. They *gambled*, that's what they did! If he could find some of the really class gambling joints, that's where Charnier might put in an appearance or where somebody might have seen him or heard of him. But where the fuck were they? He picked up the matchbook again. He didn't know where Pivonne les Bains was, but it wasn't in Marseilles, or at least it didn't say so on the matchbook. The pari-mutuel tickets were from OTB in New York; that was no clue. And if the gambling joint was out of town how would he get to it? Sure as shit, Barthelmy would never give him a car, and he wasn't sure that old Henry wouldn't turn him off entirely if he felt he was get-ting close to the target. If only he had someone he could talk to, whom he could trust, who he could be certain wasn't involved in the deal in any way. Coco, the little bitch, was too stupid. Besides that, he wasn't too sure where her loyalties lay. He had a feeling that she had a direct connection to Barthelmy's office.

Blowing a cloud of acrid smoke from the Gauloises, Doyle leaned back in the rickety chair and stared into space, thinking. His eye lit on the pink and blue print of the nude French girl on the wall and suddenly he knew where he had to go for help. The broad from the volleyball court, the broad that worked at Avis. It was still early in the afternoon and at that moment she was probably working.

With a feeling of excitement, Doyle got up, shoved the cigarettes in his pocket, took his jacket from the back of the chair and reached into the right hand drawer of the bureau where he'd stashed the .38. It was empty! He looked under the pillow, under the mattress, in the suitcase – it was nowhere. Somebody could have ripped it off, of course. Maybe Coco, maybe the woman that did the heavy cleaning, but Doyle didn't think so. He thought this had something to do with Henry Barthelmy. Angrily, he went to the wall phone and had the concierge put a call through to Barthelmy's office.

After a lot of clicking, buzzing and gabbling in French, a voice finally got on in English. It was Miletto.

'Inspector Barthelmy is not in the office at the moment. Who's calling?'

'Listen, Miletto, this is me, Doyle, Popeye. You guys got any idea where my fucking gun is?'

'Just a minute,' Miletto said. There was a pause and Doyle was positive that he was conferring with Henry right there at the desk.

In a minute, Miletto got back on. 'Your gun is safe,' he said. 'It will be returned to you when the leave the country. Have you made plans yet?'

'You know fucking well I haven't,' Doyle said, and he slammed the receiver down so hard it nearly broke the flimsy hook.

CHAPTER TWENTY

It wasn't hard to get a taxi out to the airport, but it was expensive, sixty francs, practically the same as a taxi to Kennedy. The airport was shiny and modern and looked as though it had been built in the last couple of years. But it wasn't very big; all of the airlines had their offices in the one building. In the lower level where the baggage came in were several desks for car rentals and at the third desk, sure enough, in a cute red hat and uniform jacket Doyle caught the streaky yellow flash of Francoise's tumbling hair.

She greeted him with a businesslike smile, but no sign of recognition at first. Then the smile changed and broadened.

'Ah, it is the Yankee in the public relations business. Can I help you?'

'Yeah, you can rent me a car,' Doyle said, 'but you can also give me some advice. Where would a guy go around here if he wanted to do some high class gambling? You know, not some horseroom in back of a saloon, but something with class.'

'You mean a casino,' the girl said.

'A casino, that's right, yeah.'

'Well, there is none right here in Marseilles. There's quite a nice one at Aix-en-Provence. That's about twenty-five miles away. And there's one not far out of town to the east, at Cassis.'

She looked at Doyle's wildly printed Hawaiian sport shirt.

'You will have to wear a tie, of course, and perhaps another shirt would be more acceptable.'

'Okay, okay,' Doyle said, 'I could put on something else. You got a map? Can you show me how to get there?'

The girl pulled a little folding map of the Riviera from the desk in front of her and with a felt-tipped pen traced the route for him.

'Listen, are you doing anything tonight? Maybe you can come with me,' Doyle said.

He was hoping he could make some kind of good connection

with this girl. She's the one that had the brains and the language to help him and he was pretty sure that she wasn't tied in with the cops, or the others.

Francoise gave him a cute look sideways from under her blue tinted lids.

'You are persistent, you Americans, eh?'

'No, I'm not persistent,' Doyle said, 'I just like you. I haven't met any broads as nice as you since I've been here.'

'And how many have you met?' the girl said, laughing.

Doyle grinned sheepishly. 'Well, I admit I haven't met too many. But there's something else. You see, I need some help. I'd even be willing to pay a little if you could use the dough. I need somebody who speaks the lingo and speaks English to kind of steer me around.'

'But didn't your office supply you with such help?' the girl said, with a mocking smile.

'No,' Doyle said, 'I'm pretty much on my own. But I could pay maybe twenty bucks a day and it wouldn't be an all day job. No kidding, on the up and up. No monkey business.'

The girl shrugged. 'It might be amusing. About the money, you can decide after you . . . use me, what it's worth.'

'So what about tonight? Can you go out there with me to this casino place?'

She put her hand over Doyle's hairy fist which was resting on the desk.

'Honestly, I do have an engagement tonight.'

Her touch was warm and dry and the pressure of her fingers sent an electric charge right up Doyle's arm. Idiotically, he felt himself actually blushing.

The girl took a pencil from the desk and a piece of paper and wrote something on it which she passed along to Doyle.

'This is my phone number here at the airport and underneath it is listed my home number. Perhaps we can get together tomorrow and talk about this.'

'Why don't we make a definite date?' Doyle said. 'What time do you get off tomorrow?'

'About six.'

'You want to meet at that bar, the Calypso?'

'It's a deal,' the girl said, smiling warmly.

Doyle took the key to the Renault 16 he had rented from her and went out to the parking lot, whistling 'The Girl From Ipanema' to himself. He couldn't see light at the end of the tunnel yet, but this was a start — yes it was a definite start.

CHAPTER TWENTY-ONE

The casino was easy to find. Doyle had only to follow the long, winding mountain highway that curled above the Mediterranean, passing through the bleak, unforested landscape open to the sun, and then descending in a winding pattern to the sea.

The little harbour was like a smaller version of Marseilles' Vieux-port, except that here everyone looked rich. At the eastern end of the U-shaped marina was a long, low white building, just as Francoise had described it, the casino.

Inside, it was like a quiet version of a Vegas game room, the usual tables for baccarat, chemin de fer and roulette, but no craps or blackjack. You could get chips for as little as five francs, about a buck, and Doyle bought twenty-five dollars' worth of the smallest denomination. The language was foreign, but the roulette game was easy enough to follow — red, black, double o, thirty-five to one payoff if you hit the number on the nose, and so forth. Doyle pocketed the plastic chips and walked around the carpeted casino where the players sat, intense, bright-eyed, concentrating with avid attention on their game. They were well dressed; some of them even wore dinner jackets. There were none of the usual female hangers-on that one saw in Vegas but there were a couple of good looking women players who were obviously as rich as the men. Doyle had a good feeling that his hunch had been right. This was the first place that really looked as though Charnier might have been there.

He pulled up a stool at the roulette table and put a five franc chip on the black. He was determined to play cautiously, pull back his winnings and double up. It was the system he learned from a little booklet in Vegas. In the end you never won, because the house had the percentage, but if the house was honest you could hang in a long time on fifty bucks . . .

On the other side of the harbour of Cassis, almost in view of the gaming room windows at the casino, two men were dining.

The restaurant Les Calanques, had never made three stars in the Michelin, not even two, but its falsely naive imitation of a Marseilles *cabanon* concealed one of the best restaurants between Marseilles and the Cote d'Azur. General William Ball and Alain Charnier did not speak as they spooned the thick, red *rouille* over the croutons in their *soupe de poisson*. They were sensual men to whom each thing came in its place. When the *rouille* was properly distributed and the *soupe* tasted, Charnier raised his eyebrows questioningly to the general.

'Good,' the general said. 'Very good. The best I've had.'

He took a sip of the *blancs de blancs*. 'That's good, too,' he said. 'By the way, Alain, your reasons for not going through with the shipment were understood.'

Charnier inclined his head and gave a thin smile of satisfaction.

'Good,' he said. 'I'm pleased you all continue to see the situation the same way I do . . .'

He paused sipping the *soupe*.

'Bill, has Geneva taken the necessary first step?' he asked.

Ball smiled expansively. 'Exactly as you wanted it, with a good spread against inflation and the floating currencies. One hundred thousand in South African rands, and you know what's happening to gold these days, fifty in Canadian dollars, another fifty in yen, although we're kind of doubtful about that one, two hundred thousand altogether anyway, ten percent down as per the agreement.'

Charnier nodded, apparently gratified. 'You could tell your friends that the final shipment is already on the way, that is, the base. Once it arrives here we'll need at least three weeks to cook it.'

'Understood,' the general said.

'We're expecting you after dinner at our place. A little party, very informal, you know. You'll come?'

Ball looked regretful. He stood, picked up a plastic clothes cover from a nearby chair. In it was a full dress US Army general's uniform, its braid and metal gleaming.

'Love to,' Ball said. 'No can do tonight. Official business.'

He smiled broadly at Charnier. 'Looks like your guys really want us back again over here. We're gonna discuss numbers and bases with my NATO opposite number in Paris. Anyway, thanks for the meal, Alain. Incidentally, Geneva's counting on you. They wanted it made clear.'

With the last sentence, the cordial lightness of social chitchat drained from the atmosphere. Charnier seemed unimpressed. He shrugged. Composed and confident, he smiled at Ball.

'Naturally. I have expectations of *them* too. Be sure that they also know that.'

After the general left, Charnier waved away the rest of the dinner, ordered a malt whisky, Glenfiddich, and sipped it with a Havana Upmann he took from a silver case in his pocket. He had a lot on his mind. Setting up the new lab, picking up the morphine base and solving the riddle of the man in the Renault. There was something about that hat . . . He had a hunch about it and he always trusted his hunches.

On the other side of the harbour, Doyle cashed in his chips. After three hours of play, he still had a hundred and fifty francs. He wondered if Francoise liked to gamble. He wondered if it would be a good idea to bring her out there. He wondered if Barthelmy's tails had managed to follow the zig-zag route he'd taken through the city before getting on the highway. They probably didn't even have cars, anyway.

Francoise agreed to come with him the following night. She wore a long, swirling skirt and short jacket. With it a sort of man's shirt buttoned very low and showing well in contrast to her sun burnished skin.

'Baby,' Doyle said, 'you are really all class.'

Francoise smiled but said nothing as she let him help her into the car. She pointed out the sights as they drove through the twilight toward the little fishing village that had now become a tourist centre and made him stop to see the view from the Vauufrege Pass of the islands of Calseraigne and Riou.

This was not the sort of girl Doyle was used to and her speech and obvious education tended to make him modify his own speech and behaviour. Besides, she brought him luck – although not on his primary mission, finding Charnier. He drew a blank on that one again, but he did win back the hundred francs he had lost the night before plus an additional hundred and fifty.

'You're my lucky piece, baby,' he said to the girl, who sat beside him but didn't play. He squeezed her knee appreciatively, then took his hand away, looking embarrassed.

'I'm sorry . . .'

Francoise turned a slow smile on him. 'Never be sorry,' she said. 'Isn't that what they say in your American films?'

He told Francoise a little about the elegant bearded friend for whom he was looking and asked if she thought this was a likely place to find him. Francoise said that it was.

Driving back, the distant lights flickering along the shore of the Mediterranean, Doyle felt a sexual stirring unlike any he had felt before. Instead of being concentrated in his groin, it seemed to reach right up to the roots of his hair and down to his toes. His entire skin felt sensitized. Without touching her, he could feel the radiance of her body heat next to him.

As they neared the centre of the city, Doyle thought about what his approach would be.

'Do you have to get home right away,' he said, 'or can you come up for . . . uh . . . a drink of Jack Daniels?'

Farncoise smiled. 'I don't really like bourbon. Perhaps I can come up and stay with you for a while, anyway. But I must leave tonight. I have to get up early.'

Doyle hoped Coco would notice nothing as he passed the desk, picked up his key and escorted Francoise into the creaky brass elevator cage.

As they entered the room, Doyle turned on the dim lamp on the dressing table and raced around picking up his old socks and underwear, throwing them hastily into the closet.

'It's all right . . . Bill,' Francoise said. 'A man's place has to look a little bit disorganized. If it didn't, I'd be suspicious.'

She took off her short jacket and hung it carefully on the chair. The she sat on the edge of the bed and lit an English Oval.

'Do you have an ashtray?' she asked.

Popeye quickly wiped an ashtray out with a Kleenex on the dressing table, brought it to her and sat down beside her. Francoise put her two bronzed hands on either side of his face and looked into his eyes. Hers were blue-green, flecked with yellow, Doyle noticed now, and there was an amused expression in them.

Softly, she began to sing, 'I'm Popeye the Sailor Man . . .'

Popeye rose up roaring and pushed her, now laughing crazily, back on the bed . . .

CHAPTER TWENTY-TWO

In the morning, there was only a note. She had gone while Popeye was asleep. It said,

'Darling, it was good being with you. Call me next week.'

It was signed with a sweeping F.

The next night, his luck was not as good, but he still hadn't used up his initial stake. As far as Charnier, his luck was still zero. Doyle was beginning to wonder. Was this the right move? A steady stakeout in the one place – but if not there, where? Obviously none of the other places he had visited had even a hope. He had avoided Barthelmy for three day now, although probably Barthelmy had kept tabs on him through his spies. The Consul had not called and he had not spoken with the DEA men, nor had he gone down to the Consulate to pick up his paycheck.

As the Renault mounted the winding side roads leading from Cassis up to National 559, Doyle was aware of a car behind him. He tried speeding up, but it was not easy making time on the still unfamiliar winding mountain road. The car stayed behind him, travelling always at the same pace, not trying to overtake him. It could be a tail, Doyle thought, it could be one of Barthelmy's men, or maybe it's somebody else. Then again, there's only one road from Cassis to Marseilles, so maybe it was just somebody going home from the casino like him.

It was late, and the Place des Marsellaises was dark when he parked the car across the street from the Hotel de l'Univers. Doyle thought he had lost the tail somewhere in the streets of the city when he jumped a couple of traffic lights. He pushed the buttons, locking the doors on the R 16, and started across the shadowy Place. Suddenly from behind a closed news stand a figure leapt and a fist smashed from out of the blackness into his stomach. Another fist from behind him landed a rabbit punch behind the ear. Doyle felt a greater darkness than that of the street folding in as a black car, its headlights blazing, surged from a side street and cut off his stumbling retreat. A third dark figure leapt from the car and began a smashing attack on Doyle's already fading consciousness. Desperately, with a last flicker of awareness, Doyle's hand reached for his ankle, remembering too late that the pistol was long since gone.

In the night, lit only by the distant glow of the streetlight, the men all looked black to Doyle. Another blow sent his hat sailing into the gutter. Desperately, he tried to butt the man in front of him but missed and went sprawling face down on the street, as a sharp toe caught his rib cage. Then there was a sound of running feet from the doorway across the street, the entrance to the Hotel de l'Univers. It was the Old Pro and his curly-haired assistant, but they were too late. A fourth figure came from behind and caught the Old Pro in the back of the head, a light tap with a tape-wrapped section of lead pipe. The boy was cut down with a clothesline stroke across the windpipe. Three of the men muscled Doyle inside the door of the black car. He came to briefly and braced his elbows and feet against the doorframe, but it was hopeless. He was taken out with a heavy slammed fist into his midsection.

In the car Doyle had hardly to put on an act to feign unconsciousness. He felt a trickling warmth around his ear and he knew that he had cuts on the upper parts of his scalp and across his eyebrow. Every time he breathed, he felt a sharp stabbing pain in the side of his chest where someone's toe had caught him. He lay back, trying to get some idea where they were being driven and to clear his head, but without much success.

The car turned off the main highway, on to what seemed to be a narrow and cobbled pavement, and pulled up outside a sagging and grimy hotel front but Doyle by this time was too sick to see anything. The sign over the door said 'Hotel de Niger' one star, '*tout confort*'.

Another rabbit punch behind the ear wiped him out totally as the three dark figures pulled him from the car and dragged him through the entrance of the hotel. Just before they mounted the sidewalk, Doyle's brain swam into a minimal consciousness and he blearily made out the name cut into the stone curbstone only inches from his eyes – '*Hotel de Tanger*'. It looked as though the incised letters had been trecked over by thousands of abrasive shoes.

The girls hanging around the seedy bar off the shabby lobby hardly gave a glance as the three men half-dragged in their companion – his face streaked with blood, the skin grated raw on one cheek where it had dragged across the pavement. These girls were paid for a lot of things, but one of them was *not* to notice who went in and out of the hotel.

Through his half-conscious fog Doyle could see nothing, but was dimly aware of a jukebox loudly blaring Johnny Hallyday singing 'I Love You, Baby'. There was no elevator, so Doyle was hauled, his feet flapping limply at the worn, carpeted steps, up three flights, past a half-open door where a woman nodded in a wheelchair, her works carelessly spread beside her on the table, past another door where a hooker, rid of her trick, stood with one knee up on the bidet wiping thoughtfully at her parts with a soapy washrag. At the end of the long, dark corridor on the third floor, Doyle felt himself thrown to the floor of a small unlit room atop of a block of steps. It was so black in there that even after lying on the cold floor for half an hour regaining his consciousness, Doyle couldn't tell whether his eyes were open or closed.

He didn't know how long it had been that he lay there completely wiped out. It seemed that through it all he could hear or rather feel the thumping rhythm of the jukebox three floors below. There were no other sounds. After a year or so, Doyle pushed himself to his bruised knees and started to crawl. It didn't matter in what direction since he couldn't see diddly shit. The floor was grainy and cold and slippery, like the cellar of some old French dungeon, although Doyle knew he was somewhere in the upper reaches of the hotel. He had crawled about a kilometer, when his head hit a cold plastered wall. The long crawl had taken every last bit of strength out of him. He leaned over on his hands and knees and retched onto the already slime-covered floor, barely feeling the warm steam rolling past fingers propped on the floor to hold him up. Then he rolled over on his back and began to cry.

CHAPTER TWENTY-THREE

He was dreaming a big American eagle had picked him up because he was a baby again, crying and shitting in his pants. It carried him high over a strange landscape to a nest of sticks. In the nest were other eagles. They all hated him because he didn't belong. They pecked at him and tried to gouge out his eyes when he tried to protect himself. They made grating, cackling noises like old men laughing at dirty jokes. The nest was high up, close to the sun and the sun tried to push soldering irons into each of his eyes whenever the eagles weren't pecking at them.

Then he knew he was awake because his eyes made a tearing sound as they ripped open against the drying mucus that had held them shut. A face with an eagle's beak was close to his, a dark face, and a light was shining off stainless steel teeth, that peeked slyly from the corners of the mouth. Reflexively, the muscles in Doyle's shoulders and arms tensed and they reached out to strike at the ugly beaked face above him, haloed in sunlight, but his arms wouldn't move. There was a sharp biting pressure at the wrists. His feet, too, were wired together. Suddenly his face was washed with a quick douche of warm, pungent fluid and the cackling around him grew stronger and he could see that it was not little eagles but dark, rapacious men with shiny bright eyes and bony, ravaged features. The man with the eagle's nose moved closer and Doyle could smell garlic and decaying teeth.

'You're awake Mister Popeye,' the voice said. 'You like your morning shower? We have all pitched in together to make it for you.'

The voices behind him burst into a chorus of cackling approval. Doyle strained his body, trying to get at the man, scraping the chair to which he was tied a few inches across the floor and making a strangled animal sound, part anger, part frustration. The man put one finger on his brow, stopping him and the move made clear to Doyle how helpless he was.

'Can you hear me, Mister Popeye?' the voice said again.

Popeye nodded groggily, the urine dripping into a stinging stream into his lacerated eyelids. His mouth and tongue felt thick and the inside of his mouth tasted of old blood and fresh vomit.

'Give me some water, for crissake,' he said.

'You want some more?'

There was another cackling sound and then some voices in French. Finally a dipperful of lukewarm water was poured down his raw gullet. The rest of it was thrown into his face. That felt good.

'If you are feeling better, Popeye, my associates here want to discuss things with you.'

In the background were more figures, shadows he couldn't see, coming back and forth, murmuring in languages he couldn't understand.

'They had ideas of how to make you talk,' the voice said, 'but I told them it would be useless, you would die first and then of course we could never find out what we want to know, what you've learned about our little business here, who you've seen and identified. We respect you, Popeye. Your actions in New York cost us a great deal, many, many millions, so we have great respect for you. You're a good cop, quite honest as cops go. Quite stupid, but honest.'

Doyle's eyes strained to see beyond the bright light streaming on his head from the skylight above. He had finally made contact with a representative of Frog One, that much was clear, but the information wasn't much use at that moment. The voice was cultured, and spoke American style English, with a faint French accent. It spoke again from behind the bright light.

'Now our friends have left the matter in our hands. They don't care how the information is obtained, they want it. So we have cooked up this marvellous idea.'

A voice in the background said, '*Qu'est-ce que il dit?*'

'*Il dit qu'on lui a cuisiné un piquouse dans la popote.*'

There were more cackling sounds of appreciation.

Now Doyle, through his swollen nostrils, could catch the faint acrid bite of a wooden match being lit and then something gleamed in the hand of the man with the eagle's nose. A long shiny point of a knife approached his arm and he strained back against it. The knife reached out and with one long swoop slit his shirt from the wrist to the shoulder, laying bare his sinewy but bruised forearm.

'*Jules, Mario, allez-y les gars!*'

Now there was another gleam of metal in the sunshine and Doyle's body stiffened into panic as he saw the approaching needle. An arm was wrapped around his head from behind to hold him still and some kind of binding was put around his arm, forcing his already well-marked veins into prominence. There was a sudden, brief, shooting pain and another roaring chorus of cackling appreciative laughter.

'He is a new one. You've taken his virginity,' a voice said.

Gradually Doyle's stiffened body relaxed and the light seemed less harsh, the voices dimmer and somehow more melodious. He noticed that the light, when it hit the bottom of his wet and gummy lid made patterns like rainbows and there were little halos in the air wherever the light bounced off a bright surface. Actually it was quite interesting. He watched one little ball of luminosity as it mounted from the lower left corner of his lid and swam across his eyeball like an ascending balloon in glorious colour.

'Jesus!' he said to himself, 'that's really something!'

There was an excited gabble of voices in the background as the group watched his reaction. Then he felt a great, warm feeling rising from his stomach up through the oesophagus and over the gums as a stringy spew of green bile shot from his mouth – all that was left in his stomach after the violent retching of the night before.

'You should really try to hold it down,' the voice of the eagle said. 'Otherwise you will not appreciate the good of it.'

'Fuck you,' Doyle said, and fell into a sleep that was almost pleasant, his head hanging down, his arms hung over the chair, like a Christ in a cheap crêche.

When he at last lost consciousness, the little group of men pulled back. Besides the three dark and wasted faces was another – tall, handsome, a touch of blond at the temples, an elegant young man, a young man used to driving a Mercedes. A young man seen very much on the waterfront at La Joliette.

'Well, monsieur Jacques, you see he can say nothing now for a while.'

The young man studied him curiously.

'You think it will help, *la blanche*?'

Yusif, the man who had talked first to Doyle, shrugged. 'In my experience, it always helps a little, but then you don't agree, do you monsieur Jacques?'

The elegant man, who now wore a Cardin blazer and a camel-coloured turtleneck, looked indifferent.

'Every man has his own pleasures,' he said. 'We're not interested in pleasures, we're interested in information.'

'Well,' Yusif said, 'you yourself pointed out that the usual way would probably not work. He's a stubborn one, a tough one. And then it would be amusing to see how this New York *stu'* will react when he finds the pleasures of *la pousette.*'

Jacques nodded wordlessly but with obvious distaste and turned on his heel.

'It won't matter anyway, in a few days, but we would like to know if he already has enough information to interfere with our business. How soon can you try again?'

Yusif looked thoughtfully at the limp figure slumped in the chair.

'Maybe three or four hours we'll give him a small *picquouse.*'

'You know what we want to know.'

'Oui, monsieur.'

'Then find it out, that way or any other.'

The young man left without a goodbye.

CHAPTER TWENTY-FOUR

Doyle stretched and yawned, a jaw-cracking yawn. He swung his stiff body to an erect position, but was jerked back by the pressure of the cuff on his right wrist which chained him to the iron bed in which he had been lying. He inched his bottom closer to the end of the bed so that he could sit up, his elbows on his knees, slumped over and staring at the floor.

Curiously, he examined his left arm. There were half a dozen purple dots running along his strong bulging vein, some of them circled with beads of dried blood. He was wearing what had been his white skivvies and tee shirt, but they were now almost as grey as the concrete floor below him. Lifting his head drowsily, he could see little dark heaps that he assumed were the rest of his clothes, scattered around the room. A roach crawled industriously across his toe, bound on some arcane mission. Aimlessly, Doyle flipped the little animal across the room with his fingernail. He wasn't angry at the roach, but this was *his* corner of the room.

An old woman shuffled into the room in worn carpet slippers and sat down on the bed beside him.

'I have a son, you know . . .' she said, as though picking up an old conversation.

Doyle looked at her curiously. She was familiar. He knew her. He had known her for some time. He remembered seeing her first nodding in a chair, the works beside her on a table someplace, but now her face was more familiar than that.

'He is a very nice young man,' the old lady said, 'about your age.'

'That's good,' Doyle croaked. His voice came out like an old Victrola record.

'I'm English, you know,' the old lady said, and it seemed very funny because she cackled witlessly. 'I heard you speaking English, but you mustn't, you know. No one will listen.'

There was a long silence, then Doyle said, 'Your son. Tell him about me. *Please* tell him.'

The woman shook her head in negation. Her eyes were glittery and intense.

'Don't be silly. No one will listen. I've been in Marseilles for forty-two years, even through the war. My husband was French, but he wouldn't listen. My son is gone away too. Nobody listens in Marseilles.'

With the palm of her hand she rubbed her thin arm under a washed-out, flowered sleeve. As the sleeve pulled back, Doyle could see the hard, scarred, lifeless flesh of a thousand needle marks. The old lady reached out a dry hand and touched Doyle's shackled arm, examining his fresh needle marks with interest.

'Oh, you mustn't scratch them,' the old lady said. 'They'll become infected and you'll be sick. Do like this . . .'

She rubbed his tracks with the palm of his hand and relieved the terrible itch that had begun to afflict him. He gave her a look of gratitude and she smiled at the secret they shared.

Doyle thought that she might have been quite a nice young lady at one time. 'When do they come around again?' he asked.

'Soon, soon,' the old lady answered, 'but don't shout for them, young man. No one will listen.'

From somewhere downstairs he could again hear the voice of Johnny Hallyday singing 'Yeh Baby, Yeh'. Doyle's shackled hand was resting on the side of the bed behind him. The other was resting on his knee, his wrist and fingers limply splayed in mid air. He seemed lost in a reverie again, thinking about the station house, thinking about the great coups brought off in the past.

The woman watched him for a few moments and then very quietly pulled at the elastic band of Doyle's watch, slipped it over his wrist, and dropped it in the pocket of her dress. Doyle watched with dead eyes as if it were happening to someone else.

'You know I can't remember what it was they were asking me? I know it was something very interesting . . . very interesting. They've been good to me. I really must try to help them,' Doyle said.

CHAPTER TWENTY-FIVE

Inspector Henry Barthelmy was quizzing the Old Pro and the curly haired Kid almost as thoroughly as the dark, eagle-faced men were grilling Doyle but the two detectives had come on the scene too late to see anything except a departing car, the black Citroen DS 19, much like the one driven by the inspector himself, but without the roof light. At the corner it had turned south towards the port, but that could mean anything. But it did make it more likely that Doyle (if he was alive) was being held somewhere in the city rather than in the mountains to the north.

Francoise was brought in from Avis and questioned thoroughly. Barthelmy was interested in the fact that she had been a hostess for Pan Am. His experience was that hostesses were very knowledgeable about the drug trade.

'You're sure?' he asked the girl who sat demurely with her streaky blonde hair pulled back and fastened by a red ribbon, 'you're sure that you knew *nothing* about Doyle's business?'

'Nothing, I assure you, Monsieur l'Inspecteur. We had met less than a week ago at the volleyball court at Calypso. I knew him only casually.'

Barthelmy inspected some notes in front of him.

'You were at Cassis with him, at the casino?'

The girl looked surprised. 'Yes. Why?'

'I'm just curious,' Barthelmy said. 'And you stayed with him at the Hotel de l'Univers?'

'That is my own affair,' the girl said.

'But you did.'

The girl nodded wordlessly. She seemed more offended by the invasion of her privacy than ashamed of anything she had done.

'Did you love him?'

The girl shrugged. 'I barely knew him.'

'Yet you stayed with him.'

The girl looked at the policeman sardonically.

'Inspector, really . . .'

'Do you have any idea what happened to him?'

The girl shook her head negatively.

'I only knew that he probably went back to the casino again. He indicated that he would do so. He was looking for someone, for a friend of his who had a white beard, a Frenchman with a lot of money.'

'Yes, we know about that,' Barthelmy said dryly. 'And did he find him?'

'Not that I know of,' the girl said.

Barthelmy dismissed her. He rose to his feet and bowed.

'You've been very kind, mademoiselle. I hope we have not disturbed you, but you understand. Please remain in Marseilles, as we may need to question you further.'

For the first time, the girl dropped her composure. 'Do you think he has been killed?'

Barthelmy shook his head hopelessly. 'I have no idea, except that we have found no trace of him.'

Miletto and Diron directed a team of men who checked every place that they knew Doyle to have visited – the *tabacs*, the Speakeasy, Francoise, Babette, the other girls, Coco at the hotel. They went as far as to hold Babette under suspicion of conspiracy over the attempted mugging, in the hope that she might tell them something.

Ultimately, they even found the Arab boy whose eye Doyle

had nearly put out with his ballpoint pen. He'd been picked up in a purse-snatching arrest and had told a wild story of a huge American in a porkpie hat. But this, too, was a blank wall. Barthelmy felt frustrated. He suspected that Doyle had lost faith in him and his men and had gone on his own but then, why would he not have? Barthelmy knew only too well what little reason Doyle had to have faith in the French *Bureau de Stupefiants*, or for that matter the New York Narcotics Bureau, at least as far as some of its higher members went.

But now he felt the overwhelming sense of loyalty and cameraderie of two men in the same profession. Barthelmy was a different sort of man than Doyle, but he wondered if he might not have ended up in the same place in some fashion.

At the hotel the old woman shuffled into Doyle's room, carrying a tray. On it were a set of works, the hypo, the bent spoon, the strip of rubber tubing, the small glassine envelope and a box of wooden matches – also a shaving mug and a brush. As she entered, Doyle could hear a key turning in the door, locking it behind her.

'Good morning,' the old woman said.

Doyle looked at her blearily. His face was black. The eyes were sunken, a heavy growth of beard covered his skin like a mat.

The old woman treated him as though she were a very old and kindly nurse. It was obviously a routine that had grown up between them.

'Good morning,' Doyle said. He reached for the glassine envelope, the spoon and the matches, and the motion was practised. As the woman worked up a lather in the mug, Doyle cooked up his own dose of heroin. From a long, leather case she took out a straight razor and placed it on the radiator.

'You do need a shave, young man,' she said.

But Doyle paid no attention. His eyes were focused on the flame and the melting beads of heroin in the spoon. Softly, sweetly, he slid the shiny needle into a good spot he had found between two previous marks and leaned back on the grey surplus US Army blanket, breathing deeply and nodding in beautiful relief.

'Sweet Jesus,' Doyle said.

His arms were no longer cuffed to the bed and he rolled off it, half sliding to the floor, lying out flat on his stomach, his eyes focused on the space at the bottom of the door where a sliver of dim light came through. He crawled to the wall, painfully drew himself up, and tried the door. To his surprise, it opened. For a moment, he stood there frightened of the vastness beyond. He stepped into the corridor. It was lit by a dim, ten watt bulb at the far end. Doyle leaned dreamily against the wall, and slid down into a hunkered position, staring at the bulb and the darkness, frightened as an injured animal. Then he started to move towards the light. There was a sudden bar of illumination across the corridor as the door opened, and Doyle pulled back, alarmed, but it was only the old woman's dusty face. She smiled knowingly and closed her door. Below him, he saw stairs leading downwards to the street.

Hanging to the banister, he slumped down a short flight to another dark corridor which stretched out endlessly before him. It had a door at the far end which blocked his exit. Doyle felt frozen by a junkie's panic, afraid that if he made the wrong move, he would wind up punished and deprived of his shot. His pride struggled with his need and he pulled himself ahead. The door opened slowly. Cigarettes burned in the gloom of the room, one of them larger, a cigar.

Doyle moved closer into the room, running his tongue over dry lips. The men in the room paid him no attention. Then as he drew closer to the group, a harsh blue light suddenly went on, an overhead fluorescent which bathed the scene in a cold glare. Jacques was there, sitting quietly, puffing on his Upmann. Yusif, Jules and Mario were sitting at the table. There were cards, a bottle of wine and glasses, but there was nothing in front of Jacques. It was obvious that he was questioning the three men and perhaps giving them more things to ask Doyle.

Jacques looked at Doyle as if he were the family dog arriving at the dinner table for scraps. Wordlessly Doyle extended his pitted arm. Jacques turned to Yusif, his eyebrow raised as though asking if they should feed the dog. Yusif laughed evilly.

Doyle pulled himself up as straight as he could, holding his back against the wall for support, drawing on all his reserves of pride and strength.

'Look,' he said, 'you've gotta believe me. I came here on my own looking for Charnier and maybe you, too. I was the only guy who saw you in New York but I didn't find a goddamn thing here. Believe me, it ain't my town. I can't even order a goddamn drink.' He ran his forearm across his swollen mouth. He was full of need, but he was fighting his instinct to plead.

Jacques looked at him coolly, perhaps with some increase in respect. He nodded to Yusif who got up, went to the bureau, and took out the works. Doyle's eyes focused hotly on the equipment in Yusif's hand.

'You know,' Jacques said, 'I believe you. I finally do believe you.'

He turned to Yusif. 'I don't think we need anything from him anymore. Do what you want. You'll get your money when the deal is through.'

Yusif nodded, put the works back in the drawer.

'Hey!' Doyle said piteously. 'Ain't you gonna fix me?'

Yusif looked at him with contempt. 'You heard what he said. We're not wasting any of that good *jules* on a fucked-up flic.'

He picked a leather-covered billy up from the bureau where he had stashed the works.

'Now get back in your room, or I'll let you have some more of this.'

He slapped the billy hard against his palm, a gesture with which Doyle was only too familiar, but from the other end.

'Listen, you can't do this to me.'

'Don't worry,' Yusif said. 'We'll take care of you soon enough.'

Desperately, Doyle made his way back to the only home he now knew, the dark cell at the top of the stairs. He was feverish with need but he understood the meaning of that conference. He didn't remember what he had told them, or what he hadn't told them, but he knew they didn't need him any more. What could he have told them? He knew nothing but that's what they had to know, of course, to know that he knew nothing.

And he himself had found out something too. He had found out beyond a doubt that there was one fuck of a big shipment going out of Marseilles and it wasn't gonna be very long before it moved.

It all fit. The scope of the lab at Rue Galine, where preparations for a larger shipment had obviously been made. And the kidnapping and intense questioning – they wouldn't have risked that unless there was something big in the works. So what? He was a useless hulk now. He dragged himself down the hall, his mind stretching its fading resources looking for a way out. Popeye Doyle – Detective, First Grade Popeye Doyle only needed one cut at the apple to score a hit, and he wasn't out yet. In his drug-dimmed mind the glimmer of an idea began to shine through.

CHAPTER TWENTY-SIX

As he passed the old lady's door again it opened, letting a sliver of light out, and this time he lurched towards it.

'I got to speak to you, old lady, let me in.'

She smiled. 'I can't help you. They don't let me have any of my own.'

'Let me in, goddamnit,' Doyle said, pushing past her.

In the room he pushed the woman aside, his eyes searching wildly about him.

'I told you, dearie, they don't let me have anything here. I'm sorry if they cut you off, but that's how they are.'

But it wasn't heroin Doyle was looking for – it was something else. There was nothing in the room he wanted, just a faded picture of some limey in a World War I tin hat and another of a bright-looking young man in a wedding pose that looked as though it had been taken only ten years or so ago.

'You got a bathroom in here?' Doyle said.

The lady pointed to the corner.

'Just the washbasin.'

Doyle lurched in and looked at the shelf above it. There was an ironstone mug, toothbrush, an enema bag hanging on the wall, a tiny miserable sliver of hotel soap, a towel that would never be Rinso white again. On the stained, spattered shelf running above the bowl was what he wanted, a long, slim, black leather case, a straight razor. He grabbed it, slipped it in his pocket, turned to the old lady.

'Listen, you old sweet thing, you old bitch,' he said, 'I don't know what you saw and what you didn't see, but you didn't see anything, you see? Because if you see anything, you're going to be one dead old lady.'

'I didn't see anything, dearie,' the old lady said, cackling. 'I can't see that well anyway.'

Doyle peered cautiously from the old lady's doorway, sidled out and stumbled back to his room to think. It was hard to focus his mind with that churning pain in his gut, with that sweat, with that horrible need.

Small red pimples, itchy and stinging, had blossomed at his armpits and in the crooks of his arms and in all the other sweaty parts of his body. Spasms rippled up his muscles from his toes and up his thighs, causing his legs to twitch convulsively from time to time, completely out of control. The pants he had worn when captured, now flapped several sizes too large around the waist. The tang of his belt had to be pushed to a spot where it held precariously, four or five inches beyond the final hole.

But there were moments of relative clarity when he could think, though the nausea never seemed to go away. He scoured the room for anything like a weapon that he could conceal. He thought of smashing the one chair in the room, but it was wire. Anyway a chair leg would have been too hard to hide. If they tried to kill him up there in the room, he would just have to depend on the razor and see what he could do with it. But if they took him out beyond the locked door where the men were always waiting and playing cards, if they took him to the street, he might have a chance to make a break for it. Maybe if there was a crowd or something.

The room was barren. There was only the old iron bed, the tin pitcher in which they brought him water and the tin basin that he poured it into. Everything else he used was strictly on loan, and so was his life at that moment, because it wouldn't take them long to get rid of him now that he had become useless.

CHAPTER TWENTY-SEVEN

He was curled in a ball, sweating and jerking in the immediacy of his need when they came to get him. It was just Yusif and Mario. They knew they wouldn't need any more help with this pitiful rag of a creature who used to be some kind of a man.

'Get up, filth,' Yusif said, prodding him savagely in the kidneys.

Doyle felt a sudden embarrassing warmth on his leg as his sphincter let go and sprayed his thigh with warm urine.

Yusif held his nose. 'God, you're a pig. Look at this pen you live in.'

Doyle had never felt the need so great, yet he was acting a little bit too. He knew he had reserves of strength somewhere. He had to have them. He had to get free. But at this point it would be to his advantage to play possum.

'I can't get up, Yusif,' he pleaded. 'My muscles are all cramped. Just give me one little shot.'

'You won't need it where you're going,' Yusif said. 'On your feet, *flic*.'

The two men grabbed him by his tortured arm and hauled him to his feet, where Doyle stood, swaying uncertainly.

'Now *filez*! Move out,' Yusif said.

Mario broke out into a silly giggle. 'Look at him. He looks like a scarecrow. I wonder what they would say about him in New York now.'

'He's a piece of shit,' Yusif said. 'Don't worry about him.'

He looked contemptuously at his friend. 'And you, you're almost as worthless a piece a shit if we didn't give you the stuff every day.'

Mario looked hurt. 'Don't say that, Yusif. I'm not a piece of shit. You know I can't help it. It was in Annam, Dien Bien Phu. We all got the stuff there. How could I help it? In the Legion they would piss on you if you didn't use it.'

'Save your stories for Mother Goose,' Yusif said. 'Let's get this job done.'

He prodded Doyle towards the door. Doyle controlled his enormous need to reach for the slender shape in his pants pocket. It was too early to betray any sign of strength. Wearily, he shuffled down the short flight of stairs past the old lady's door, open a crack, where he knew she was watching. He wondered if she felt sorry for him, if she felt anything.

They walked down the corridor into the small room where Jules sat playing solitaire and drinking *pastis*.

'Take care of things, Jules. We'll be back soon.'

Jules nodded wordlessly. Then, as they were at the outer door he called to them.

'Do you need any help?'

Yusif laughed. 'Help? You must be joking. We just need one to drive and one for whatever. To babysit for this piece of *merde*.'

Outside, they wound down the vaguely familiar staircase as the whores gazed at him with indifference from doors of their rooms. If he screamed, Doyle knew nothing would happen. They would simply turn their backs and close their doors. Probably ninety per cent of them were users, all paying off to the big guy, all of it feeding ultimately to the same channel.

He walked stiffly, still twitching, out through the brightly lit corridor, past the bar where the eternal Johnny Hallyday records were still whining, and into the night air. The cold breeze off the sea, the *mistral*, was blowing and its brisk dampness was not exactly like a shot in the arm to Doyle, but it helped. It sharpened his dulling senses a bit. Now his nose was running and his eyes were tearing. He stopped for a moment and pleaded.

'Wait a minute. Let me just blow my nose. I'm dying here.'

Yusif sighed. 'Go ahead, *merde*.'

Doyle reached into his pocket where the filthy handkerchief

was wadded. Next to it nestled the long, black case. Fumbling for the handkerchief, he managed to pull the cap of the case loose and let the razor hang free in the bottom of the pocket. Doyle had no idea what time it was and never had had since the old lady stole his watch, but it must have been late. The store shutters were all rolled down, and most of the lights were out. There was almost no traffic in the streets. Doyle didn't even know if Yusif was carrying a gun or a shiv or what. Probably nothing, with him in the shape that he was now.

The Citroen was already parked at the kerb, sleek, black and chromium lined, looking strangely out of place in these shabby environs. Wordlessly, Yusif opened the door, shoved him into the softly luxurious back seat and gestured to Mario to take the chauffeur's position. Mario jumped in, started the motor, and Doyle was aware of the strange, hissing noise and lifting sensation as the Citroen mounted on its air cushions.

He sniffled compulsively and reached for his handkerchief again. This time holding it wadded in his hand, because inside it was the long shape of the folded razor. Yusif got in beside him and reached across him to lock the door on the far side. Doyle hunched around so that his back was to the door and that he was facing Yusif. His right hand twitched compulsively on the filthy handkerchief with the weapon inside it.

Slowly, smoothly, Mario put the Citroen into gear and rolled off. The car rolled quietly over the cobblestone streets, hardly vibrating on their irregular surfaces. Doyle had almost forgotten his need now – the constant nausea, the aches and the itching. But charges of adrenalin were helping. Perhaps it was the new wonder drug. His eyes were brighter, not just with need, but glowing with a sort of excitement that he tried to conceal behind lowered lids. He felt almost like a man again. If possible he wanted to be in a place where he could get help before he made his move. He had to wait for the right moment. He only hoped that they wouldn't be able to take off directly for the country or some isolated site. In that case he would have to change his plan.

Through the window, Doyle could see the high illuminated statute of Notre Dame de la Garde, the towering statue that surveyed all of Marseilles. It was on their right as the car moved out and Doyle knew they were moving north, probably to the coastal mountain road, the lonely road up towards Cassis. There would be no one travelling it at this hour, a perfect drop, better than the Bath Beach section of Brooklyn. But to get there, the car had to head east towards the Canebière, then turn north. This was territory that Doyle knew and he knew there was an all night sandwich joint at Place Charles de Gaulle where the frogs killed some hunky king. He timed himself carefully. The car made the turn past the Samaritaine. Suddenly he fell into a fit of coughing and sneezing as Yusif looked on him with disdain. Under the cover of the hacking and whooping, Doyle was able to reach down and open the long, wicked straight razor.

The car swung left into the Canebière which was now void of traffic, but there were taxis at the stand in the far corner of the Place. Holding his hand low, Doyle leaned forward carefully. Yusif was hardly looking at him. Suddenly, with a reserve of strength and agility that he would never believe he could call up, Doyle made his move. The blade flashed dully through the half light and swept across the dark, hawklike visage of the Algerian. There was a wet spurt as the blade cut across the man's eyeball. Yusif shrilled one horrifying scream and Mario hit the brakes.

Doyle shoved the bleeding, already blinded figure of the Algerian into the corner of the car and leaned forward with the blade at the throat of the driver.

'Keep moving,' he said, as he fumbled for the door of the Citroen, which was open on Yusif's side. The Algerian was now screaming and blubbering and clutching at his face, almost unable to function. Doyle braced his back against the doorpost of his side and shoved at the Algerian with both feet. The door opened soundlessly and there was a crumpling sound, a gurgling sigh and the tearing of cloth as the eagle-faced man pitched from the doorway to the pavement.

The car by now was opposite and just north of the plaza. Doyle leaned forward again and without a word moved the razor blade smoothly across the grimy neck of Mario, the

Corsican chauffeur. The blade sliced soundlessly through the carotid artery.

Mario gave a small sigh, like a child sobbing in his sleep and slumped over the wheel. Blood spurted in a brilliant pulsing stream from his slashed neck.

The car careened crazily on the empty street and then slowed down as Mario's foot fell lifelessly from the accelerator, smashing noisily into the huge storefront of the Monoprix, shattering the giant glass window with a sound like a crystal waterfall.

CHAPTER TWENTY-EIGHT

Doyle was momentarily stunned by the impact and he sat back against the comfortable, grey upholstered cushions of the Citroen, breathing shallowly with his eyes staring ahead and unfocused. The sound of shouts and running feet from Place de Gaulle revived him. He pushed open the door of the Citroen and ran across the Canebière into the warren of small streets leading to the sea.

His right arm felt wet and sticky and when he looked down he was surprised to see that his shirtsleeve was soaked to the elbow with the bright arterial blood that had spewed from Mario's slashed carotid.

'Fuck 'im,' Doyle mumbled to himself. 'Bastards had it coming.'

He felt lightheaded and strange. Little phosphorescent balls of different colours danced across his vision, but for the moment the cramps were gone, leaving only the nausea and the lightheadedness of a person in a state of near-starvation. Now he could hear the hee-haw claxons of police sirens converging in the streets behind him, and he knew somebody had called in the bloody accident.

'That ought to give them something to think about, those fucking frog cops,' Doyle said aloud to himself. Almost without thinking, he was stumbling, feet dragging and hopping erratic-

ally towards the port and then westward, towards the *Hotel de
la Police*.

*Gotta get straight somehow . . . Gotta see old Henry and
piss in his face ... I guess they'll know Charnier's here now ...
sonofabitch he's really here . . . what was the name of that
hotel? . . . fucking place was a nest full of vipers . . . that's a
laugh, vipers . . . those goddamn scrumbags in Henry's office
didn't even know what it was about ...*

He felt blown across the city like a dry, fallen leaf, moving
erratically, but always in the same direction. Gradually, as he
moved the *Hotel de la Police* seemed like a home to him. Going
there, he felt he was going back to the only friends he knew, to
Miletto and Diron and even old fuckface Henry. But *could* he
trust even them? Who had blown the whistle on him? Who had
set up the snatch? Well, there was nowhere else he could go
anyway.

At the iron gates of the Hotel de la Police, Doyle tripped on
the sill and lay spreadeagled on the cobblestones for a moment.
After several seconds, he crawled to his knees and began to
move on all fours blindly towards the entrance to the police
station. From the other side he could hear the braying claxon
as cars went out, no doubt to check on the accident.

Diron and Miletto were leaning on the granite steps outside
the station house taking a smoke break when they noticed the
scarecrow crawling and stumbling across the courtyard. Miletto
said, 'That old clochard. He must be really desperate to go to
jail. Maybe he's looking for a warm cell for the night, crawling
past the policeman on guard.'

'Well, you know,' Diron said, 'the nights are getting colder.
I suppose the old bums don't like to sleep in the streets anymore.'

Perhaps it was the bloodstained sleeve that focused their
attention more closely, or something vaguely familiar about the
haggard and emaciated features. Staring in wonder as his brain
slowly reconstructed the vision in front of him, Miletto absently
stubbed out his cigarette on the granite step.

'My God,' he said, 'I can't believe it! But I think it's . . .'

Diron, too, seemed to get the message at the same time

and ran forward to clutch at the torn shirtsleeve of the ragged figure.

'Is that you, Popeye?' he said, unbelievingly. 'Is that really you? My God, what happened to you?

'Miletto, help! It's Popeye!'

To the guard daydreaming at the gate, he said, 'Go inside and get Inspector Barthelmy right away.'

'But the Inspector,' the guard started to protest.

'Get in there, you idiot, fast.'

It was not a usual tone of voice for Miletto. This was not a usual situation. Between them, Diron and Miletto hoisted the limp figure on their shoulders and half walked it, half dragged it into the headquarters building and down the corridor towards Barthelmy's office.

Barthelmy came out and met them half way, with the guard at his heels. Looking at the wasted face, he felt sick at heart.

'What happened, Popeye?' Barthelmy asked. 'My God, what happened?'

The two detective inspectors dragged him into Barthelmy's office and put him down gently in a swivel armchair.

'Your arm is covered with blood. Are you wounded?' Barthelmy said, pulling back the shirtsleeve. The series of infected scabs, needle marks and pimples, a familiar sight to Barthelmy, told the whole story as the inside of Doyle's arm came into view.

'*Merde!*' Barthelmy said. He tore at the other cuff and revealed a matching array of holes. Doyle's head began to loll in the chair. Miletto looked at Barthelmy for guidance.

Barthelmy's face was a mixture of pity and hard determination. He looked towards the interior of the station and pointed his finger towards the rear. It was clear that he had come to a decision concerning the ruined American narc. The two detectives half dragged the bleary and mumbling Doyle to an interrogation room deep within the bowels of the building – a soundproof room with steel doors and a tiny window. There was a cot in it and a light high in the ceiling, barred by wire-reinforced glass. The bed was bolted to the floor. There was a washbasin in the corner and an iron chair and a heavy oak table. That was all the furniture.

To Doyle, it had a familiar look. It reminded him of the room he had spent so many centuries in, in the Hotel . . . the Hotel . . . what the fuck was the name of that hotel?

As they lay him in the bare canvas cot, Doyle was seized with a sudden chill. His legs drew up in violent spasms and his face turned green and clammy.

'Gimme . . . gimme . . . gimme . . .'

Barthelmy snapped out of a daze of guilt-ridden compassion.

'Get a mattress in here,' he said to Miletto. 'Some blankets. Get some water, but make sure it's in a tin pitcher, nothing that can break.'

He pulled a couple of ten franc notes from his pocket.

'When you're finished with that, hop in the car and run over to the Gare Saint Charles. There's a place there that's open, a news stand where they have candy. Get all the candy this will buy – chocolate, hard candies, anything.'

Doyle lay unheeding, curled into a foetal coil, shivering with cold. There were confused flashes, movements, frowns, and Doyle had a feeling that he was, in a sense, safe. But he needed a fix so bad, even a small fix. He realized that he had been moved and was now on a steel medical table. It was padded like a bed and he was covered with a blanket. Tubes had been run into his nose and throat. His face was the colour of scraped bone, the chin wet with green bile and drool. Three medical attendants were working at him. Barthelmy watched from the foot of the table. When Miletto entered with a string bag full of groceries, he was motioned to the side. One of the medical attendants turned to Barthelmy.

'He's all yours now.'

'Right.'

'Remember, no records on this.'

'Of course,' the man in the green tunic said.

Barthelmy looked at Doyle for a long moment and then left with the medical man as Miletto started to unload from his bag sixpacks of Coca Cola, French bread and candy bars.

Doyle wasn't sure how much time had elapsed when he came slowly awake. Standing nearby was a grim, freshly-shaved Barthelmy. His eyes looked with sorrow at the man on the steel table, but Doyle turned away, shivering and ashamed.

Barthelmy opened a Coca Cola and handed it to Doyle.

'Drink,' he said.

Doyle looked at him cautiously, took the Coke in both hands, and started to drink. His arms were shaking, his face screwed up into a grimace and he spit the Coca Cola on the floor.

'That's bitter,' he said.

Barthelmy took the bottle, poured the rest of the Coke into a glass, then tore open four packets of sugar and poured them into it, stirring it with a spoon.

'Listen, Henry, I need a doctor . . . an American doctor.'

'Doctors keep records,' Barthelmy said. 'Do you want that? A junkie cop – they'll throw you off the force.'

He handed the extra-sweet Coke to Doyle, who drank it greedily and handed the empty back to Barthelmy. A shudder ran through his body.

'More, Henry, please.'

Barthelmy repeated the formula and handed the Coke to Doyle. He started to drink in greedily, then spewed it out onto the white sheet. His huge emaciated frame jacknifed forward in the first rumble of a convulsion, and the glass fell shattering to the concrete floor.

'Mother of Jesus,' Doyle said hopelessly. 'Can't somebody do something?'

Barthelmy put his head out the door and yelled 'Miletto!'

Miletto returned, his arms full of towels and a fresh set of sheets. Together the inspector and his assistant started tying the large towels around Doyle's arms and legs in the form of a crude straitjacket.

'Hey, don't do that, Henry,' Doyle said helplessly as his body stiffened in pain as a muscle spasm raked from his ankle to his groin.

Miletto went out again and dragged in a thick mattress, placing it on the floor. Together he and Barthelmy lifted Doyle's wasted body from the steel table and placed it as gently as possible on the mattress. The American detective's body shuddered again and bubbles appeared in the corner of his mouth. His eyes were clouded with need and then starting in a whimper, rising and building, coming from some terrible depth, Doyle began to scream.

CHAPTER TWENTY-NINE

A long time had passed in the windowless room. It was impossible to say how long, except that the bag of groceries seemed to be empty and Barthelmy, who was sitting against the far wall watching, seemed very tired. Doyle stared at the grocery bag.

'It's cold,' he said. 'Henry, it's very cold.'

'Yes.'

Barthelmy got up and took an extra blanket from a pile in the corner, draping it over Doyle. Doyle tried to get up and then fell back weakly.

'I feel like I spent a week licking the fuzz off a pool table.'

'It's been three weeks,' Barthelmy said.

Suddenly a memory flickered in Doyle's disordered mind. And anger appeared in his eyes.

'Where the fuck *were* you guys?'

'We looked,' Barthelmy said, 'but . . .'

'Where in Christ's name *were* you guys?' Doyle said furiously.

'I had fifty-two men looking for you full time,' Barthelmy said. 'Nearly a third of my force.'

'If I had fifty-two men in New York looking for a guy, I'd find him in three hours,' Doyle said.

'Marseilles is not New York.'

'You bet your ass it isn't,' Doyle said.

He stared frantically around the room again and pushed himself on one elbow.

'It's a skag city, that's what it is. I'd like to bust it down brick by brick with you fuckers in it.'

'Relax,' Barthelmy said.

The exhausted New York detective lay back for a moment on the mattress and looked at the inside of his eyelids. Suddenly a picture flickered across his view. It was like an old faded colour slide. It was a picture of a curbstone with a name incised onto it – Hotel de Tanger!

Doyle began to murmur even before he opened his eyes.

'Henry, I got it, I got it!' With a struggle he raised himself on one elbow.

'It was the Hotel de Tanger! That's where the fuckers held me! Hotel de Tanger! I saw it written on the curbstone.'

Barthelmy looked interested. He tugged his black notebook from his pocket and wrote the name down. Then he wrote it down again on another page with a brief notation and handed it out the door to an officer on duty there.

'That's good. It may be just what we need,' he said to the man on the floor.

The blanket fell from Doyle's shoulders as he tried to rise again, and suddenly he was aware of the scabs on his arm and the fact that New York was far, far away.

'Jesus,' he said. 'I look like a pincushion.'

Barthelmy's sad eyes wrinkled with sympathy. Doyle shuddered, pulled the blanket around him and lay down again in a foetal position.

Afraid to face the inspector, he spoke to the wall. 'You're not asking me to go . . . cold turkey, are you Henry?'

Barthelmy's voice was soft with compassion but firm.

'Yes, I am.'

'Jesus, Henry,' Doyle protested, 'I mean I've seen a lot of guys go cold turkey. They try to put their heads through steel doors. For a five-dollar bag of skag, they'd cut their mothers' throats.'

'*Voilà*,' said Barthelmy, 'I'll call your mother.'

Doyle looked back over his shoulder.

'Leave my mother out of this,' he said.

'She'll be proud of you,' Barthelmy said, cutting into the knotted fibres of Doyle's self-pity with a hard knife.

'Lay off,' Doyle begged.

'Madame Doyle,' Barthelmy said, 'may I present your son, the hero?'

His arm swung in an elaborate broad gesture at Doyle's pathetic form. Doyle rolled himself over, his body shaking now with rage, and pushed himself to a sitting position, even rose to one knee.

'I said leave my mother out of this!'

'Didn't I ever tell you,' Barthelmy said, 'when I was in New York I think I had her once. It was in what you call Red Hook.'

Doyle lurched towards the taunting figure in a rush, anger bursting from him, his clouded eyes assuming a purpose and clarity as he vainly tried to throw punches, but Barthelmy backed away a few steps and gripped his wrists. It took very little force to stop the hopeless, enraged onrush. He held Doyle's wrists and forced him back onto the mattress, gripping the clenched fists, until Doyle let his arms go limp, acknowledging his weakness.

Barthelmy's voice softened. 'Don't quit now, Popeye.'

Doyle fell back on the mattress, his eyes acknowledging that he understood the French cop's tactics. His eyes rolled towards the paper sack on the table.

'You got a candy bar in that bag?' he asked pathetically.

It was a long time later. Doyle was alone in the room. He held the blanket closely around his shoulders and leaned against the wall, looking at the ceiling, door, the overhead light, the walls around him. He began to roll back and forth then, bracing his feet against the wall, he took a hard, running block at the steel door. It shuddered, but didn't move. There was only a sharp pain in Doyle's shoulder for his efforts. It was a pain he hardly felt as he backed against the wall and slammed hard at the door again. But he knew it was hopeless. He slid down against the door into a hunkering position, ripped the paper off the French candy bar and started to gnaw eagerly at it. It helped the nausea, but not much, and the muscle spasms seemed to be less violent now.

He slept, maybe a half hour, maybe two or three hours. Then he was sitting against the wall and Barthelmy was talking to him. He had a notebook in front of him.

Popeye looked at it curiously.

'Well? Did you bust that place yet? Did you collar those motherfucking greasers?'

Barthelmy shook his head dejectedly.

'There is no such place. Are you sure you remembered it correctly? It wasn't some kind of drug hallucination?'

Doyle raked the French detective with a scornful glance.

'I never imagine *nothing*, Henry. That was the name of the place. It's like burned on the inside of my skull. I couldn't ever forget it. That curbstone, six inches from my eyes, goddam it!'

'Well we can't find any record of it.'

'You sure you're not covering up for somebody?'

It was Barthelmy's turn to look scornful.

'Do you believe that?'

Doyle shrugged, but there was a small apology in his eyes.

'Popeye, you must remember something? A look, a sign, a smell, anything.'

Doyle looked at him. There was an undertone of slyness to his answer.

'Listen, I just had the shit beat out of me. They didn't give out business cards in that place.'

'Did you smell the sea?' Barthelmy persisted.

Doyle rose from the mattress and began to pace the floor.

'Did I smell the sea? What the fuck kind of a dumbass question is that? No, it smelled like a baboon's sock.'

He walked to the corner and stood there for a minute.

'Did I smell the sea . . . Shit!'

Barthelmy's voice was slow and patient.

'You want to find Charnier. Then you must tell me where you were.'

Doyle whirled. 'You tell me where *you* were. What kind of a bush outfit is this anyway? Those fucking tails you had on me – their idea of a disguise is they limp across the street on one foot and then to change they limp back on the other. And listen, ain't you got any stoolpigeons in this town?'

He was shouting at Barthelmy's back as the French inspector sat, his pencil poised for any information that might leak but Doyle couldn't see the grim smile on the inspector's face.

Barthelmy got up, went to the table to the food, buttered a piece of French bread and handed it to Doyle.

'Here, eat,' he said.

Doyle bit into the broken-off baguette. It tasted like plaster.

'Shit,' Doyle said. 'I want a hamburger, a PJ Clarke's hamburger, big and juicy with the blood running and all and an onion on it, a big Bermuda onion. Lots of salt and a good cold Rheingold.'

There was a knock on the steel door and it was Miletto.

'Send for two, no six hamburgers for our friend here,' Barthelmy told the lean, grey-haired man.

Doyle looked over his shoulder at the corridor outside. Barthelmy caught the look.

'Forget it,' he said. 'You're staying in here.'

'Listen, I'm gonna need some help, Henry. I'm gonna need a doctor, an American doctor. He could take care of me.'

'Forget it,' Barthelmy said. He closed his notebook and picked up the chair to leave.

'Hey listen, Henry, stick around a while,' Doyle said desperately. 'I mean, wait until the hamburgers come. Or listen, change the order, make it Hershey bars, real Hershey bars with almonds, not this frog oatmeal. The real stuff – how about a Milky Way. How about a Snickers with nuts – nuts, Henry.'

Barthelmy took the chair with him and left, closing the door and bolting it behind him. Doyle was alone. He yelled after the departing figure, 'Henry!' But there was only silence.

He pounded on the unyielding steel of the door with his fists until they were bruised.

'HEEEEENNNRRRY!' he screamed. 'Come on Henry, I know you got some stuff in the office. Henry, I seen it up there. Come on, who the hell would know? HEEEEENNNN-NRRRRY!'

CHAPTER THIRTY

Time had passed, how much Doyle had no idea. Maybe two days, maybe three days, maybe a week. Barthelmy was sitting opposite him at the heavy wooden table. There were two glasses on it, half filled with brandy and a bottle stood between them. Barthelmy cupped the brandy in his hands and inhaled deeply.

'This is very good stuff. You should appreciate it, Popeye.'

Doyle knocked back an ounce of Remy-Martin, shuddering at its hot impact.

'I never drink this stuff back home. But you know, it ain't bad, it ain't bad at all! Fucking cognac, eh?'

'Only the best for you, Doyle,' Barthelmy said.

'You know, when I was a kid,' Doyle reminisced, 'I thought drinking was a sin. You know, the nuns. You a Catholic, Henry?'

'Retired,' Barthelmy replied, dryly.

'Retired, huh?' Doyle said. He chuckled. 'That's pretty good. You just put in your papers, huh? You get a pension?'

Doyle reached out for the bottle and poured, almost filling the snifters. The bottle was about one-third empty now and Doyle was feeling the effects.

'Well, you should know a few things, Henry. In addition to being a Catholic, I mean besides the nuns and the confession, I was a ballplayer. Baseball. I even had a tryout with the Yankees. You ever hear of the Yankees, Henry?'

'As in Yankee, go home?' Barthelmy inquired.

'Yeah. Only . . . no. They were a baseball team. They sent me down to the minors and I wasn't half bad if I say so myself. The problem was, they had this other kid, fast as a bastard, a shortstop he was then. Could hit a fucking ton . . . Anyway, I seen this kid in spring training and right away I decided to take the cops' test. You know what his name was? Mickey Mantle. You ever hear of Mickey Mantle?'

Barthelmy sipped conservatively at the brandy.

'No, I can't say that I have.'

Doyle looked at him in mock astonishment.

'What, you never heard of Mickey Mantle? What about Willie Mays?'

Barthelmy shook his head no.

'Duke Snider?'

'Not even him.'

Doyle slurped a large swallow from the brandy glass and wiped his lips with the back of his wrist.

'Whitey Ford? Never heard of him either, I bet. He was a nifty little southpaw.'

Barthelmy raised his eyebrows. 'Southpaw?'

'Yeah, a lefty.'

'Like a communist?'

Doyle waved his hand in disgust. 'Jesus Christ, no. He threw the ball with his left hand which is like his south hand, see? His paw, you know, like a dog.'

Gesturing with his left arm to illustrate the point, he looked down and noticed that the tracks had faded to little white scars, and he felt a sudden uncontrolled rush of tears.

Time must have gone backwards now. Doyle felt himself alone in a shell again, squashed in a corner, a mattress under him, the blankets kicked off, his arms and legs again bound with towels. He groaned quietly, not a sound to be heard by others, just something full of hurt and pain and despair. He began to jerk and twist, forcing his face down into the mattress. Again his leg jerked involuntarily and then again. Suddenly, he was completely in convulsion. He started to vomit on the mattress with his face in it. He lifted his head to get it out of the smelly wetness, but another spasm smacked him forward, face into the vomit. He began to cry with pain and shame.

The light outside seemed bright, very bright, as it cascaded in through the broad skylight of the shower room. Two cops were holding Doyle erect in the shower as the water pounded on his naked body. He felt weak, but it was clear the worst was past. They had shaved his face already and the police barber stood to the side, ready to trim his shaggy hair. Barthelmy stood by approvingly.

To Miletto he said, 'Get him a toothbrush and some Colgate toothpaste.'

Doyle raised his face to the cold stream of the shower letting the water run into his mouth and throat.

Later in the day, Doyle and Barthelmy stepped out of the station house. It was a hot day, very hot for that time of year but Doyle was wearing a heavy wool suit and a hot turtleneck sweater. The harsh sunlight punished his eyes and his face was the colour of a fish's belly. Suddenly his lips began to tremble.

'You're not sending me home, are you, Henry?' he said.

'Not yet,' Barthelmy answered.

He led Doyle to the waiting Citroen and after a moment's hesitation, Doyle got in. On the seat were blankets and towels. Apologetically, Barthelmy ran the cuffs over Doyle's right wrist and attached it to the door-handle.

'Hey listen, come on, Henry,' Doyle protested.

Barthelmy said nothing, but piled some of the blankets on Doyle. Doyle's face began to pop out in rivulets of sweat. Barthelmy handed him a towel and signalled to Miletto to start the car.

'What the hell are you doing?' Doyle asked.

'You were cold,' Barthelmy said. 'Now we warm you up and maybe we'll give you a little ride around Marseilles too. Perhaps you will see something that will remind you of where you were.'

The car, without siren or flashing light, moved slowly through the streets. It seemed as hopeless as it had in the beginning. Every face could be Jules' or Jacques'. There were millions that looked like them. Just as any Frenchman with a beard could be Charnier. Doyle looked hopeless.

'I tell you, I haven't a clue what the name of the place was. They just finished working me over. I wasn't seeing too clear.'

'Anything,' Barthelmy said patiently. 'A detail.'

'I don't remember a thing,' Doyle said flatly. And it was clear to Barthelmy that he was lying, but why?

The car rolled slowly up the Canebière past the X-rated movies. Doyle noticed that 'The Mechanical Bananas' had been replaced by a film called 'Emannuelle'. It meant nothing to him. But on the next corner a beautiful golden-skinned woman with long black hair stood. She was licking an ice cream cone. Doyle looked at her hungrily.

'Oh brother, would I like a little of that.'

Barthelmy smiled. 'A woman would finish you off now, Popeye.'

Doyle turned to him with disgust. 'Not the *woman,* the *ice cream.*'

Barthelmy told Miletto to pull the car over to a sidewalk and bought the American a pralinée ice cream cone which he handed through the window. Doyle took it with his free left hand and devoured it sloppily as the car cruised through the city. Later he wiped his chin on his sleeve and brought out the question that had been bothering him.

'Listen, tell me the truth, Henry. I was set up, wasn't I?'

There was a long pause. The car must have rolled a half block before Barthelmy answered.

Finally, he said, 'In a way, yes.'

'Whose orders?' Doyle said.

'New York, your superiors. They wanted you to be bait, to draw out this Charnier, as you call him.'

'And you went along with that?' Doyle said.

'There was a lot of bad publicity about this case, my friend. And we have superiors, too.'

Doyle chuckled bitterly. 'You're a bigger asshole than I thought you were.'

'Oh?' the French detective said.

'Don't you understand? Those bastards in New York wanted me dead. They don't want to find Charnier, especially alive. He'd tell everybody which one of them he bought to get away. So they send me here to work with you and then they tell you to get me out in the street where Charnier can blow me away. That's beautiful.'

He laughed again darkly.

'Why didn't you figure this out earlier?' Barthelmy said.

Doyle's voice turned even more bitter. 'Because I'm a bigger asshole than you are.'

CHAPTER THIRTY-ONE

They were back in Doyle's cell, the interrogation room, but it was more cheerful now. There was a little pot of flowers on the table and the door was open. Chairs were left there now as a matter of course. Doyle was doodling bearded faces aimlessly on a pad in front of him. Raoul Diron entered the room with a small tray of hot chocolate, croissants, and a copy of the Paris *Herald.*

'*Bonjour,*' he said.

Doyle looked up passively from his doodling as Diron greeted him with a small formal bow.

'You're a regular little asskisser, aren't you, Raoul? A regular politician,' Doyle said bitterly.

Raoul smiled, but clearly the young detective didn't understand the reference.

'I've been watching you real good, fella. I bet you didn't know that, did you? I guess if old Henry said "Shit" you'd squat.'

He broke off a piece of croissant and dunked it in the hot chocolate.

'Let me tell you something, Raoul. You ain't never gonna be much cop that way. You become a cop on the street, not in some fucking narco office filling out papers, kissing ass with the bosses. You go right out on the street. Shit, when I was on the force three months, I'd already made seventy-six collars. Used to go to the academy daytimes and hang around Times Square at night. If it moved, I busted it – hookers, degenerates, Murphy-game artists, junkies – you name it, I busted it. I hung around some joints where you could get crabs just playing the jukebox, but I got a lot of collars.'

He shoved the rest of the croissant into his mouth and gulped the scalding hot chocolate.

'You know, I was the youngest sergeant in the history of the department,' he continued. 'Nobody ever made sergeant faster. You know how many arrests I've made? Eleven thousand. How many collars you got on your record Raoul? Twenty-five, fifty?'

Raoul's English wasn't too good. He missed most of the words, but he certainly understood the tone. Doyle stabbed a finger in the direction of the French detective.

'I've been stabbed six times and shot twice. I got medals they ain't even minted yet back home in the drawer.'

A shiver ran through his body and he drank the rest of the sweet chocolate as if it were fuel. He was almost talking to himself now; as if he were reminding himself of who he was before the poison was needled into his veins. He held his hands out for Diron's inspection.

'Look at these hands. I got three knuckles left. Broke 'em all up. That's when I was young and I still thought you could hurt a punk by hitting him in the head. You gotta hit 'im in the belly. Kill the body and the head dies, you got that, Raoul? Shoot low, sheriff, he's crawling . . .'

Doyle fell back in the chair, depressed now, tired of talking, his hostility ebbing. He picked at some crumbs from the croissant.

'Ah, fuck it,' he said. He turned away from the detective and the younger man patted him on the back as if to reassure him and left, locking the door behind him.

Doyle opened the pages of the Paris *Herald*, turning first to Art Buchwald, then going through the paper page by page, even reading the situations wanted, the holidays in the Costa Brava, the baseball scores that he had long since lost track of, the international financial news, the price of the dollar, the price of gold, the reviews of the plays in Paris and London. There was nothing in the paper about Marseilles. The only thing about New York told about a big round-up of mob people by District Attorney Gold in Brooklyn. Doyle could bet his ass he would've known some of those guys.

He picked up the stub of the pencil that he'd been doodling with, made a vain attempt to solve the crossword puzzle, but words were not his strong point. He threw the pencil down angrily in frustration and again began to try to reconstruct what he really could remember of the events. He began to number items that he could remember.

1. The building had at least three storeys; that was probably all. 2. There was a bar in the basement full of whores. 3. The whole building was full of whores and junkies. Christ, a cop ought to be able to find that. 4. It was an old building – he remembered that, with thick stone walls that dripped with dampness. 5. The rugs had some kind of oriental design and they were worn through to the threads.

What else did he have? 6. There were Johnny Hallyday records on the jukebox. Shit, there were Johnny Hallyday records on every jukebox in this goddamn country. 7. There was an old English lady. He wondered if she were registered with the British Consulate. 'Not very likely,' as she would say.

What about the gang that held him? 8. One of them he knew, was a Corsican. The other two joked all the time about it. That was Mario, but Mario wasn't around anymore. Doyle laughed to himself. 9. Then there was old eagle-beak. He was some kind of Arab or Algerian. His name was Yusif. The third guy Jules' identity eluded him for a minute, but he remembered the fourth guy that only came sometimes to give orders. That was the guy that might be the connection to Charnier. He was tall, kind of blondie, goodlookin' kid, looked very high class, wore expensive clothes, blazers, turtlenecks, Gucci loafers, even had a manicure. They called him Monsieur Jacques.

The door opened and Miletto walked in with containers of coffee, a big *bagnat* and some more candy bars. Fed up with the French version of hamburgers, it had been Doyle himself who requested the *bagnat*.

'How are you feeling?' Miletto asked.

'Bad,' Doyle said.

'Eat,' the French detective said.

'I'll try.'

He stared at the food and then up at the ceiling light.

'It hurts, eh?' Miletto said sympathetically.

Doyle looked at him oddly. 'I'll tell you something, Miletto. I really racked my brain and you know, I never been any place in my life where somebody wasn't hurting somebody.'

His eyes were tired and battle-weary like an infantryman who has been too long in the line.

'Ah, the hell with it,' he said. 'I don't even know what it's all about.'

He sipped the coffee and Miletto left quietly, as Doyle stared vaguely into the dark corners of the room.

Later, they let him walk around a little outside in the hall. He even walked up to the front door of the station under the watchful eyes of Miletto. Some of the detectives were lounging around in the shadow of the courtyard steps. Doyle walked out of the dark interior and blinked in the sharp sunlight, huddled in his heavy overcoat. He was very pale and much thinner than he'd been.

Sitting on the steps, taking in the sun, Doyle noticed the Old Pro and the curly-headed kid, his tails. He started to smile at them and then turned away. His eyes were shiny now, over-bright, and there was a half-smile that never left his tight lips. If he had seen himself, he would have marked himself down as flaky, definitely flaky, not the sort of man you would trust on an errand.

At night they left his room unlocked, trusting to the guards at the gates to keep an eye on him. He even had his old clothes back; they had sent to the hotel for them, his keys, his wallet, his empty holsters. Somebody had loaned him a cheap watch, so Doyle had some idea of the time again.

It was around two am when he got up, put on his clothes, slipped into a pair of crêpe-soled shoes, and walked down the hallway towards Barthelmy's office. As he expected, there was no light from inside. Doyle fumbled in his pocket and pulled out his key ring. On it was a small selection of lock picks. He selected one from it and tried it quickly and expertly on the lock of Barthelmy's door. No problem. The door swung back on well-oiled hinges. From his pocket, Doyle took a small penlight to show his way to the display cabinet behind Barthelmy's desk. He opened the first one with practised ease. The lower shelves were an arrangement of drugs on display – hash, opium, vials of heroin, syringes, the works. Doyle stood looking at the items, began to sweat. His face twitched with emotion and his hands began exploring the upper shelves, where there was a less-organized collection of evidence, mostly weapons, including guns.

A shadow fell across the outside office door, but Doyle didn't notice it. A hand reached in to the door which had been left open a crack and pulled it gently back. There was a change in the air pressure or some other thing that gave a subconscious signal to Doyle's strained senses. He looked up. Barthelmy was standing in the doorway, framed in the light from the hall, looking at Doyle.

Doyle dropped to a crouch, fumbling on the ground, hiding something, then rose to greet the angry French detective. Barthelmy rushed at him and Doyle tried to grapple him but the Frenchmen was too quick. He caught him under one arm, twisted it around, and pushed it upwards in the old police lock, the grip that Doyle had applied so often to others.

Frantically he threw his elbow back, trying to catch Barthelmy in the stomach but he wasn't quick enough or strong enough. It was a struggle between two street cops, but Doyle was not the man he'd been. Barthelmy finally got Doyle's arm well behind him, jerking it up and tossing him hard, face first against the display case which rattled under the impact.

'Hands on it,' Barthelmy said. Doyle didn't move and Barthelmy kicked him savagely in the ankle.

'You bastard!' Doyle said.

Barthelmy slipped a pair of cuffs on the angry American cop, keeping him pressed face down against the drug display, gave him a quick frisk. Onto the table behind him he threw Doyle's pickpocket set, a handful of change, a Zippo lighter, the penlight, some candy bars, cubes of sugar. He patted around Doyle's shoulder and then down his legs. At the ankle he found the gun, pulling it from the ankle holster. Breathing hard, he backed off and then a small smile came to his face. He held the gun out.

'Is this *all* you wanted?'

'Yeah,' Doyle said bitterly.

He pushed himself up from the display case and sat on the floor breathing heavily from the effort of the tussle.

'Miletto said you were holding it here after I got into that hassle.'

He unwrapped a candy bar and started to eat it. Barthelmy watched him and his eyes flickered from the seated detective to the display case full of dope. Doyle caught the look and grimaced, ashamed of himself. Barthelmy looked at him sadly.

'You liked it, didn't you, Doyle?'

Doyle concentrated on eating the candy bar.

'Bullshit! You think I like sticking needles in the arm?'

'You don't have to be ashamed of liking it,' Barthelmy said. 'A lot of people do.'

'Get outtahere,' Doyle said. 'Like it, shit!'

His eyes switched to the gun still held in Barthelmy's hand. Barthelmy used it to shove Doyle's things over on the table.

'You won't need a gun,' he said. He slipped it into the file drawer, this one with a combination lock on it, and twirled the dial. Then he came and took the cuffs off the bitter New York detective.

'What do I do without a gun?' Doyle said. 'Depend for protection on your great tails?'

Barthelmy nodded firmly. 'You have to. If I catch you with another gun, I bust you.'

And Doyle knew that it wasn't an idle threat. He stood there for a minute remembering how Barthelmy had helped him out of a jam. There's no way he could have been part of the set-up, not after that. For a moment his tough façade softened.

'You know, I *did* like it, Henry,' he said.

Barthelmy looked at him with respect. It wasn't an easy admission for anyone to make.

Doyle's voice turned hard again. 'I'll never forget that the sonofabitch *made* me *like* it.'

CHAPTER THIRTY-TWO

The first thing Doyle did when he was checked back in a semi-normal state at the Hotel de l'Univers was to call Francoise. She was working at the Avis counter in the airport. Her voice came through the wires warm and urgent.

'Is it really you, Popeye? My God, what happened to you? I thought you were dead somewhere. The police were looking everywhere for you. They questioned me for hours. What is it all about? And how are you, are you all right?'

The concern in her voice was clear and Doyle felt a rush of blood to his cheeks and a stirring in his groin unlike anything he had felt in what seemed like centuries. This girl really sounded concerned! First the tender loving care from the *Bureau de Stupefiants* and now this sweet worried voice. It was more popularity than Popeye could stand.

'I have to see you,' he told Francoise.

'Of course,' she said. 'When? When can we be together?'

'How about after work? You can come to my place, okay?'

There was no coyness about her.

'I can be there by seven o'clock. Is that all right?'

'That's great uh . . . *chérie*.'

The word had a strange sound in Popeye's mouth.

'Oh, and listen, what do you like to drink? Some wine maybe? Some of that *pastis*? Some champagne?'

Francoise laughed. 'No, no, don't worry. I drink very little. Perhaps a little Scotch. That would be fine.'

'Okay, see you later . . .' Popeye said, 'chérie.'

All this sweetness and light was catching. 'A "little" Scotch,' she said. Shit, he had to go about twenty bucks for a bottle of Scotch. He took a traveller's cheque from his folder and cashed it at the desk downstairs. The grumpy concièrge managed a snaggle-toothed smile and even worked up a few words of English.

'Nice to see you again, monsieur Doyle,' he said.

Coco, who was helping with the accounts in the back room, popped to the door.

'You are back, Popeye, and you do not call me?' she said, pouting. 'We were very worried about you. You look terrible. Have you been sick?'

'Yeah,' Popeye said. 'I've been real sick.'

'Ah, Coco come up and make you feel better,' she said.

'Yeah, well, uh, not tonight, honey,' Doyle said. 'I got some business meetings to take care of.'

'All right, you call Coco when you need her. *Tu comprends chéri*?'

The concièrge looked up with interest at the endearment. Apparently his gossip network wasn't up to date.

'Yeah, I'll call you, sweetie,' Doyle said.

It cost him almost twenty dollars for a bottle of White Label. It was beginning to be a race as to whether he would find Charnier or go bankrupt first.

On the way back, he asked the concièrge to send up some ice and some bottles of Perrier. The order was delivered by Coco, who kissed him with tender concern first on the cheeks and then full on the mouth, her warm tongue probing deep inside, while her free hand brushed lightly across the front of his fly.

Christ, Doyle thought, it's either feast or famine.

He turned her around and guided her towards the door with a gentle shove. 'Not tonight, sweetie, I've got work to do.'

Her eyes strayed towards the Scotch and ice and Doyle coloured with embarrassment.

'I can't explain it now, but it's important work. Detective business.'

Coco smiled brightly. 'Yes, Coco understands. You are the zero zero seven.'

'Right,' Doyle said. 'Agent double-oh seven, that's me. See you later.'

Pouting, Coco left the room, closing the door very slowly behind her, as though to give Doyle time to change his mind.

Promptly at seven thirty Francoise arrived, looking like a golden goddess in a crisp yellow cotton dress with a man's shirt collar and a deep vee at the neck. Her tawny hair was tied back with a matching ribbon and she wore very little makeup. Doyle could see that she was much younger than he had first placed her, not much more than twenty-four or five.

She rushed into his arms as soon as he opened the door and gripped him in a very tight hug. He felt as though those firm young breasts were going to push right through his rib cage. Then she leaned back and looked in his eyes.

'You don't look the same, Popeye. You're so pale. You've lost weight, no?'

Popeye nodded wearily.

'Your eyes – they look strange. Are you all right?'

Popeye shrugged, went to the bureau and poured some Scotch over a couple of ice cubes for both of them.

'Soda?' he asked, the Perrier bottle poised.

'No, no,' she waved her hand, 'I'll just have mine on the rocks as you say.'

Doyle sat on the edge of the bed and patted the place next to him.

Francoise dutifully came over, took the glass from him and sat beside him.

'Cheers,' she said, and watched him carefully over the rim of the glass as he sipped the Scotch and soda.

She really had great eyes, Doyle thought. They were big and they had a way of looking deep inside of you. He put his hand behind her head and kissed her very, very gently. She pulled back and looked at him with surprise.

'Is that really you, Popeye? It's not your style of kissing, is it?'

'You just look so great, I wanted to do something,' Popeye said quietly.

'Well, whatever happened to you seems to have changed you quite a lot,' Francoise said thoughtfully. 'You want to tell me?'

Popeye kissed her again, this time with a little more heat. He kissed the hair on her forehead and then her fresh, flower-like ears, cool and soft under his lips.

'I do want to tell you,' Popeye said, 'later.'

His hand reached up and began to unfasten the little bone buttons at the top of her dress. Francoise smiled languidly.

'Do you want me to help?'

'No,' Popeye said. 'I'd like to do this all by myself.'

Francoise lay back on the bed and watched him with a tender smile as he fumbled with the long series of buttons leading to the hem of her dress. Underneath she was wearing only a brief bikini panty and her body was bronzed from head to toe without a single pale mark to show where clothing might have obstructed the ultra-violet rays.

Later, they lay in bed with the sheets pulled up to their chests, her gold-toasted colour making the contrast with his fish-belly skin even more vivid. The tracks were fairly well healed now and would only have been noticed by a practised eye and the pimples were gone from his armpits and the corners of his mouth. But there were still hollows in his cheeks and between his ribs and the slightly crazed look of a junkie in need had not completely left his eyes.

Francoise offered Popeye one of her Winstons but he signalled that he now actually preferred one of his Gauloise Bleus. The love-making had been sweet, tender and had lasted long enough for the ice to melt in both their glasses. Only in the end was there a violent, twisting climax, and Popeye felt as if a string run up his urethra had pulled his entire insides out through his pulsing member. When they had finished, Popeye said, 'Boy, baby, you really cleaned out my tubes. That was the best ever.'

Francoise smiled. 'You are very different,' she said. 'Very, very different and I like it. You seem sweeter, more tender. I don't know what this sickness was that you had but at least it had some benefits, although you do look as though you could use a good rest and some sunshine,' she said looking down at his worn-out body.

Doyle smoked thoughtfully for a few minutes, organizing his thoughts. If this broad was some kind of plant, Popeye thought, then he had lost every shred of street sense that he'd ever learned. He decided to take a chance and level with her.

'You know that I'm not a businessman, that I'm not in public relations, don't you?' he said.

Francoise shrugged. 'After all those questions from the police, it seemed clear that there was something more involved than a missing Yankee businessman. And those men asking the questions, they were from the *Bureau des Stupefiants*. I'm not stupid. You're connected in some way with the narcotics division of your police. That is what I suspect.'

Popeye nodded with approval. 'You're a bright one, all right.'

She shrugged. 'It was not very hard to figure out. After my talk with Inspector Barthelmy, I think he suspects that I was a courier, but I can assure you that I was not.'

The last phrase came in a bitter tone. Popeye looked up with interest.

'If you could see my brother . . .' Francoise started to say and she let the sentence trail off.

Popeye looked at her with compassion. 'He's a junkie, right?'

Francoise nodded wordlessly. 'It's hopeless, you know,' she said, after a pause. 'We've lost him and we'll never get him back.'

'And these frog cops try to tell me there's no addiction here,' Popeye said.

'There really isn't much,' Francoise said. 'My brother got the habit when he came to see me in New York, but it's considered the smart thing to do in Paris these days. *Trés snob*. The cocaine and the marijuana I don't mind. I even use them myself sometimes, but this white stuff, it's worse than poison.'

'That's what we've been trying to tell your French cops over here,' Doyle said. 'But they don't seem to get the message.'

Francoise looked at him, her eyes bright with excitement.

'You blame *them*? Who do you think started this whole drug traffic in Marseilles?'

'The Mafia?' Doyle asked.

'Yes, the Mafia, but it was your own CIA that gave them control of the docks. It was back in the fifties, when the CGT, that's the communist union, was taking over all of France and your people backed the strike-breakers and hoodlums along with a whole labour union movement of their own. It was then that these Corsicans got control of the docks and began the drug trade. Until then, there was nothing here.'

'You sure of that?' Doyle asked.

The girl shrugged. 'I don't care if you believe it or not, but if you do a little research, you will find that I'm telling the truth.'

There was a long silence, while Doyle thought about what the girl had said as he sipped at the Scotch and soda, now gone flat and warm.

'Will you help me?' he said finally.

Francoise turned towards him and her eyes were hard and businesslike.

'I'll give you all the help I can.'

'Okay,' he said, 'the first thing I want you to do is help me find a place that used to be called the Hotel de Tanger. It's not called that anymore. I looked it up and I asked and the cops asked. But there must be some way of finding it. I'll tell you everything I know and maybe between us we can dope it out – I mean,' he corrected himself hastily, 'we can *figure* it out.'

CHAPTER THIRTY-THREE

The next couple of days were spent in going carefully over every clue that Doyle had been able to put together. The presence of the whores in the place limited it to one of a few areas, probably either the old section of the Opera or the Panier or some of the streets up towards the Canebière. There were brothels in other parts of town but not the sort that Popeye described, with a bar and jukebox and so on. There were a couple of places out on the Avenue de la Republique. 'I'll ask around some of the men at the airport. They know where these sort of places are,' Francoise said. 'There are quite a few, but not as many as you would think; possibly not more than twenty-five places would answer that description.'

'Shit,' Doyle said, 'I've checked out hundreds of places in

my time to try to run a clue down.'

Popeye had Francoise call a couple of the phone numbers he had taken from Charnier's New York hotel room. One was a pizzeria called Antoine's. 'It's very chic,' Francoise said. 'It's possible your friend might hang out there. A lot of movie people go there.'

Another number seemed to be a bakery shop, but after some questioning, Francoise discovered that the shop had only had that number for six months, whereas Doyle had picked up the numbers from Charnier well over a year earlier.

'You realize,' Francoise said, 'that the numbers here change very frequently, sometimes every year, so that these numbers might all be meaningless at this point. You don't, by chance, remember the name of the street where the hotel was that you were held?'

'No, dammit,' Doyle said. 'I wasn't in any condition to observe stuff like that.'

'You know, they have the phone numbers listed in Bottin according to the street addresses, as well as the names.'

'Well that would be great if we knew the street,' Popeye said, 'but we don't.'

'I think I'll spend a day at the Bureau des Archives,' Francoise said. 'I might be able to find out something about where the Hotel de Tanger was, but I might have to go back very far in the records.'

Doyle pulled a hundred franc note from his pocket. 'Use this, if you have to, maybe it'll get you a little extra help. It works in the States, anyway.'

Francoise smiled. 'It works here, too.'

That afternoon Doyle went to get Francoise at the archive room in the Hall of Records. It was a vaulted, galleried, huge rectangular room, very calm, very sedate, redolent with age and history, the walls lined with leather-bound books, paper-bound folders, envelopes, file boxes. Free-standing bookshelves packed with ledgers, documents, scrolls and files subdivided the room. Silence shrouded it like a blanket of foam.

Francoise was sitting at a desk in the middle of the room with a heap of books and ledgers going back to the twenties.

She was sweaty and there were smudges of dust on her face and the back of her hands. Doyle came up quietly beside her and kissed her very gently on the forehead. In some way, she looked more beautiful than she ever had. She looked at him with eyes that were far away in distraction, concentrating on the problem.

'You know,' she said, 'there were no phone books before 1924. There weren't enough telephones in the city. And also I discovered that a lot of hotels were listed then and are listed now only under the proprietor's name, but not by the name of the hotel. This will take a long time.'

'Can I help?' Doyle said.

'Yes, you can go through these books and see if you recognize the name of the hotel or any other name.'

She put a pile in front of him, and Doyle pulled a chair up next to her's.

On the third day Francoise looked up with interest.

'Here is an entry that says "Bordagaray, Collette, Hotel de Tanger."'

'Sonofabitch, daylight!' Doyle cried exultantly.

The archivist at the front desk looked up with annoyance at the noise.

'Look, there it is, goddammit!'

'Yes,' Francoise said. 'But there is no address listed.'

'Shit!' Doyle pounded the table in frustration, generating little clouds of dust.

'You know,' Francoise said, 'if the place was a brothel?'

'Well, Jesus, it wasn't a church,' Doyle said.

'If it was a brothel, the owners often kept the addresses private.'

'Okay, then let's see if we can find this Collette Bordagaray. Maybe she's listed in one of these books.'

'It's a good idea,' Francoise said.

'Maybe she's related to Frenchy Bordagaray. He played for Brooklyn. Wore a moustache. Couldn't hit a curve ball.'

Now they both turned to the main listings in the old phone books and began to run their fingers methodically through the

B's. This went faster, since they knew just what they were looking for and it didn't take long to find that no such person was listed as far back as 1924. Of course, if it went back earlier than that they were sunk anyway, as far as the records were concerned.

'Listen,' Doyle said, 'if she was running a whore house there had to be a police record, right? I mean a whore house was illegal in those days.'

'That's true,' Francoise said.

'Let's go over to headquarters and take a look there.'

'That might work,' Francoise said, 'except that during the war no records were kept between 1941 and 1946, at least not by us.'

'Who kept them?' Doyle said.

'The boche.'

'Okay, let's go over and see if we can get a little help from our pal Henry.'

He slipped another hundred franc note to the archivist who accepted it without looking up or thanking him.

At the *Hotel de la Police* Doyle started to present Francoise to Miletto who was alone in the office.

'I believe we've met,' Miletto said dryly.

'That's right,' Francoise said. 'And how are things going in your work?'

'*Comme si, comme ça,*' Miletto said, taking a key from the wall rack and leading them down the corridor to a dusty room not unlike the Hall of Records.

'If it exists, it's in here, probably on this shelf,' Miletto said, indicating a row of books about chest high.

Doyle pulled a book out at random.

'Christ, this stuff is in German.'

'Well,' Francoise said, 'the name would be spelled the same and that's all we need. Besides, I can read German.'

They divided the books between them, starting with 1946. Francoise worked backwards and Doyle worked from 1946 to the present. After two hours of eye-straining work in the musty, darkness of the records room, Francoise looked up with a smile.

'I think I have it.'

She pointed a finger, now grimy with the ancient dust accumulated on the books, and Doyle came running over.

'For crissake, they've got five addresses listed for her. Those krauts! Those bastards wrote down everything.'

Carefully, Francoise copied the addresses down and closed the books.

When they returned the key, Miletto asked without much curiosity, 'Did you have any success?'

Doyle shrugged. 'Naw, couldn't find much. I'll let you know when I come across it.'

Doyle and Francoise checked out a Renault R 16 and with a map of Marseilles in his hand and Francoise at the wheel they began to check the addresses. The first place was a huge hole in the ground with a sign saying that work on the new Bourse had been suspended because of the discovery of ancient Roman ruins on the site.

'Well this sure as shit isn't the place,' Doyle said.

At the next address, a huge department store called Baize, new and shiny, stood on the former site of one of Colette Bordagaray's houses.

Disgustedly, Doyle crossed the second address off the list. The third address was known to Francoise.

'That place was blown up during the war and it's been covered over with a new highway now, so that is not it.'

It was sunset when they finally found themselves in the area south of the Opera quarter over towards the French Foreign Legion headquarters at Saint Nicholas. The sign said Hotel de Niger, but even though this wasn't the name he remembered, Doyle knew they'd found the right spot. Now he could even hear the persistent 'Yeh, yeh, yeh' of Johnny Hallyday. He slid down in the car so that the girls lounging on the steps in front of the seedy hotel couldn't see him.

'Keep moving,' he said to Francoise.

She drove around the corner and stopped.

'Is that the place?'

'Yeah,' Doyle said. His voice was hard and flat. 'That was the fucking place, all right.'

'Shall we call Inspector Barthelmy?'

Doyle's eyes had that crazy bright look again.

'You just go to work, honey. I'll take it all from here. I'll drop you off at the bus so you can get out to the airport on time.'

'I can take another day off if you want, if you need me.'

'I need you like crazy, baby,' Doyle said, 'but not tonight.'

CHAPTER THIRTY-FOUR

The reaction at the *Hotel de la Police* was enthusiastic at first. Barthelmy sent Diron with the address to check against the real estate registers.

Barthelmy smiled at Doyle with approval. 'I see that you can really be a good detective when you want to, Popeye. I wasn't sure you realized there was anything to it besides smashing people about and shooting pistols.'

'You see too many movies, Henry,' Doyle said sourly, but he felt a sense of pride at the accomplishment.

Miletto returned in a few minutes with some notes scribbled on a piece of paper and handed it to Barthelmy. Barthelmy looked at the name written on the piece of paper and his face fell.

'Are you sure this is the place?' he asked Doyle.

'Am I sure? You're fucking right I'm sure. It's a fucking rat's nest. There isn't one person in that joint that isn't in it up to here. You name it, they're doing it there – dope, murphy games, the place has probably got about a ninety per cent VD rate, lush-rollers, the works.'

Barthelmy shook his head regretfully.

'This man, Du Verrier, who owns it is very influential, if you know what I mean. He is closely connected to Mayor Deferre.'

Doyle looked up, his eyes coming to a hard focus.

'He's also closely connected with the SAC, the parallel police. Do you know who they are?' Barthelmy said.

'You mean he's a cop?'

'Not exactly. But when de Gaulle was being attacked by terrorists, he formed his own little group, some very tough men who could act, shall we say, unofficially against the people who were bothering him. Some of these men were from the *milieu*. They were men with police records, gangsters. Many of them had learned about killing in the underground during the war, but then couldn't stop when the war was over. Now they have this group which is very closely connected to the government, people in high places.'

'Your hands are tied, right?' Doyle said.

Barthelmy shrugged. 'It would be no use, even if I wanted to do something. Informers would get the word out and I would not only be stopped, but I would be fired from my job. I'm as upset about this as you are, but it's something we just can't buck.

'Besides, I think we can find the men we want and get a line on this shipment without necessarily moving against the hotel.'

'That's what you say, Henry,' Doyle answered. 'I've been expecting something like this.'

He grabbed his hat and slammed from the office.

Walking with purposeful intent, he headed east towards the Canebière and then up to the Monoprix, which was still open. In it, he bought a length of rubber tubing and a plastic jerry can. There was a shopping arcade across from the Monoprix and Doyle ducked into it and out through a side entrance and around the corner before any tail who was on him could have caught up.

A half hour later Doyle was standing in front of the Hotel de Niger. Lights were on in some of the rooms where various activities, legitimate or otherwise, were taking place. The jukebox was playing at full blast, but all that could be heard was the constant thump, thump, thump of the rhythm section. A couple of the whores were leaning against the door smoking cigarettes and watching the sparse pedestrian traffic.

Doyle stood in the doorway across the street and surveyed the scene. He checked his watch. It was only nine thirty. He figured he had at least an hour and a half to wait.

At eleven o'clock Doyle was in a phone booth. During their forays through the city, Francoise had finally shown him how to use a coin-operated phone. The trick was when you heard the bip, bip, bip signal to push the coin in past the little spring loaded doodad. A weird system, no wonder he had had trouble understanding it. Carefully he dialled the number 919040. After some confused shouting at the police switchboard, he finally managed to get through on the emergency line to Inspector Barthelmy, who was already at home in his little villa on Rue Bobilier.

'This is Doyle. Sorry to get you up, but I couldn't reach you at the office. What are you doing, fuckin' off?'

'Where are you, Popeye?' Barthelmy said sleepily.

'I'm at that place we were talking about, you know, the Hotel de Niger, Rue Rappatu, got it? You remember the address, don't you? It's that place that that guy from the SAC owns.' Doyle cackled wickedly into the receiver.

Barthelmy sounded very concerned, as Doyle expected. 'Stay where you are . . .'

'Oh, I'll do that, sure, Henry, sure, when you come, bring a lot of water, a lot of it.'

He hung up the receiver with a laugh, just in time to cut off Barthelmy's farewell '*Merde!*'

Doyle moved again to the doorway opposite the hotel with his 10-litre can and after watching for a while walked across the street, swinging the can like a milkmaid. Most of the lights had gone out by now. The scene was winding down. Doyle went up the steps and into the bar. Most of the chairs were upon the tables, prior to closing. He unscrewed the cap on the can. The bartender turned just in time to see Doyle, who was already pouring petrol on the floor. Doyle walked past him through the curtains.

'Exterminator,' he said, laughing crazily, 'you've got rats.'

He sloshed the can through the back hall and then started up the stairs, leaving a trail of petrol behind him. The desk clerk, dozing on a canvas cot, was roused by the footsteps and saw Doyle charging up the worn carpeting.

Doyle doubled back on the stairs, trailing the can behind him. At the bottom he took the Zippo lighter from his pocket and whirled the flint. To his surprise, it caught the first time, and he threw it about five yards to the side of the stairs into a pool of petrol. It went up with a whishing sound. The desk clerk, now wide awake, leaped flailing at Doyle, but Popeye pushed him off with one arm, his other hand reaching down automatically for the place where the hold-out pistol used to be.

'Sonofabitch!' he muttered at its absence.

The flames started to climb the walls. Doyle kicked the banister and ripped away one of the rails. It was as good as a policeman's billy. He rushed up the stairs again and kicked open each door as he came to it, looking inside. Whores were in bed, some alone, some not, some nodding out. The smell of smoke was strong. A junked-up sailor staggered from a room rolling down his sleeve over the bleeding vein.

Doyle was looking for Jacques the elegant Frenchman, for Jules the third jailer. He wasn't settling for anything short of a clean sweep on this caper.

'Okay, you fuckers,' Doyle yelled inanely, 'everybody out! This joint is coming down!'

The hallway was beginning to fill with people, yelling and screaming, milling about in their nightclothes as the flames began eating towards them. Oblivious to the danger of being trapped, Doyle pushed through one floor, another floor, through the little room where the men played cards and into the cell where he'd been held, but there was nothing in it now except bad memories. The look of it, however, sobered Doyle. He turned and ran quickly down the stairs. Patches of flame spotted the bottom flight as he leaped several steps at a time.

The sound of sirens was cutting through the night. Doyle pushed past the bleary inhabitants milling towards the door. They were trying to comprehend what was happening, carrying weird objects they had suddenly decided were priceless: a fox stole, a canary in a cage, a pair of new shoes, a bottle of *pastis*. Soon the night air was filled with the howling and braying sounds of the police cars and sirens of fire engines as they came roaring up the Rue Rappatu.

Firemen began to unroll their hoses and raise their ladders, as the police cars blocked both ends of the street and squads of policemen collared and questioned people. Barthelmy arrived a few minutes after the others, having three miles to drive from his home. He jumped from his car, hitting the street on the run. Miletto and Diron, whom he had picked up at the *Hotel de la Police*, were with him.

Doyle peered through the smoke to see Jules slipping from the building, carrying several large paper sacks under his arm. Doyle pointed to the fleeing Algerian and shouted, 'Grab him, Henry!'

But that served to alert the fleeing man, who dashed for the corner of the hotel and ran towards the back of the building. Doyle charged after him.

Just before the swarthy man reached the alley leading into the warren of streets beyond, Doyle brought him down with a flying tackle. Using his torn-off stair rail like a nightstick, Doyle cracked down on the Algerian's wrist and then straight up into his face, the old cop-on-the-beat technique he'd learned at the academy. As the Algerian folded, Doyle punched him against the wall, ripping at the paper sack. Syringes, rubber tubes, balloons of heroin and hash fell to the ground. Instinctively Doyle's fist closed around one of the envelopes of dope cascading out, and he stuffed it into his pocket.

He looked up from the pile of evidence just in time to see a fireman carrying the old English woman and he angrily exploded at the memory of her.

'Bust that bitch!' Doyle yelled. 'She's a junkie Jonah! And hold this sonofabitch for me, he's really got it coming.'

Barthelmy signalled to Diron to take the old lady in custody while Miletto gathered up the contents of the paper bag. The Hotel de Niger was blazing now. Doyle, hunching like a wild animal, radiating restless energy, glared at the flames. There was no sign of Jacques, and he was the real contact. 'That bastard frog has slipped me,' Doyle said furiously.

Barthelmy wheeled on him. Doyle straightened up, coming out of his frenzy.

'I'll talk to you now, Doyle,' Barthelmy said in cold fury. 'Get out of here and go to the car.'

Doyle looked at him almost contemptuously and then strode out to the street. Barthelmy trotted behind him.

'You lied to us, you cheated, you fucked up again,' Barthelmy said, but Doyle was oblivious, remorselessly intent on getting to the Algerian, who was being held handcuffed by Miletto.

'Imbecile!'Barthelmy shouted. 'How do I explain this . . .?' He swept his hand at the fire.

Doyle shrugged. Shoving Miletto aside, he grabbed the Algerian.

'Charnier, that motherfucking pigmeat . . . where is he? Do you hear me? Where? . . . Where? . . . Where?' Each question was punctuated with a blow.

Miletto started to move in to stop the agitated American, but Barthelmy held out a hand to stop him. He knew that Doyle needed this release before coming to his senses, needed it to expiate the horrifying experience of having been an addict, needed it to get revenge on the people who had made him one.

The Algerian began to buckle at the knees under Doyle's berserk attack. He began to babble in French. The more Doyle hit him, the more he shouted. Now he was half lying on the ground. Barthelmy moved closer, alert to what the man was saying. He was babbling everything he knew about the big drug operation, every shred he could dredge up out of his memory, his terrified eyes still fixed on the towering figure of Doyle, panting with rage.

Doyle swung his foot back to polish him off with a good one in the ribs, but this time Barthelmy stopped him.

'Popeye, we have it, we have it. It's enough.'

But it was like trying to stop a tornado. It took both Miletto and Diron, one on each arm, to drag Doyle off.

Slowly, Doyle surfaced from his red rage, his body still hunched in a fighting stance, the fists like rocks, the eyes glaring wild, the chest heaving. Barthelmy touched his arm gently.

'We have it, Popeye. The dry-docks, tonight. He gave it to us. He gave us everything he knows.'

His tone was authoritative and gradually brought Doyle around.

'Okay, Henry, you hate me, right? I finally had to get it with my fists. That's not good detective work.'

Barthelmy held him in his gaze a long time. Finally, shaking his head regretfully, he turned to Miletto and said, *'On n'apprend pas à un singe à faire des grimaces.'*

'What the fuck does that mean?' Doyle asked Miletto.

'It means,' the grey-haired cop said, 'you can't teach an old dog new tricks, and maybe sometimes that's just as well.'

CHAPTER THIRTY-FIVE

It was a black night as the thin sliver of moon disappeared behind the mountains. A police car, lights out, rolled silently to a stop near the approach to the dry-docks of Ja Joliette. There were little pools of light thrown by lamps attached to the various structures in the sprawling yards, but the light was contained to a tiny circle; the rest was in blackness. The doors to the car had been unlatched before it was driven through the gates and the four occupants were able to leave the vehicle silently and deploy in the darkness, approaching from opposite directions the Dutch freighter which was squatting, bow first, in the only occupied concrete basin.

The ship was obscured in the night. But as the men moved closer and could see down into the steep well of the drydock, they could make out a small circle of light under the stern end near the sea gates. Shadowy figures were moving there, back and forth swiftly, sometimes under a shower of tiny sparks drifting down over their heads.

Barthelmy signalled to Raoul and Miletto to cover him from the top of the ship's berth while he prepared to descend a long flight of stone steps leading to the floor of the dry-dock. He held up his palm, signalling to Doyle to stay back and wait.

'No way, baby,' Doyle muttered under his breath.

Barthelmy sighed and made no objection as Doyle followed him on his rubber-soled shoes down the steps.

The vessel was resting on concrete blocks three feet high. The faint noises from the harbour echoed in the acoustic trap of the dry-dock, and any accidental sound made in that concrete hole would be magnified tenfold.

Keeping in the shadowed corner of the drydock, Barthelmy and Doyle advanced cautiously, hoping that the crackling sound of the acetylene torch working under the stern would cover any slight noises. Above them, Miletto and Diron moved along the edge of the dock, bent low, taking advantage of any cover.

The floor and walls of the basin were damp and slimy with sea-grass. High above their heads was the water-mark, signifying the point at which the ship could float again, and the sea-gates could be opened to release it into the harbour. The floor was a hazard course of loose timbers, refuse, chains and rusted tackle. The two detectives were able to pick their way through it by the dim reflected light from the cutting torch.

Above them, long heavy wooden beams extended from the freighter to the wall to keep the ship upright. As they neared the area where the twin propellers projected from the ship's bottom, Barthelmy and Doyle stopped for a moment to study what was going on at the stern above them.

On a wide plank between mobile steel ladders, a burner, his oxyacetylene torch flaring away in a shower of sparks, worked at cutting off metal pods secreted behind the propellers. Each pod was about two by four feet, encrusted with barnacles and attached to the hull by steel bands. Already several had been released from the hull and were being loaded by a small group of workers into a crane cage.

The cable from the cage led upward to a mobile crane at the edge of the dock. Behind it a truck stood ready to take the load of pods to their destination.

At some distance, parked carefully out of sight near a huge travelling crane was a Mercedes 220-SL. Beside it a man with a white beard waited patiently.

Jacques, elegant as ever, but wearing a workman's blue smock to protect his Cardin jacket, was supervising the operation of the cage in the dock. Doyle recoiled in surprise on spotting him. He began to move toward the young Frenchman, but was held back with a gesture by Barthelmy, who then looked up to check on the whereabouts of Miletto and Diron.

Each signalled his presence with a slight wave of the arm, which was acknowledged by Barthelmy, who gestured that they should stay in close. He turned and signalled to Doyle to avoid looking into the blinding glare of the burning torch so that their eyes could become adjusted to the darkness.

As they drew closer, they saw that a guard was standing on the plank scaffolding with the welder, covering him with a World War II grease gun with a long magazine. The men around the stern were working quietly and efficiently. Their muttered conversation was casual and even spotted with occasional jokes. Doyle put his lips close to Barthelmy's ear.

'The bastard thinks up the cutest ways to move the stuff,' he said. The welder now had released the last pod and was lowering it to the loaders below.

Barthelmy pulled Doyle's head close and signalled towards the exit. 'We leave now,' he said.

Doyle turned to him, his temper flashing instantly. Barthelmy shook his head and held up his hand in caution. Then he pulled Doyle close.

'We want the laboratory too, don't we, and Charnier? So we follow.'

Reluctantly Doyle nodded his agreement.

Above them, Miletto, leaving Diron watching the truck, was working his way around. As he made a dash for the protective cover of a travelling crane, his eyes fastened on his objective, he tripped and fell over a rail. A guard on the truck turned, noted the sprawling figure and opened fire. Bullets smacked into the cobblestones around Miletto as he rolled quickly into the shelter beneath the crane.

Below all hell broke loose. Barthelmy unlimbered his Walther PPK, a relic of World War II, and opened fire on the guard on the scaffolding above. But the big old automatic jumped insistently to the right as it was fired. It was of very little use at that range. The guard himself turned quickly and responded to the firing with a stream of bullets from his automatic weapon. Doyle, aching for a weapon, and Barthelmy dived under the hull.

Jacques and his crew, including the welder, flattened themselves on the crane cage, which immediately began hauling them up with the pods.

Topside, Diron and Miletto were pinned down as two more guards started banging away at them. Charnier slipped into the Mercedes, knowing he must leave the situation to straighten itself out. After all, there could be other deals, other shipments, but if he was caught, it was all over. He knew that he should not have been on the scene anyway. The size of the deal, and the urgency of the men in Geneva and perhaps a desire to be closer to the excitement had impelled him, against his better judgement, to come down and witness the work.

Trapped under the hull, Barthelmy and Doyle were helpless. Slugs dug into the concrete at their feet or ricocheted off the steel hull with staccato pings. They had to watch as the steel crane cage swung above the dock, straight out and then onto the truck, whose engine started up with a roar. Jacques began shouting orders. The Mercedes was screaming away in a tight turn and vanishing into the night. Diron and Miletto, pinned down by crossfire, were helpless to stop it.

The rusty ship bottom inches from their heads, Doyle and Barthelmy hugged the concrete blocks. They were soaked by the residue of water. Every time one of them made a move, a fresh burst of bullets sent him wriggling back to shelter. The sound of non-stop firing topside emphasized how helpless their position was. The guard on the scaffold could cover both sides of the freighter, containing them neatly.

Doyle turned and looked back along the hull.

'If we don't get out from under here, that hotshot's gonna put us away,' he shouted.

There was no longer any need to whisper.

Barthelmy nodded agreement and signalled that they should both try to make a retreat along the keel towards the bow. But as they started to scramble back, they were stopped by the sudden sound of cascading water.

They saw torrents of seawater bursting from the sluice gates at the end of the drydock. The threatening sweep of water rushed towards them. Above, Jacques and his men, covered by machine-gun fire, were furiously turning the wheels which controlled the sluice gates.

Miletto and Diron were doing their best to stop the action, but their pistols were futile against the continuous spray of automatic fire. Miletto shifted slightly for a better shot at the men turning the valves. He exposed only a quarter of his upper torso, but it was enough. A guard zeroed in and the force of the bullets spun the grey-haired detective around and he stumbled back and pitched into the rising waters in the basin, unseen by either Barthelmy or Doyle.

Suddenly the hail of fire from the guard on the scaffold stopped. He realized that the rising water would trap him, and he made a frantic descent into the thigh-deep seawater.

Now Doyle and Barthelmy were free to make their run for the steps at the end of the basin. The guard was sloshing desperately toward another set of stairs at the dock side. Barthelmy stopped long enough to take a shot at him, but the distance was too great and he missed. The guard turned, pulled a pistol from a shoulder holster and fired back, forcing Doyle and Barthelmy to duck for cover again.

The seawater was increasing to flood, boiling over the detectives, sweeping them off their feet. The two men were soon battling for their lives. Barthelmy's gun was knocked from his hand by a piece of timber now swirling and thrashing dangerously in the oncoming torrents of water. Other loose debris began to smash and whip savagely around the two in the raging torrent. A sudden undertow sucked at them, dragging them back beneath the hull.

Above, the firing stopped as the truck took the same route the Mercedes had, racing for the gates of La Joliette, while Diron emptied his magazine helplessly after them. Jacques and his group, sheltering behind the tailgate, fired constantly until the truck disappeared into the night.

Below, new hazards threatened Barthelmy and Doyle. The supports holding the freighter upright began to loosen as the ship shifted in the rushing waters. Long battens torn from the dock sides clanged with enormous force against the hull. In the dark confusion the two men could barely see each other.

Diron, now free to help them, ran desperately along the dock edge keeping pace with the two as they were carried like flotsam towards the end of the basin. He grabbed up a heavy rope and began to uncoil it feverishly.

Barthelmy, coming up for air, caught sight of Diron and waved desperately at him. He failed to see a massive batten slicing toward him through the water, but Doyle spotted it.

'Henry, look out!' he shouted. The heavy timber smashed against the Frenchman's skull. Knocked unconscious, he sank into the black flood. Doyle swam desperately after him, trying to estimate where the water would sweep him. After two dives he came up, holding the inert form around the neck.

Battling against the current with his free hand, but holding onto his prize, Doyle struggled toward the rope Diron had lowered down the side of the dry dock. He managed to grasp it and Diron pulled with all his strength to guide his human load toward the steps.

Doyle finally reached them and began to climb exhaustedly, pulling Barthelmy after him. Diron descended to help.

Totally exhausted, Doyle sank down on the ground beside Barthelmy, whose eyes began to flicker open. For a long moment, neither said a word. Then Barthelmy's face twisted into a weak smile of thanks.

'If I'd had a gun . . .' Doyle said, panting from the exertion, 'if I'd had a gun . . . I could have helped you more!'

Barthelmy was trying to say something. 'Where . . . where is . . .'

Doyle understood. 'Where's Miletto?' he asked Diron.

The detective searched a moment for the English words. 'Shot.' He nodded towards the flooded basin. 'Down there.'

'Oh, shit . . .' Doyle said regretfully. He got up to take a look.

CHAPTER THIRTY-SIX

Doyle lay back in the lumpy bed. A big bathtowel was wrapped around his middle, and he rested with his head against the bolster, staring at the palm-leaf chandelier. Françoise, dressed only in her beautiful tan, moved busily about the room.

'I think your suit is almost dry, but it may need a touch of the iron,' she said, inspecting the damp clothes hung near the window. Underneath she had placed copies of the *Provençale* to catch the dripping.

Doyle watched her through half-lidded eyes. He supposed she had the most beautiful and perfect body he had ever seen. She was a moulded doll without a blemish, except for a brown mole as big as a dime under her right arm.

'Françoise,' he said drowsily, 'you are really bee-yootifull. Bee-yootifull, baby.'

'Thank you,' she said.

'You know, we could really have something terrific going between us.'

Françoise removed Doyle's drip-dry shirt from the hanger and folded it. 'We've been through all that, haven't we?' she said. 'You know it's an illusion. This is just something that pleases us now. In five years . . .'

'In a hundred years,' Doyle said, 'I could go for you, baby.'

Through the window, street sounds floated up – the honking of horns, the wailing of sirens mixed with the hooting of steamships in the bay. Doyle looked past her smooth form at the fading sky. On his arms the needle marks were now only faint white ghosts, but the itch returned from time to time. With the flat of his hand, as the old lady had shown him, he rubbed absently. The chilling events of a few hours ago in the dry-dock floated back into his mind.

'Jesus!' Doyle said.

Françoise looked around in concern. 'Are you all right?'

'Yeah,' Doyle said disgustedly. He got up, shaking with a

recurring spasm of need, and padded into the bathroom, where he splashed cold water on his face. It did little to relieve the tension. He went to the window and stood beside Françoise, looking at the street below. There were only a few people hurrying on late errands, a boy on a bicycle with a long *baguette* strapped to the handlebars.

Doyle paced nervously up and down the room beginning to sweat. His arms began to itch again, then his nose. He rubbed the needle marks ferociously.

Françoise lay down on the bed and watched him, aware that it was a battle he had to fight on his own.

Doyle looked into the mirror. The face staring back was fevered and drawn, the face of a stranger. His hands were shaking badly. He had thought that was all over. He went to the bureau and tore the wrapping off a Hershey bar, stuffed the candy into his mouth and chewed furiously. It wasn't enough. From a drawer, he took a couple of tablets of sugar, cracked them with his teeth and washed them down with water from the tap.

There was a knock at the door. Doyle grabbed his soiled raincoat and slipped it on to hide his nudity. Françoise jumped into the bed under the covers with her back to the door.

'Yeah?' he said.

It was Barthelmy.

Doyle opened the door a little way. Behind Henry was a tall man with iron grey hair. Barthelmy's arm was suspended in a sling.

'Popeye, this is Inspector de la Croix.'

Doyle nodded. The man bowed formally but did not offer his hand. His eyes flicked briefly toward the bed where a swatch of yellow hair was visible.

Barthelmy said, 'The Inspector wants your passport. There's a plane for Barcelona in the morning for the connection to New York. They'll give you the passport back when you get on the plane.'

It was clear that Barthelmy didn't like what he was doing, nevertheless Doyle started to close the door on the pair.

'Listen,' he said, 'I'll give it at the office.'

But Barthelmy shouldered his way into the room. The Inspector followed him, looking with cool distaste at the seedy furnishings and disarray. He turned to Barthelmy and released a barrage of French.

What he said was this:

'One undercover man dead because of Doyle, one fire that could have burned down Marseilles because of Doyle, two very suspicious deaths that you say are not connected with Doyle, but we know very well are, worthless types it's true, but still French. Now this drydock business and one good man killed. That's all. He goes – out!'

Barthelmy turned apologetically to Popeye. 'Do you want me to translate?'

'No,' Doyle said.

'They called your boss in New York.'

'I'll bet they're disappointed over there that I'm alive. This guy must be a pal of theirs.'

'Your passport, Popeye,' Barthelmy said.

Doyle went to his bureau, opened the drawer and took out the green American passport with the eagle on it and handed it over dispiritedly.

'Henry, this ain't right. We're so close to that sonofabitch now I can taste it. You can't cheat me like this, Henry.'

Barthelmy shrugged, the all-purpose Gallic gesture. He handed the passport to the impatient inspector.

The inspector said, *Je ne veux pas le voir. Même dans la rue!'*

'He wants you to stay in the hotel, Popeye,' Barthelmy said, 'until we say you can leave.'

De la Croix turned and strode out of the room without a glance at the haggard detective, with his skinny white legs sticking out underneath the tattered raincoat. At the door, Barthelmy turned and gave Doyle a short glance of apology. Popeye thought there might even be a hint of a promise on the French cop's face. Then, rolling his eyes toward the impatient inspector, Barthelmy turned and left.

Françoise rolled over and leaned her head against the headboard. 'Well . . .' she began, but Doyle launched a frustrated kick at a pile of soiled clothing on the floor.

'Shit!' he said. Then his gaze fell on the bureau where the contents from his soggy jacket had been piled. His eyes took on a hard glint.

He fanned out the objects with a swing of his broad palm, found the package of heroin he had pocketed at the Hotel de Niger. He held it up to the chandelier and shook the little balloon. Inside the white powder was dry and skittered from corner to corner.

Françoise watched silently, steadily.

He stared at the tempting translucent envelope for a long moment, sweating. Then, with a savage surge, he strode back to the dresser, took the knife and stabbed the packet open, spilling a bit of the powder on the top.

He looked dully at what he had done, wet a finger and put a few grains on his tongue. The taste was bitter, very bitter.

Both he and Françoise were frozen in a dead quiet. Then he turned, strode to the bidet and flushed the temptation away. The sound of rushing water was like a triumphal symphony to him.

In the drydocks at La Joliette, two frogmen emerged from the refuse-strewn water. Between them they supported the body of Gerard Miletto. There was a purplish hole in his forehead, and other bullet holes were hidden by the clothing. The Dutch freighter had settled again to the floor of the basin. Dock workers were re-attaching the wooden supports and big pumps were sucking the water away. Barthelmy watched the operation, his face taut with grief. The frogmen passed the sopping body to the waiting ambulance attendants.

Barthelmy's arm was out of the sling, but his hand was still bandaged.

The big sun of Marseilles was shining overhead. The dock was a peaceful place after the terror of the previous night. The area had been cordoned off by the police. The officers and crew of the Dutch freighter were lined up alongside the drydock and Diron was taking down their names in a notebook. Barthelmy looked over the crew distastefully.

The burly blond captain of the freighter approached him, complaining vociferously, but Barthelmy chose to ignore him for the moment as the ambulance slowly passed along the line of crewmen. Raoul Diron lowered his notebook, muttered a silent prayer and crossed himself. But the captain continued his posture of outraged innocence unabashed. He remained bumptious, aggressive and indignant.

Barthelmy faced him coldly. *'Vous n'avez rien remarquer dans le cours de la voyage, capitaine?'*

'My French more bad than goddamn English,' the Dutch captain said. 'I say nothing until goddamn consul get here. I know no thing of the last night!'

Barthelmy switched to English. 'You must have been able to tell from the way the ship handled that something was stuck to the hull. You expect me to believe you noticed nothing?'

'We come,' the captain said, 'for fixing the rudder. I not know anything of the other.'

Conversation was interrupted by the tooting of a car horn.

Barthelmy turned to see Doyle at the end of the drydock, standing beside a taxi beeping for attention.

'Will you wait here please, captain,' Barthelmy said.

The captain indicated his freighter. 'I go back Dutch territory.'

Barthelmy's voice turned harder. 'You are on French territory now, captain. You will *stay* on French territory.'

He signalled Diron to keep an eye on the disgruntled captain and went to meet Doyle. The American was grinning boyishly.

'Popeye . . .' Barthelmy said, starting to remonstrate.

'Aw c'mon,' Doyle said, 'if I'm with you, what can I do bad?'

The French inspector sighed with resignation and turned back to the drydock as Doyle paid the cab. The American caught up to him.

'What did you find out about this tub?' Doyle asked.

Barthelmy looked rueful. 'The captain claims he knows nothing. According to him, he made one stop in Singapore. He says it was "to fix a bad rudder".'

'I'd like to make him eat that fuckin' rudder.'

'He says he knows nothing about last night either,' Barthelmy added.

'You believe that?' Doyle asked.

'Of course not.'

'What are you gonna do now, Henry?'

Barthelmy looked irritated. 'We wait. When his consul comes, we take the captain to headquarters and hold him. We question him. When the consul leaves, maybe we question him some more.'

Doyle smiled, appreciating the implication that Barthelmy was capable of doing things that worked very well in the squad room in Brooklyn.

Before Barthelmy reached the waiting captain, Doyle grabbed him by the arm. Barthelmy winced with pain.

'Oh, sorry. I forgot about your arm, Henry,' Doyle said. 'But listen. Don't lock this bum up right now.'

Barthelmy looked at him with interest.

'Look, he hasn't been paid yet, I'm sure of that. A guy like Charnier doesn't pay a dime until he's checked out the goods. I know this Dutchman won't leave town until he gets his cash.'

Barthelmy looked sceptical. 'It could be waiting in Holland. It could be on deposit in Geneva.'

'No,' Doyle said, 'it's gotta be cash and it's gotta be here. Charnier wouldn't take the chance of stiffing the guy. He knows the captain could tell you some nice stories.'

Barthelmy was doubtful. 'I don't know . . .'

'Look,' Doyle said, 'if you wait to follow the Dutchman all over Europe, that skag will be in five-dollar bags on Amsterdam Avenue by the end of next week. Let the guy walk and he'll take us right to Frog One.'

Barthelmy stood with his arms folded, looking at the captain and pondering Doyle's idea and its implications.

'You owe me one, Henry,' Doyle said. His tone was cold, but it couldn't hide the pleading underneath.

Barthelmy looked at his American friend speculatively. Doyle *had* saved his life – and besides the proposition made sense. The French inspector nodded once. Doyle turned away so that the Dutch captain could not see his expression. His face had broken out in a broad grin of momentary victory.

For the rest of the day Barthelmy assigned an agent dressed as a yard maintenance man to see the Dutchman didn't make any unexpected moves. Late in the afternoon the Inspector and Doyle set up an observation post in a tall-ceilinged room in an engineering shed in the dockyards. It afforded them a perfect view of the Dutch freighter below. They had equipped themselves with bread and sausages, some of Doyle's favourite *bagnats*, a bottle of Côte du Rhône and a six-pack of Coca-Cola. They also brought walkie-talkies, a set of powerful Nikon binoculars and a mattress. Their jackets and ties were off and Doyle had taken his shoes off as well.

There was a crackle from the walkie-talkie. Barthelmy picked it up, answered, listened intently, then signed off with satisfaction. He turned to Doyle.

'Our men are covering the harbour in case he tries to make a rendezvous by boat.'

Doyle was watching the freighter through the binoculars. Barthelmy walked to the window. He could see a group of shipyard workers tinkering at the stern. Doyyle dropped the binoculars from his eyes.

'Dutchy is taking his time, ain't he?' he said. He handed the binoculars over to Barthelmy. Doyle looked over his shoulder. The Dutch captain was standing on his bridge, still in uniform. Barthelmy put the glasses down.

'When will they be finished with the work, do you think, Henry?' Doyle unwrapped a Snicker and nibbled at it.

'Sometime tomorrow, according to our information,' Barthelmy said.

Doyle looked at him with a meaningful smile.

'The quicker the better.'

Barthelmy nodded and then shrugged helplessly.

Charnier hurried through a long industrial shed located behind the cemetery of St Pierre, beyond the Chemin de l'Armée d'Afrique. It was a good location that the chemist Simonpieri had chosen. It was not far from the Pharmacie Militaire and near the tramway depot, a place where unusual smells were not likely to be noticed, and yet near to town and sources of supply, a place sparsely populated, and yet industrial enough for the comings and goings of trucks, even at strange hours would not be noticed.

And supplies did come in at strange hours, since the lab was working around the clock to fill the order delayed so many times. The lab had a jerry-built look, but to Charnier's practiced eye it was a marvel of efficiency. Unlike Cesare's ancient laboratories in which he stirred his mixtures with a spoon and dried the product on the balcony, this lab was equipped with mechanical mixers adapted from hand-held electric drills, baking ovens powered by propane tanks so that there would be no increased usage of city gas to tip off the police, and efficient freezers hijacked from a shipment destined for a new fish-market.

The morphine base was cooking in long tin tubs immersed in a water bath. These were much less likely to burst than the usual glass flasks. The heroin would probably not be as pure as Cesare's, but the production was high. However, in order to reach a proper degree of purification, it was necessary to re-peat the same process five or six times. The whole thing was tedious, dangerous, and it used up precious weeks. Three men worked on a sixteen hours on, eight hours off schedule. They slept in cots in a shed to the rear of the plant.

Guards armed with Uzi Israeli automatic weapons stood near the entrances and several overhead windows. Most of them had been assigned only recently as the shipment began to accumu-late in large quantities. The scene had a surrealistic look since all the people were wearing World War II gas masks to pro-tect against the fumes. Even so, the three processors had faces pitted by the acid fumes. One had grown a beard to conceal the scarring effects.

Charnier stood looking over the shoulder of a masked worker and shook his head sorrowfully. He turned to Jacques.

'They never come up to the old craftsmanship,' he said. 'If we had the workers from the old days, you would see how fast we could turn this out, without any stupid accidents such as we had before.'

The chemist Simonpieri noticed the two men, joined his thumb and forefinger into an O and nodded enthusiastically, signalling that the shipment was coming along well.

Charnier and Jacques left by a rear entrance, stopping at a workmen's sink to soak some paper towels and thoroughly wash the acid residue from their skins. Outside they climbed into Jacques's Mercedes, parked in a little *impasse* off St Jean du Desert.

'What do you think, Alain?' Jacques looked concerned.

'I think they will get it done on time, but it will be a close thing. We must try to improve our techniques for the next shipment,' Charnier said. 'This inefficiency is costing us millions.'

CHAPTER THIRTY-SEVEN

In the room over the engineering shed Doyle and Barthelmy were aching with fatigue. Doyle rubbed his red eyes and put down the binoculars for the hundredth time.

'That goddamn Dutchman is taking his own sweet time.'

Barthelmy was stretched out on the mattress, an arm thrown over his eyes to block the light.

'You know, Popeye, things will get very difficult if we don't see anything by tomorrow. I don't think I can cover you for more than two days of "recuperation". Then . . .' He gestured with a forearm across his throat.

Doyle sighed. He knew that Barthelmy was right. 'Listen, Henry, maybe I could get a disease or something.'

Barthelmy grinned. 'To the Commissioner, you *are* a disease.'

'Yeah,' Doyle said ruefully, 'and I'd like to give it to him.'

He lit a Gauloise and stared again at the Dutch ship through the binoculars, watching for some sign, some signal that the exchange was about to take place.

It was hardly likely that the payoff would take place in the middle of the night. The arrival of a car in the deserted dockyard would be too obvious. But Doyle was so intent on closing in for the kill that he persuaded Barthelmy to alternate shifts with him through the night.

In the morning, Barthelmy saw that the water was steadily flowing into the ship basin. Longshoremen were pulling away the beams and a wisp of steam floated up from the freighter's funnel. He touched Doyle lightly on the shoulder and the American was instantly awake. He took the binoculars, peered at the dock, nodded with comprehension and began to pace the loft restlessly, casting irritated glances out of the window. He felt crowded by time. He knew that Barthelmy could cover for him only a little longer.

In the laboratory behind the St Pierre cemetery, the process of refining the morphine base was nearing its conclusion. A number of large packages, wrapped in paper and marked with red tape indicating the ultimate client on the other side, were piled up. One lab worker had started carrying them through a side door, stepping carefully over the thick electric cables which had been clandestinely connected to the tramway repair yard.

Beyond the shed was a garage where a Fiat van was being loaded with the bundles, under Jacques's supervision. The tall steel doors of the garage entrance were guarded by a huge black in a turban, his face carved with five rows of tribal scars. The little Uzi looked like a water pistol in his fleshy hands.

At La Joliette the drydock was completely filled. The freighter floated peacefully, only a few lines still attached to keep it from bumping against the sides of the dock.

Barthelmy, watching from the window, turned away with a disappointed expression.

'I think we've had it, Popeye.'

Doyle was shaving at a rust-stained basin in the corner with the straight razor he'd lifted from the old lady. He'd taken a fancy to it and besides, he still packed no gun.

'That Dutchman's got to bite, I tell ya. I just know it. This is one I can really feel.'

178

Wiping his face with a discarded tee shirt, he went to the window and raised the binoculars.

Barthelmy at his shoulder said, 'He's got very little time left.'

'It's enough, Henry,' Doyle said. 'Take a look.'

Below, the Dutch captain in full civilian rig, was making a call from the pay phone on the dock side. The blond officer looked uncomfortable in the tight-fitting suit which obviously had been purchased years before and rarely worn. He spoke briefly, paused a moment, replaced the receiver and puffed patiently on a cigar, waiting. After a minute and a half the telephone rang. The captain answered it quickly, listened, nodded happily, replaced the receiver and began to saunter toward the gates. Doyle grinned and threw his arms around a surprised Barthelmy.

'Whoopee!' he said, 'he's movin'!'

Barthelmy caught Doyle's mood of exhilaration.

'Nothing's gonna stop us, man, nothing,' Doyle said.

Barthelmy grabbed up the walkie-talkie and paused, as if he knew a message was about to come in. And in half a minute, it did rattle off some rapid French. Doyle began gathering up his stuff into his Samsonite case.

'Are you sure you got all the roads covered, Henry; you got units stationed at all the intersections he might take?'

Barthelmy shrugged. 'I'm covering as best I can with the number of cars and portable radio units that we have. But I don't think we have to worry. According to that message, we can expect him in 15 minutes at the dock of the Chateau d'If.'

'Huh?' Doyle said, amazed.

'My dear Popeye, we have had what you call a "bug" on that telephone for more than a month. In fact we've been auditing every pay phone in the dock area, since this is the logical place to pick up tips on drug shipments moving by sea. The portable unit connected to the bug just informed me that the exchange is to take place somewhere aboard the Chateau d'If launch. But even the captain himself doesn't know exactly who his contact is or how it will take place.'

'Is the boat crowded?'

179

Barthelmy shrugged. 'Sometimes, sometimes not. You can be sure of one thing. The captain will not escape with his money. But our goal is to catch the contact man.'

'I will arrange that the motor of the launch will be out of commission for fifteen minutes after the arrival of the captain, maybe more if we need the time. Our agents will get aboard, disguised as tourists, fishermen and so forth. I'll alert men to proceed by fast boat to cover the dock area on the Chateau d'If. Several will be in the tower and several more in fishermen's gear on the Fereole Islands where the boat makes a stop on its return. Our captain will be under observation at all times.'

Doyle was impressed. 'That's good work, Henry. You guys can really move when you have to, but he's going to be rubbin' shoulders with an awful lot of people between now and when he gets off that boat.'

CHAPTER THIRTY-EIGHT

It was a sunny morning and a substantial crowd had turned out for the short boat ride to the Chateau d'If. Most were tourists from other parts of France, a few adventurous family groups from Marseilles itself, merchant seamen, some foreign tourists but not many – Marseilles not rating high as an international tourist attraction – some students with backpacks and fishermen with creels and rods who planned to get off at the Fereoles. The crew-cut blond captain, with his fat pink neck and his tight-fitting, chalk-striped suit, now formed part of the group.

A crewman whistled for attention and made an announcement in French. There was a murmur of disappointment through the crowd.

The captain knew little French, but understood there had been a delay. He looked impatiently at his watch and began to pace nervously, brushing past the importunate balloon and peanut vendors, past the black African souvenir sellers of carved ivory tusks and dangling necklaces and staccato skin drums.

The Dutchman couldn't resist casting a speculative eye over

the crew and the waiting passengers but there were many who might be his contact. Two-thirds of the group carried bundles in paper, cloth, canvas bags, knapsacks, any one of them big enough for the substantial wad of money he was expecting.

The captain, like the Japanese before him, had been instructed to be among the last aboard. He stood aside as some newcomers arrived then the captain of the tourist boat signalled that boarding of the launch could start.

The Dutchman went to the cart presided over by an elderly gypsy and bought a *Mystère*, with a wooden spoon for eating the ice cream confection.

Slowly the crowd filed across the gangplank onto the sixty-foot launch, equipped with parallel rows of benches across its beam. A sheltered cabin covered the forward half, protecting against spray, and most of the passengers avoided the last damp rows at the stern. The Dutchman took a last spoonful of the ice cream and threw the cup into the water.

A young man in a beige turtleneck and a blazer was buying a packet of pistachio nuts from an Algerian vendor. Occasionally his eyes, covered by giant aviator-type sunglasses, would flicker to the line of people boarding the craft, inspecting each passenger carefully and watching if anyone seemed to be taking a special interest in the Dutch captain. None appeared to be. Jacques, cautious nevertheless, walked carefully away from the area of the loading stage then strolled casually, dropping pistachio shells as he went. He surveyed the benches and terraces of surrounding cafes for possible observers.

At the very last moment, just as the whistle signalled the departure, Jacques bought a ticket at the wooden counter and hurried aboard, a canvas Adidas flight bag hung casually over his shoulder. The boat chugged backward into the centre channel of the port, then headed out towards the twin guardian towers of St Jacques and St Nicolas. Jacques had made his way forward under the protective roof and sat in a centre aisle seat.

Barthelmy and Doyle, in the upper windows of the tower of

the Chateau du Pharo, overlooking the Old Port, watched the departure through a telescope and the Nikon binoculars.

'You think he's aboard already, Henry, the contact? Maybe I should've been down at the dock, I might have spotted him.'

Henry shook his head. 'You can be sure the contact would not be Charnier himself; that would be foolish. It's work for a lesser man.'

'Yeah,' Doyle protested, 'but there was another guy that I could recognize – the guy that questioned me at the hotel.'

Barthelmy shrugged. 'By the same token, *he could* recognize *you, n'est-ce pas?*'

'I coulda hid somewhere,' Doyle argued.

Barthelmy said, 'Let me run this case. It is likely that your contact man has a highly developed sense of danger. If we made a move too early and we were wrong, the whole affair would go up.'

Doyle, impatient to take an active part, pounded the knuckles of his right fist into his palm.

'There's no way that sonofabitch is gonna get away again, I tell you Henry. It'll be over my dead body.'

Barthelmy smiled grimly. 'Or somebody else's?'

The Dutch captain, sitting in back, was getting drenched with cold spray from the Bay of Marseilles, but he was used to that. He looked at the passengers on either side of him. A pair of young honeymooners were looking into one another's eyes and occasionally glancing at the approaching saltbox of a tower. To his left was an old lady in a shawl busily fingering her rosary.

Beads of moisture began to appear on the captain's pink brow that were not due to the salt spray. Where was his contact? Had he been double-crossed? Was he being set up? These were desperate men he was dealing with. Would they do him in, rather than make the big payoff?

No, the captain thought. It wouldn't make sense. They had a regular channel now for the dope; why should they spoil it for one deal? But suppose the *courrier* wanted to take off with the money? In American dollars it was a quarter million. A man could live forever on that. Suppose the contact decided to knock off the captain so that there would not be any feedback to the organization for a couple of days? For God's sake, the Dutchman thought, *hurry up*!

Jacques sat comfortably, smoking a Balkan Sobranie, inspecting his well-kept nails and occasionally glancing through the spray-beaded windows.

There was a sudden halt in the thrumming vibration of the diesel as the launch captain cut the engine and let the craft drift in towards the big stone jetty of the Chateau d'If. Standing on the small wharf and crowded back up the narrow walled passageway was a crowd that had already done its tour of inspection and was waiting to be taken ashore.

Was his man perhaps somewhere in that crowd the Dutchman wondered. Should he ascend to the museum? He had been told on the phone just to get on the boat, to sit in the last row, behave as though he were an ordinary tourist.

Some passengers got up and began to crowd toward the opening in the bulwark where the gangplank would be thrown. A deckhand pulled a pin and opened the gate preparatory to disembarkment.

The Dutch captain remained seated, looking nervously about, and shifted over in the vacated space to leave room in case the contact intended to sit next to him. A rope was thrown ashore and the boat was warped towards the small dock. Finally convinced that no one was to join him in his stern seat, the captain got in the line of passengers.

Jacques, among the last to get up, moved casually with the crowd as it headed towards the exit. He stood behind the captain. Only the young honeymooners separated the Dutchman and the gangplank. With a slight jostle, Jacques slipped the Adidas flight bag unobtrusively under the captain's arms.

In the tower of the Chateau du Pharo, Inspector Barthelmy's radio sputtered into action.

'The captain's been contacted!' he said excitedly to Doyle. 'A tall young man with wavy brown hair, five foot eleven, tanned complexion, well dressed. Does it mean anything to you?'

'You bet your sweet ass it does!'

'He passed a flight bag to the captain and disappeared into the crowd. But my men have him in the kidneys.'

'What?'

Barthelmy smiled. 'That is to say, there is no way that young man will slip away. The captain, of course, is being followed, too, but we can be reasonably certain he will return to the ship. The important one to hang onto is the contact man, *n'est-ce pas?*'

'Fucking-A right!' Doyle said. 'That dude is Charnier's numero uno stooge. Stick to him and we got Frog One, the lab, and enough shit to send half of New York to the moon!'

CHAPTER THIRTY-NINE

Barthelmy had staked out all routes leaving the Vieux-port and had people mounted at key intersections of area traffic. The Inspector had ordered out every possible unit – including motorcycles, sidecars, vans. Plainclothesmen dotted the streets of downtown Marseilles and some were detailed as taxicab drivers. Helicopters were on the alert. All available means would be used to track Jacques.

Diron, Barthelmy and Doyle followed the action by radio from the Citroen and tried to keep within reach of the quarry. It was obvious that Jacques was an old hand at covering his tracks. He twisted, turned and doubled back, forcing Barthelmy's tails to switch frequently. A taxi driver followed Jacques for a short distance up the Canebière before handing the tail over to a delivery boy with a wagon full of Tunisian halvah.

Hurrying through the Marché des Capucins, the dapper young man emerged on the Boulevard Garibaldi, where he swung aboard a trolley-bus. A tail in sailor uniform barely had time to swing aboard behind him as the vehicle rumbled off, but before the trolley-bus picked up speed, the agile young Jacques leaped from it to the ground. Signals from the roof of the

Hotel Noailles reached a hippie at the corner of the Canebière and Rue Garibaldi, who slouched along in the trail of the elusive Jacques.

As the pace of the surveillance increased, Doyle became more tense, more impatient, more eager to get out and do something himself. He was not used to sitting and kibitzing via short wave. Barthelmy looked at him with understanding.

'He's sharp for his age, your friend.'

'Yeah,' Doyle said.

The radio crackled with instructions as the elegant young man was passed from a middle-aged storekeeper to a priest, who was excommunicated in favour of a window cleaner. Nobody stayed on the trail more than two or three blocks at a time.

Jacques was advancing in a westerly direction that brought him closer and closer to the old tramway depot behind the cemetery of St Pierre. Finally, in the Impasse de Vignes near the Hippodrome, he picked up the parked Mercedes. Convinced that he was in the clear, he drove the mile or so to the laboratory.

Jacques pulled the Mercedes up to the big shedlike building and honked twice. An electrically controlled garage door opened and swallowed the sleek grey car. Two of Barthelmy's men were watching from their tramway repair van.

Now Barthelmy directed his tails and assigned as many cars to surround the area of the laboratory. Although the language escaped him, Doyle was impressed with the efficiency of the hunt.

'We have them bottled up now,' the Inspector said to Doyle. 'As for your Charnier, it is questionable whether he is there. It's not usual for someone at that level to be present at the laboratory, but perhaps because of the size of this delivery, and the fact that it must be very near to shipping time you may be in luck . . .' he paused, 'if your man is, in fact, even in Marseilles.'

As they drove towards the rendezvous, Barthelmy checked off the block points on his detailed map of the city.

Doyle was completely absorbed in the operation. 'What

about that place you just mentioned, that cemetery?' Doyle said, looking at the map. 'Couldn't they escape through that?'

Barthelmy shook his head. 'The entrances to the cemetery on their side are kept closed and there is a high wall around it. There is no way of driving through.'

Barthelmy's car stopped at the roadblock at Sainte Jeanne d'Arc and made a final check as to whether all units were in place. The railroad underpass was blocked with two large *paniers* parked nose to nose. As Barthelmy signalled, one pulled back so that the Citroen could glide through.

It was decided to follow the usual policy to make a fast assault with a small team of picked men to avoid any advance warning by local people or watchful guards posted along the way, with the uniformed men and cars scheduled to follow shortly afterwards.

Eight burly and determined-looking detectives, none in uniform, met Barthelmy, Diron and Doyle. Synchronizing watches, Barthelmy instructed four of them to approach the building from the rear via the *Impasse de Bedarieux*, while the rest would approach through the Rue Jean Aicard, passing directly through the tramway yards. These men were tough and armed.

It was hard for eight men in raincoats, some concealing automatic weapons or tools, to look casual as they passed through the yards, but they tried. Luckily, the area was nearly deserted. The workmen, unless they were in the pay of Charnier, were not likely to react. Diron covered the rear and kept a sharp eye in case any worker moved towards the main building telephone.

At the rear of the tramway yard, past the rows of parked trolley-buses, a plainclothesman in a parked taxi pointed to the electrically controlled gate of the laboratory. Barthelmy stopped to survey it and turned to Doyle. 'What do you think?'

'Looks like that big garage door would be impossible to crack,' Doyle considered. 'But you see that little side door that's just got some wire glass in it? I'd head for that one. It looks like those two screened windows along to the right, if you hit 'em a couple of times with a crowbar, will give pretty fast. You sure you got the rear of the building covered?'

'Of course,' Barthelmy snapped, but Doyle was flattered that the Frenchman had asked his advice.

Watching the hand of his watch, Barthelmy raised his arm. The team tensed. The arm fell and the assault group raced forward and began to smash at the three vulnerable points with crowbars.

Doyle and Barthelmy were right behind the team at the door. It took only a few seconds to pound a hole through the glass and reach inside to the latch. The first blow alerted the lab crew.

Charnier grasped the situation instantly and took control. He shouted for Jacques, workers, guards to grab up the paper-wrapped bundles, eight twenty-five kilo packages, each a good load for a man. Taking the big black man with the tribal scars and automatic weapon with him, Charnier raced for a side entrance.

Police cars were screeching into the courtyard and into the *impasse* behind the laboratory. Cops were swarming all over the building, smashing down doors. But the place was a labyrinth of nooks, staircases, and balconies.

Doyle and Barthelmy leaped up a short flight of stairs and spotted a guard hidden in a niche. Before he could raise his Uzi, Barthelmy brought him down with two shots from the big Smith & Wesson. Doyle wished he had been resupplied with his weapon.

Barthelmy charged through a doorway, Doyle and several cops close behind. They were in the lab itself. After the shadowed area of the passageways, they were momentarily blinded by the blaze of electric light in the brilliantly illuminated workroom. Guards on the balcony began firing down in a desperate holding action. Almost enough dope had been prepared to assure the shipment. It was worth millions and each of the guards wanted to protect his share.

Barthelmy and Doyle hit the floor and the others took cover. Doyle crawled into a niche near the window as bullets sprayed around them. Beyond it he caught a glimpse of two figures, the white-bearded drug-merchant and the black ducking along an open balcony across from the courtyard.

Barthelmy was flattened behind a table and firing away a good fifty yards beyond him and there was no time for explanations.

Doyle picked up a small iron workbench and smashed it through a window opening and vaulted over. He rolled backward out of the building, landing with a grunt. Then, bent low, he raced for the foot of the stairs towards which Charnier and his man were heading.

The last guard on the balcony exposed himself to take a potshot, only to be cut down by Diron behind an iron pillar. Just then, Barthelmy observed Jacques slipping through the balcony doorway. He charged up the steps after him, across the overpass, down the far side of the building, into the garage. A worker was fastening the tailboard of a truck as Barthelmy followed by Diron exploded in.

Bullets from two guards knocked concrete chunks from the wall behind them and the detectives dived for cover.

Jacques hit a button and the big steel doors began to slide open. He sprinted for the truck. Diron and Barthelmy fired after him but he managed to grind it into reverse to clear a disabled truck blocking his way. Barthelmy hurtled for the control box and hit the close button.

Jacques, his cool gone, stamped his foot to the floorboards and the light truck sprang like a tiger forward, the iron jaws inexorably closing. The truck rammed them and crumpled like a concertina. Jacques went through the windshield, a log smashing through an icejam, the glass raking off his face.

The two remaining guards dropped their Uzis and walked slowly toward the two policemen, their hands raised.

CHAPTER FORTY-ONE

Charnier and the black had a hundred yards start on Doyle and were headed for the cemetery wall, unaware that he was behind them. Doyle could see the black man's Uzi, and knew he had to stayed covered. This wasn't easy, as the large paved area had only a few parked vehicles and concrete posts. Doyle narrowed the gap to about thirty yards and then was forced to stop. There was no more cover between him and the high cemetery gate topped with broken bottles. Charnier, prepared for all eventualities, reached into his pocket for the gate key.

Now the pair went through the gate and Charnier slammed it behind him. Doyle broke out into the open and looked desperately around for help. He could hear firing from the lab building.

To his right was a small electric yard wagon. Doyle jumped on it, switched on the ignition and stepped on the accelerator. The iron wagon was no race car but fast enough for his purpose. He aimed it at the gate of the cemetery, and jumped off just as it hit. There was a snapping noise as the lock sprang. The engine began to smoke and strain its wheels, pushing against the masonry wall like an angry baby rhinoceros. Doyle leaped aboard again and turned off the switch.

He edged the gate open with his toe, but there was no one in sight. Anxiously Doyle scanned the rows of tombstones, behind which could have been hiding the black African guard or Charnier himself, who Doyle was certain was armed too. He was about to give up when his attention was attracted by the distant sound of clanging metal. Then he saw a gate on the far side of the cemetery swinging open and the two figures slipping away.

Now his heart felt that old familiar pump of adrenalin, like in so many action situations before in New York. This was it! He was a man on his own, ready to finish a job he'd come out to do.

Running over the soggy turf and the bones of centuries of Frenchmen, Doyle raced for the far gate. He burst through the archway. For a moment the streets appeared deserted. Then, peering down to his right, he saw a trolley-bus stopping for passengers, among them Frog One. There was no sign of the black bodyguard.

Already winded, and realising a mad dash would attract Charnier's attention, he broke into a brisk walk. He hoped the vehicle would be making stops, and given a traffic jam time, he might be able to catch up. Behind him he could hear the braying of police cars.

He wished he had a goddamn walkie-talkie. He wished he had a vehicle, even roller skates. His breath was coming in wheezing gasps, but he was closing in, chanting to himself, '*You won't get away this time, you sonofabitch, you won't get away.*'

He was sparked by an almost insane energy to push his body to the limits. He realized that if the trolley-bus skipped a few stops, he'd be lost.

Passing a workmen's *tabac*, he saw a bicycle leaning against the wall. Commandeering it, he threw a leg over and spun off after the vanishing trolley-bus. He heard a shout as the bike owner came running into the street, shaking a shirt-sleeved arm after his disappearing *Velo*.

Good, Doyle thought, I hope they call the cops. Maybe I'll get some help.

The tramway was headed for the centre of town. Doyle was gaining on its tail. But as the bus entered the Avenue de la République, it ran a yellow signal, and Doyle had no intention of braking for a red light. He sailed into the intersection, swerving just in time to avoid a head-on collision with a furniture truck.

The bicycle shot out from under him and rolled to an unfortunate end underneath the truck. The angry driver waved his fist like a mechanical man, as Doyle took off on foot.

Every breath he took burned like acid and red dots jumped before his eyes. It was obvious there was no way he was going to catch that trolley-bus at this rate. Casting an eye wildly around, he welcomed the sight of a waiting taxi, and leaped for it.

The goddamn doors were locked. Doyle pounded angrily on the closed window and pointed ahead. The driver shrugged and indicated something on the roof light which Doyle knew meant off-duty.

Ahead the trolley-bus was momentarily blocked in traffic. Frantically Doyle searched his pockets and came up with a hundred-franc note. He dangled it before the windshield and some sort of agreement seemed to blossom in the reluctant driver's eyes. Charnier had spotted the frantic sweat-stained figure at the door of the taxi, and over the distance the message hit him. The New York cop!

He whirled and made his way through the crowded coach to the driver, noisily cursing the departure of a huge trailer truck which had been blocking the avenue.

In the taxi, Doyle was having difficulty in making himself understood. He pointed ahead. 'Follow that fuckin' bus!'

The driver looked puzzled. '*Comment?*'

'The trolley-bus, follow the fucking trolley-bus, you stupid frog idiot.'

'*Comprends pas.*' The driver still hesitated, but the honking horns behind him forced him to put the car into gear and start moving in the direction Doyle was pointing.

'What's the matter, are you deaf, you stupid prick? Follow the fuckin' trolley-bus.'

Doyle said it with increased volume. It seemed to have some effect. Comprehension glimmered in the driver's eyes.

'*Ah!*' he said. '*Le trolley-bus!*' He accelerated.

Inside the bus Charnier reached into his pocket for the neat Brown & Richardson 32. The gun was a legal one, covered by his membership in the SAC. He tapped the harried driver on the shoulder and showed him the pistol. The driver's eyes went wide with fear.

'Do not panic, my old friend. I'm not interested in hurting you and I'm not interested in robbing you. But I do not want you to stop for any more passengers and I want you to drive this bus as fast as you can through this traffic.'

One of the four remaining passengers glimpsed the pistol.

'*Mon dieu! Le barbu a un pistolet!*' His wife beside him screamed.

Charnier whirled on the four. The couple were panicked. But a black labourer and a tall soldier looked capable of making trouble.

'Everybody out!' Charnier commanded. Open the door.'

The driver hit the control lever, and the four hurried out.

'Now let's go,' Charnier said, with a thrust of the pistol.

The driver pressed the pedal to the floor.

After two blocks, Charnier gave the driver a hard nudge with the gun. 'Faster! Can't you go any faster?'

He could hear the insistent sound of approaching sirens, sirens that Charnier knew instinctively were for him.

'I am sorry, monsieur,' the terrified driver said. 'There is a governor on the motor and this is the best I can do.'

Charnier's eyes cast vainly about in both directions for an alternative means of transport, but there was nothing in sight. He could only urge the driver to keep going as fast as he could.

At this point, Charnier bore little resemblance to the poised, assured heroin operator. His collar was soaked with sweat and his hands were trembling. He had a deep apprehension that the American was his nemesis . . . stupid, lumbering, but unstoppable.

The trolley-bus came to the long approach that led to the Quai des Belges and for a wonder, there were few cars, mainly due to a stoppage of traffic on the far side occasioned by subway construction.

'Now drive fast, do you hear?' Charnier barked. 'And don't stop for any traffic lights, just go, if you want to live.'

Charnier looked back. The little taxi was beginning to pull up alongside. Not even suspecting that Doyle was unarmed, he remembered the American's reputation for shooting first and asking questions later.

His palms felt clammy and he tightened his grip on the tiny Brown & Richardson.

'Just keep going, fast!' Charnier said desperately, and put the gun to the driver's neck.

As they approached the intersection, the way seemed clear for a dash across the Quai des Belges. If he could get to the far side, into the warren of small streets around the Opéra, he'd shake them off.

Charnier's moment of optimism was ill-founded. He couldn't see that the reason the Quai des Belges was clear was that a police roadblock had almost sealed it off along the Canebière, the Rue Pavillon, the Rue Pytheas. The one side not blocked yet faced the Old Port and at that moment cars were racing from the Corniche John F. Kennedy to fill that.

Suddenly a wholesale fish truck roared away from the kerb to make a light. Too late, the truck driver saw the bus bearing down on him. He hit the air brakes and pulled mightily at the wheel.

For a tense moment the two vehicles ran in wobbly parallel course, the bus screaming to avoid the juggernaut. It went wildly out of control and smashed into the iron pole supporting the overhead wires for the tram. The iron support post swayed and, as though in slow motion, toppled to the street, dragging the network of trolley wires with it. A shower of sparks went up like fireworks.

Doyle's taxicab skidded to a stop. As Doyle leapt from the taxi, the black Citroen of Barthelmy slid to a stop behind him, siren wailing, blue light flashing. Barthelmy was out instantly.

'What are you doing, you idiot? Don't you know he's armed? You haven't got a gun!'

'Thanks to you, motherfucker,' Doyle bellowed. He grabbed Barthelmy's arm and pulled him, running, towards the bus.

Charnier had been knocked from his feet, but now struggled up, still gripping his gun. The driver was slumped unconscious over the wheel.

'That's him,' Doyle pointed.

Barthelmy looked stunned. '*That's* Charnier? But it's impossible. That is . . .'

'Who?' Doyle demanded.

'Raymond du Verrier! He's a political bigwig close to the mayor, and a big businessman here in import and export.'

'You can say that again,' Doyle cracked.

A fallen wire bounced and trembled on the top of the stalled bus, crackled and snapped sparks left and right.

Four policemen, guns drawn, ringed the bus.

'Let's get that current cut off,' Doyle said, 'and get that sonofabitch outta there.'

Barthelmy started back to the car radio.

'No, wait a minute,' Doyle said, 'if we take this sonofabitch, if we really nail this "bigwig", it won't do any good, will it? He'll get sprung, direct from the top.'

Barthelmy shrugged. 'It's very possible. He's a powerful man.'

'Do you really want to stop this shit? Are you on my side or theirs?'

Barthelmy hesitated. 'I'm on your side, but . . .'

'All right. If it's something you can't help, they can't fire you, right? I'm the one that chased him, I'm the foreigner that caused this accident.'

'So?' the Inspector said.

'Just take your gun and tell old Charnier to come out with his hands up.'

'But the wires?'

Doyle's eyes lit up maniacally. 'You're getting it!'

Barthelmy understood. He stepped back horrified.

Then Doyle spoke in a new voice, very evenly. 'C'mon. You've seen the results of his work. You know what he is. He sells poison . . . He's a murderer. And you're a cop, Henry.'

Barthelmy felt like he'd just heard the elegant summation of the Prosecution.

Barthelmy's face reflected bitter comprehension. He walked to the bus doors, sprung open a crack now that their air-pressure control was inoperative.

'Shooting will do you no good, Monsieur du Verrier,' Barthelmy spoke through the crack. 'The whole area is blocked off. If you'll come with us, perhaps we can arrange something. Please come out quietly.'

Charnier looked frightened. He should have kept the passengers on, to use as hostages.

But there seemed to be an offer or some kind of promise in the police officer's request. Reluctantly, he pocketed the pistol and started for the door. As he grasped the metal handle, he was jerked into an epileptic stiffness. His palms were seared to the bone. On the roof the fallen wire danced.

'Oh, my god!' Barthelmy exclaimed in mock concern. 'Turn off the main current!' 'Quickly,' he shouted to Diron, 'send word to cut off the current.'

Diron spoke on the portable unit. Within a minute the shower of sparks died.

Barthelmy and Doyle approached the bus, pushed the doors open wide. Charnier's body slid to the cobblestone pavement, the face purple behind the white beard, the hands burnt black.

Barthelmy and Doyle exchanged glances.

'Poor Charnier,' Popeye said with no trace of mourning.

'*Pauvre du Verrier*,' Henry murmured, evenly.

CHAPTER FORTY-TWO

The two detectives were sitting on the *terrasse* of the Samamaritaine watching the fishing boats and yachts in the Old Port. Doyle was drinking a Cinquante-et-un *pastis*, Barthelmy, White Label and soda. The Inspector looked at his watch.

'We have only a little time to make the plane and there was someone you wanted to see at the airport . . .'

Doyle nodded, sipping absently. 'You know, Henry, this isn't such a bad burg when you get used to it.'

Barthelmy looked around curiously. 'Personally,' he said, 'I detest it. Paris is the only city.'

'I don't know,' Doyle said. 'Here you got nice weather. I kinda got to like that fish soup and this here *pastis* . . .'

'. . . and some of our women?' Barthelmy smiled.

Doyle nodded. 'Definitely,' he said. 'It all seems very peaceful now. Maybe I'll kind of miss it.'

'You're not anxious to get back to New York?' Barthelmy asked.

Doyle looked bitter. 'There's a lot of guys that are not going to be very happy to see me back and I may be lucky if I make it through the gates of Kennedy.'

Barthelmy smiled again. 'Then perhaps you should stay here.'

'No,' Doyle said. 'New York is like a big, mean old bitch to me. Mean, but beautiful. I don't guess I could be happy any place else.'

Barthelmy checked his watch again.

'Well, we better get going or you won't have any time at the airport.'

They walked to the Citroen, where Diron was waiting at the wheel.

At the airport, Doyle checked through his Samsonite cases.

'Listen, could you excuse me for a minute, Henry? I got to see somebody downstairs.'

'Now, you won't try to make a run for it and stay in France, will you?'

Doyle grinned sheepishly. 'No, this time I'm really going. You trust me?'

Barthelmy shrugged agreeably, and Doyle trotted to the stairway leading down to the car rental desk.

She was there in her red cap and jacket, the long tawny hair tied back with a blue ribbon. An impatient German in a grey homburg was shuffling his feet, waiting for the paperwork to be completed so that he could pick up his car.

Françoise looked up and saw the American crossing toward her. She turned toward the rear of the little booth and called to her colleague. 'Geneviève, will you take care of monsieur Schwaber?'

She left the German with his pen poised in mid-air, and ran across the floor to Doyle, who waited for her with open arms.

Both seemed a little surprised at the fervour of their embrace.

'I am so sorry you have to go,' Francoise said.

'You're sure you don't want to come with me?' Doyle asked, only half kidding.

Francoise took the remark as it was intended. 'No, *chéri.* 'This is where I belong. I tried it in America before. It's not for me and I'm afraid France is not for you.'

Doyle smiled wistfully. 'With someone like you around, I could get to like it. But maybe you're right . . .'

She took his hand and walked him beyond the baggage carousel.

'Where're we going?' he said.

'There's a little room back there where we rest sometimes,

196

where you and I can be alone for a while.'

Doyle blushed.

Twenty minutes later, he arrived back at the upper level. Barthelmy met him at the departure gate.

Barthelmy said, 'I have a present for you.'

'Oh shit,' Doyle said, 'you shouldn't have.'

Barthelmy held out a bulky manila envelope.

Doyle felt the weight. 'My pistols! . . . Just what I always wanted.'

'You seem to do very well without them,' Barthelmy said. 'They're cleared with security here.'

Doyle's smile was grim. 'I think I'm going to need them plenty, just as soon as I get back . . . and Henry, I want to thank you for giving me the name of that sonofabitch there that had you set me up.'

Barthelmy put his hand on Doyle's. 'And I want you to forget where you heard it.'

'Well . . . uh . . . Oh revoy,' Doyle said, extending his hand.

But Barthelmy took him by the shoulders and kissed him quickly on each cheek, French style, his mid-morning stubble scraping Doyle's face.

'*Au revoir*, Popeye.'

Doyle picked up his attache case and started off.

'Oh, and one more thing,' Barthelmy said through the departure gates.

'Yeah?'

'Your fly is open.'